D0434949

A Flicker in the Clarity

A Flicker in the Clarity

Amy McNamara

for Medbh

HarperTeen is an imprint of HarperCollins Publishers.

A Flicker in the Clarity
Copyright © 2018 by Amy McNamara
All rights reserved. Printed in the United States of America.
No part of this book may be used or reproduced in any manner whatsoever without written permission except in the case of brief quotations embodied in critical articles and reviews. For information address HarperCollins Children's Books, a division of HarperCollins Publishers, 195 Broadway, New York, NY 10007.
www.epicreads.com

Library of Congress Control Number: 2017959285
ISBN 978-0-06-230834-4 (trade bdg.)

Title Lettering by Maricor Maricar
Typography by Catherine San Juan

18 19 20 21 22 PC/LSCH 10 9 8 7 6 5 4 3 2 1
❖
First Edition

eleven-story tumble

SOMETIMES YOU HAVE TO DO SOMETHING CRAZY in order to stay sane. This is what I'm telling myself, because I'm on the fire escape, blindfolded, feeling my way up to the roof. Before tonight I would have said I could do this in my sleep. Em and I have climbed out my window and gone to the roof a thousand times. But the blindfold changes everything. I adjust my grip on the railing. Inch forward on the rough iron strips from one set of steps to the next.

This is Emma saving me from myself. An hour ago I was lost in gloom after looking up colleges and costs. Then Em showed up like a stray sunbeam. The air changes when she's around, feels more charged, ionic, which was just what I needed right when I needed it. We balance each other. I'm the calm to her crazy, and when she sees me sinking in the murk she grabs me by the hand and yanks me out.

We started the blindfold trust game in seventh grade. Mandi came up with it at one of her giant sleepovers—standard middle school girl-on-girl torture. *Monkey brains or spaghetti?* But Em and I took it further and never let it go. We may as well call it *Blind Evie,* because she never lets me lead. We do it at my place, shove the battered furniture around, move my mom's various piles and stacks, make as many obstacles as possible. Then we grab hands and spin, until we're giddy, dizzy.

I am easily lost.

Today when she showed up, I was freaking about the future. My grades aren't great, and my chances of a scholarship seem slim. I don't say how unfair it feels that poor kids have to be *on top of it* all the time because Em can mess up. Her parents have it covered. But it's like the higher the stakes, the less I care. Only that's not right, because I care so much I can hardly breathe when I think about it. The future's a formless blob and our fantasy of going to college together doesn't seem likely. Art school, which is secretly the only place I *want* to go, is way more than my mom can afford, not to mention that it doesn't promise the kind of career where I could pay off thousands of dollars in student loans.

Emma drew on the inside of my wrist while I talked, her breath tickling my skin. Two stick girls in the center of a heart, holding hands. Supposed to be us. Only Em can't draw—like, at all—so it's a mess on my skin, a heart with an affliction. I love it anyway.

Then she snapped the marker shut, stood up, and said, *Time to shake things up,* which is her response to everything.

So here I am, clammy-handed, gripping a gritty metal railing, finding each step by whacking it lightly with my shin. My legs are going to look like old bananas. That is, if I manage not to end up on the pavement below.

"A little farther . . . ," Emma says, her bubblegum breath on my face. "Almost there!"

She sounds closer than I thought. I reach out for her—it's instinct—but she moves, and my hand swipes wildly at empty air.

Emma's somewhere above me now, cackling like a downed power line, tight, explosive. She's thrumming with the insanity of what we're doing.

I have to relax. My body knows how to do this. I'm never

scared up here when I can see. The trick is to stop trying to think it through. Memory doesn't matter, it's what I touch that counts.

I creep forward, one hand on the flaking iron, the other waving like a feeler, until there's no more metal going up. I crouch and find a vast flat spot, the gritty rubberized surface of the roof, my whole arm making contact with safety. All I need to do is crawl forward and I'm done. I tell myself not to think of the great empty nothing behind me. Except telling myself that makes a movie in my mind, gravity pulling me like a snowflake, arms and legs out, falling through the air.

No.

I'm so close. Behind the blindfold I squeeze my eyes shut tight, then tighter. This is me shaking things up.

I launch myself out, but scramble frantically onto the blessed wide roof.

"Oh my GOD!" I shout, yanking off the bandanna. Above me, the dusky sky looks like a dirty gray lake.

Emma's a few feet away. She does an excited little dance, cheers, and drops onto the sooty rooftop next to me. Her thick braid brushes my cheek and she looks as relieved and thrilled as I feel. She needed this too. She's been acting weird with me, with Roman, agitated, like she's ready to leave everything behind.

"Wasn't that the *best*?" she whispers, grinning wildly at the sky. "That *rush*! Right? Oh my God, Evie, you totally needed that!"

I can't tell if I'm about to laugh or cry.

"My heart," I gasp, my hand against my hammering chest. "Feel it! It's like an animal's trapped in there."

Emma presses her silvery fingertips to my sternum, her eyes bright with respect.

We clutch each other and scream with laughter. I feel like a criminal who tunneled out of jail. My body's electric and sparking. We're near the edge, but we're together, and Emma's looking at me like I'm someone exciting. Maybe she's right about doing what scares you. I don't feel bad anymore; I'm a collection of limbs, animal, alive. My brain's overloaded with adrenaline, all the other stuff knocked offline.

"You are no mouse," she says.

Mouse. Part of the Bly School's idea of community building. A year of wilderness and environmental skills training on field trips to Bear Mountain leads to earning your animal in eighth grade on a final scouting retreat. And I got *mouse*. By nearly unanimous vote. Em's a fawn, which—okay—she has a long neck and big eyes, but come on, *mouse*? Thanks, social hierarchy. I was still pretty short and that was the year of my terrible haircut, but it hurt to have been so clearly seen and labeled.

"Tell no one," I pant, rolling my head to the side to look her in the eye so she can see I'm serious. "Jack thinks we're crazy to come up here. If he hears about the blindfold, he'll kill us both." Jack's not into crazy risks.

"Poor Snack." She smirks. "He was flirting with Alice this morning." She widens her eyes at me and laughs. "Must mean his heart's not too broken."

My stomach twists. Jack's almost as important to me as Em. After a solid year of flirting, he tried to kiss me. It was clumsy, sudden, and I ducked it, which Emma finds hilarious. I haven't admitted to her how much I wanted that kiss, how sick I am I screwed it up.

"Alice?" I groan. "Seriously? He totally ignores her."

I press my back flat against the rooftop and take a deep breath. I'll never forget the look on Jack's face that night at his house. Hurt. Confused. Embarrassed. We were on a brownie break in the middle of watching *The Shining*. Em had just left to meet up with Roman. Right there, in his kitchen, while I was pouring milk in glasses, he put an arm up on the cupboard, leaned in, and tried to make it real.

I panicked. Ducked away from him and laughed. Then we watched Jack Nicholson cackle like a madman and hunt down his family with three cold feet of space between us on the couch.

There's obviously something wrong with me. Emma flips through guys like photos on her phone and when Jack finally makes a move instead of going with it, all I can think is, *What if it wrecks our friendship?* Which happened anyway when I nervous-laughed right in his face. There's no easy way out of that one.

"Alice!" Emma laughs.

I blink up at the night sky. Love's dangerous. It flattened my mom. Em says I overthink it. Guys our age only want sex. But I don't know. It seems like another way to lose yourself, and I'm already lost enough.

"Whatever," I say, convincing neither of us. I press my cold palms against my hot cheeks.

She wedges her head closer to mine with a happy sigh. "Evie Ramsey, you are a secret fucking superhero."

Which makes it worth it. This is how it is with her. Wild, crazy, beautiful, like being caught in an unexpected storm.

She lets out an ecstatic "*Whoooo!*" and grabs my hand.

We're small beneath the sky.

Ask me about love and I'll say there's not much between your heart and an eleven-story tumble.

frozen

EM'S AN HOUR LATE.

I check my phone.

Nothing, of course.

I shift from one frozen foot to the other.

The taco place has cycled through a first dinner rush and is filling up again. I'd go in and order so I could stay inside while I wait, but I barely have enough cash for food once she gets here.

I can't keep texting her. I've already burned through my phone plan this month and the overage fees are no joke. I should shut it off until I'm on Wi-Fi again. But I don't.

She's with Ryan, again. She's supposed to be with me.

A cute couple walks up, his arm on her shoulders. He holds the door for her and they go in. For some reason this is the thing that makes me mad.

"Come *on*," I hiss, stomping my feet and blowing on my frozen fingers. I don't usually get mad—Em's always late; that's what books are for—but this is getting ridiculous, and I'm beyond my ability to deal with stuff today. Everything she said she'd do changed. We were supposed to go to the park for lunch. We didn't. We were supposed to start our Junior Investigation projects together after school. That didn't happen, either. Somehow she convinced me to deliver her breakup news to Roman. Being on time to hear how it went kind of seems like the least she could do.

I'm covering for her more than we actually hang out. Since she started cheating on Roman with Ryan there aren't enough hours in the day left for me. And today was one where I could have used a few. Jack and Alice are a *thing* and somehow seem to be everywhere, and, after an excruciatingly endless prepping-for-college-applications assembly, Em skipped out, leaving me to go to the first Spain-trip meeting after school, even though she knows there's no way I can go. We can't swing those "extras." I didn't snorkel in the Caymans at the end of eighth grade, either. It can suck being a poor kid in a rich-kid school, but I'm used to it.

Ryan better be worth it. She won't let me meet him because she knows if she does, he'll figure out how young she is. Emma looks more like twenty than seventeen. I mean, I guess it's a good sign that she thinks he'd care. The last time she hooked up with a totally random guy like this was right after her brother, Patrick, died, and that guy got off on how young she was. Em has this delicacy thing going on that draws people to her—delicacy in all senses of the word: sensitive, rare, delicious, and a little fragile. I don't know what I exude, but it's not that. I'm *useful*. Or something.

I lean against the wall near the window of the taco shop. Roman. I felt bad for him, and that's saying something. Roman, Devon, Cassius, and Max are all part of this circle of senior guys who think they're the hottest hookup material Bly's got going. But when I told him Em was done, he staggered backward a little. A step or two. Looked ruffled. I was so surprised I reached out, but he brushed my arm away and said, *She sent* you? *She couldn't come herself?*

I knew it was messed up when she asked me. When I hesitated, she looked kind of exasperated and said, *Hand him this.* Then she wrote, "Hey Roman! We're done!" on a sticky note. I don't like conflict, but I couldn't do that. It was too mean. I should have told her to do her own dirty work, but in truth some part of me liked the idea of having a little power. Guys like Roman Schaeffer don't even see me. I will never go out with a guy like him, much less get to dump one. And he's no saint. I've heard stories.

He saw me when I told him she was done, though. He looked at me with hurt in his eyes, deeper than anything I ever expected to see on his smug face. I felt mean. That look hovered there, cloudy between us—a moment of realness—before he snatched it back, clearing his throat and flipping up his hood. No more questions. He glanced my way one more time, then swaggered off, as if whoever he'd been waiting for was a no-show, as if we never talked.

I check my reflection in the window of the taco shop.

I'm not repellent, I'm just not Emma. I'm more like an extra, the people they need to make a scene feel real but who don't catch your eye while you're watching the stars. My knees are bony and my waist is straight. I wear glasses. I should probably wear them more, because I squint a lot, and Em says it makes me look kind of annoyed or weirdly intense, but I forget to put them on.

Wind tears down from Union Square and whips more of my blondish-brown hair from its braid. I tuck a few strands back, but my fingers are stiff with cold.

My phone buzzes. Finally. I whip it out of my pocket so fast I drop it, then wince as it skitters on the frigid sidewalk. I'm lucky. My screen's intact.

But it's not Em.

I deflate.

My mom's texting to tell me the Hanovers need a last-minute sitter.

I check the time again. I've been standing here an hour and eight minutes.

Screw it. I'm going babysitting. The Hanover twins are out of control, but the family lives in one of the swanky renovated double apartments above ours, and whenever they go out, they come home blitzed and pay big.

I look inside the taco shop one more time to see if she's in there, if she slipped in without seeing me and is sitting in the tiny space, wondering where *I* am. Waiting for Emma leads to magical thinking. The cute couple stares back at me instead. They're on stools in the front window, his leg flung over hers. They make me feel guilty about dumping Roman for Em. She said they were using each other, there was nothing between them, but what if he really, really liked her? Kind of looked that way. The guy in the window wipes a dot of sour cream from the corner of the girl's mouth with his thumb. The gesture's so intimate something in me twists.

My feet are frozen and Emma's not in there. She doesn't wait for me. That's not how it works. I text the Hanovers and tell them I'm on my way.

Halfway down the steps to the subway, my phone buzzes again.

This time it's Emma's dad.

Em with you?

I hesitate a second. It's kind of like I'm out-of-body or something.

Then I sell out my best friend.

Sorry! I write. At least she *has* a dad to worry when she's not home. **No idea where she is.**

I run down to my train, try not to think about what I just did.

because . . .

HER TEXTS WAKE ME UP.

Wtf??

Why???

I'm trying to figure out what to say when my phone vibrates again.

One more word.

Traitor.

songbirds, sweet tears, magic apples, and other lies

"EVIE HAS MY KNEEPADS but I'm not gonna ask her for them because *I don't want to see her face.*"

Emma knows I can hear her. Her voice cuts through the morning din as people flood the hall, changing classes. One period in and the day's already a series of small hells. Advisory was all about making college-visit plans and the best Spanish tutors to hire before the trip in May. I sat there taking notes, feeling stupid and left out.

Jack's intel by way of Alice is that Em came home high and with her shirt on inside out. Em's parents are Catholic, Catholic, Catholic. All my attempts to apologize have been met with silence, and I've barely slept.

Now this.

I look up at her for a millisecond. I get it. I picked the wrong night to take a stand and got her in major trouble. But there's a difference between mean and mad. Em and I get mad at each other sometimes, but we're not mean. Yet here she is, planted in the middle of my path, her mouth like a megaphone, her eyes glassy like she might even be high now, that plastic smile creeping across her face, and one skinny arm flung around Alice's shoulders.

Alice.

That girl's a cabbage. Pale, bland, only palatable after something extreme like shredding, boiling, or a good chunk of butter. That sounds mean, I know, but Alice is always hovering around, not really saying anything.

I try to let out the breath I'm holding, but when I do I make this weird choking sound and have to cough instead.

She looks over at me blinking fast, doe-eyed, like some innocent.

I used to kind of like her, the way she doesn't seem to care what anyone thinks, but suddenly Alice freaking Weir is everywhere, first with Jack, and now leaning in toward Em while she talks crap about me at the top of her lungs.

Her kneepads. A forensics team would have trouble identifying and repatriating everything we have of each other's. Emma took my toothbrush once because she liked the shape of it better than hers. The toothbrush I'd been using. I have her stupid kneepads because she skipped volleyball last week and I forgot mine.

Heading home sick is what she had me tell Coach Jackson, but sick actually meant rushing to Union Square to hang out with Ryan. Something's brewing with Em again, and how, I'd like to know, will the cabbage handle that? Alice has no idea what she's getting into. Emma's a storm, the wild kind that drops a cloud of dark so fast, streetlights blink awake even though it's the middle of the day.

Her life was perfect. A mom *and* a dad, her older brother, Patrick, the dogs, their good-smelling house that glows at you from the windows like it loves you as much as you love it, like no one inside is worried, lonely, or poor. Then Patrick drove drunk and died. He was not supposed to go down like that. Emma flew out of her orbit and into a wonky ellipsis.

To most people, Emma's magnetic, a magic projector, a milky-skinned girl with dark hair and rosy lips. Patrick's girlfriend, Mamie, called her Snow White. After Patrick died, nobody really knew the extent of the damage because she dabbled in perfect, got the best grades of her life, was a point guard superstar. People see what they want in her. They think she's all songbirds, sweet tears, and magic apples.

Not me. I never did. Em looks like she's in charge because she sets the course, but I'm the tiller, or rudder, or the whatever-ma-thingie you need to keep something windblown balanced and off the rocks.

I know she has insomnia and is scared of the dark. I know that until she was ten she wanted to be a saint and looked everywhere for a miracle. I know she's bored most of the time and worries it's a sign of a deeper flaw. And I know some of what Emma lost when Patrick died, because I lost it too.

I fumble my locker open. She can have her kneepads. But then Alice murmurs something, and when I look at them Emma's plastic smile stretches wider. Her laugh is high and loud.

Forget the kneepads. I slam my locker shut and look at my feet a second, as if spotting a body part is going to help me reassemble after Em's verbal and visual shrapnel. I have to get out of here. I shoulder past them, jacked up on adrenaline, and head up the stairs to the fourth floor. Fighting with Em is blowing me apart. I hold my bag to my chest and make for the art room like a fugitive to a safe house.

between storm and monster

I SKIP MY NEXT TWO CLASSES and stay in the empty art studio painting a map of my fight with Em, almost all water, purple, black, and my deepest blue.

I glance at the call for submissions Ms. Vax thrust at me on her way out to take the morning classes to the Whitney. The flyer has my name scrawled across the top, underlined and circled, like the minute it crossed her desk she thought of me. It's for something called TeenART. *Simple to apply, just scan and send!* she said, stopping in the doorway to breathlessly pitch this *unbelievable opportunity.* It includes grant money for supplies, space in a studio, and an internship with a working artist. Kind of cool, for sure, but Ms. Vax doesn't get it. Doesn't get me. I sigh and nudge the flyer to the far edge of the table until it drifts, like a leaf, down into the recycle bin. My maps aren't for anyone else. I make them for myself.

She's the one who started it. In seventh grade she showed us the three-hundred-year-old *Carte de Tendre*. Made by a French woman—a map of love. History, Ms. Vax explained, is a story people tell, and maps are one of the tools for telling it. We act like they're fact, but they are more like documents of interpretation.

That shook me to the core. It was the first time I realized no one's actually in charge. We're all just making it up. I thought maps were supposed to be true. The idea that they could be subjective tripped me up. I started eyeing everything with suspicion, as if the previously sturdy edges of the larger world, spaces made by adults, the places I was expected to grow into, were suspect, blurring.

Then I started making my own.

I shift on my stool and mash the bristles hard against the paper—black rocks of judgment. Upthrust, defensive, all spiky peaks and narrow troughs. This map is super dramatic, how I feel. Storms swirl the middle, froth the blue. It's as true as anything else. Besides, where Em's concerned, the real dangers lie past the edge, where the world falls away.

That might be where she is now, out there, or on her way.

I stare at the paper and chew the end of my brush; the sun through the windows and the white lights overhead are harsh critics. Behind me, radiators clank and hiss.

I glare at what I've made. I'm used to being lost, letting inky lines lead me, but I don't like feeling desperate, and right now I don't know how to make anything happen—on my map, in my life. Maybe this is a family condition. I'm the daughter of Died Young and Left Wrecked.

These are mean thoughts. My dad didn't want to die, and who am I to judge my mom for how she deals with losing him? I tear a hangnail with my teeth, then lean in and fill the unknown space with monsters, put my anger on the page. I twist the brush for muscled necks and sharp claws. Mix the blackest green for scales. It does nothing to fix this hopeless feeling. Everyone knows the monsters you imagine waiting for you have little to do with what lies ahead.

I roll my neck, fold a leg under, and add myself to the page, a speck in the oval, stalled out in a flat, windless bit between storm and monster.

How'd I get here? Standing next to Em is like holding a jar full of fireflies, your face temporarily bright with all that caught and flickering light. People are drawn to her. I am drawn to her.

A few hot tears prick the corners of my eyes. I blink them

back and look at the mess I've made. I'm in the wet gray center, my head a pale splodge. The knobs of my shoulders and knees are lighter yet, and the rest of me hidden, sunk through the middle of a tiny white and red lifesaver. Why'd I make that thing so small?

I close my eyes against the lonely dot, suspended—no Emma, no wind, and too much time to think. Then I toss the map.

Didn't help to make it.

Scared me instead.

lonely dot, suspended

I WALK HOME THE LONG WAY so I don't run into her and Alice.

Or Alice and Jack.

As soon as I'm in my building I text, **Please can we talk?**

For a second a reply bubble flashes three dots like she's typing back. I freeze in front of our elevators, hopeful, scared, staring at my phone.

Then . . . nothing.

I try again.

Em?

My phone vibrates a few seconds later with an angry red exclamation point.

Undelivered!

She locked me out.

a dim bulb in a marquee made of sparklers

OF COURSE, OF THE TWO ELEVATORS, the one that comes is the one with the broken light. Jack refuses to ride it. Em too. Our building's so neglected they both think it's going to fall or chop someone in half like that elevator did in Midtown. But it's here, so I take it, a dark ride lit only by the floor buttons, anemic moons illuminating and extinguishing themselves until it stops at our floor.

Our apartment's cold when I walk in, the radiators silent. My mom says the owners do it on purpose to shake out rent-control tenants so they can renovate and rent to richer people. When I asked if they can do that, if it's even allowed, she went to bed.

Money sucks. When I broke my wrist a few years ago, we bought nothing we didn't absolutely need for months, because our insurance didn't cover it all. Like my cast was some luxury. My mom tries to hide it, but things are tight. Taking to bed has its appeal. I picture us together, covered in spider webs, blinking quietly at the ceiling. Blinking's free.

"Enough!" I say as forcefully as possible. When you're home alone as much as I am, sometimes you talk to yourself. My voice startles Marcel the wonder mutt. He rolls his girth off the couch and shuffles over to lick my ankles. My mom's terrified of dogs, so Marcel's a miracle. He looks like a mistake, the result of a star-crossed love between a German shepherd and a barrel-shaped terrier. He has one torn ear, sad eyes, and he's perfect, and I love him.

Em's the only reason he's mine. She and Patrick rescued him from the side of the road upstate with their parents one weekend. She says the minute she saw Marcel she knew he was for me. If I'd been planning the whole Evie-gets-a-dog-despite-her-mom's-phobia coup I might have chosen one a little less intimidating than a motley wolflike creature, but even Patrick said Marcel was waiting for me to come into his life, and he was right. Love at first sight.

My mom made me give him back. I begged her, wrapped my arms tight around his fluffy neck, but she called over to the Sullivans' house and asked in a shaking voice if Patrick and Em could please come and take him back.

When Patrick walked in he looked so sorry for me. It's the only major fight I've ever had with my mom, and I cried myself to sleep. But Emma didn't give up. She kept Marcel and brought him over every day after school until she wore my mom down.

Marcel follows me into the kitchen while I turn on the oven for heat. We lie on the floor together a minute while I resist the urge to hide out in my room, the only place in the apartment that doesn't feel dark and overlooked. After he licks my face a million times I stand and call the management company about the light in the elevator. I am one hundred percent sure no one listens to my messages, but I have to try. I can't be like my mom. I love her, but along with various bills, she's been letting official-looking letters from the building owners pile up, unopened. One of us has to do something.

By the time she walks in I'm at the table with my laptop as if I'm a regular girl on a regular day and not a secret murk person barely blinking at my screen.

"Sorry I'm so late," she says, dropping her purse on the table next to me with a quiet sigh.

If I'm a mouse, my mom's something smaller and less visible. She hugs me from behind. I close my eyes and inhale lemon drops. She works in accounts payable at the Brucker Candy Company, and the citrus sugar gets into everything.

The February rain has frizzed her hair into a fuzzy mist around her face. She runs her fingers through it.

"Em back in school today?" she asks.

"We're fighting." My voice is tight. If I look at my mom I'll cry, so I shrug instead and click open random documents on my computer like I'm super busy and it's all cool. "She's not talking to me. It was a bad day."

"Oh dear! Oh honey, I'm sorry."

She sits next to me, the corners of her mouth down. I should have kept my mouth shut. Now she'll feel bad too, and where does that leave us?

"Even the best of friends have to fight sometimes. It will blow over, I'm sure. Can you spend more time with Jack?"

I don't answer. My eyes bulge trying to focus on the page I opened and not the scene at lunch with Jack—Alice rushing up behind us at the coffee cart all breathy and flushed, tippy-toe kissing him.

Before I could process what was happening she said, *Order me a latte? I'm texting with Em.* Whipped off Alice's tongue, Em's name came at me like a knife, handle over blade, flashing in the too bright midday light. Bull's-eye.

When I looked at Jack it was clear that I don't matter anymore. His whole face was hers, all eager-puppy, done with me.

Major internal bleeding.

I left without my coffee. It was either that or collapse on the corner like Keats on the Spanish Steps, only Keats coughed up actual blood and left behind all those crazy-good poems about love.

I'm dying of something different. Self-inflicted. I didn't stop when Jack called after me. Couldn't.

If Em didn't hate me, she'd say Jack doesn't matter, that if he's into the cabbage, he was never the guy for me. She'd say it's better, because now he and I can go back to being friends. And if none of that worked, she'd tell me to stop overthinking *everything* and hook up with someone already. Em's way ahead of me with the whole sex thing. She thinks I'm missing out, I need to be more relaxed. Like her. But I'm not like her. I tried her kiss-him-first-fall-in-love-later method once and I didn't like it. Maybe it sounds stupid, but if I kiss someone, I want it to mean something.

My mom tries another tack.

"Did you eat?"

She reaches past me for the mail. I have the parent letter about the junior class trip already safely hidden under my laptop. The trip's the last two weeks in May, right after juniors finish exams. Since it's not mandatory, they don't cover it for scholarship kids.

I tilt my head toward my laptop. "I was going to make us pasta, but I lost track of time."

"What's that?" She squints at my screen. "*Decompression sickness*, you're studying the bends?"

"For my Investigation."

Junior Investigation is a yearlong project they make us do at Bly. It's supposed to prepare us for college by pulling together curriculum across several subjects, which is another way of saying it's a boatload of student-directed work. I wish the assignment were to draw a comparative diagram of pain caused by the bends versus being iced out by your best friend. Contortions all around.

She sets down the mail and picks up one of the books I'm using for my paper like it's interesting. I can feel it in her silence, she wants to be here for me, but she doesn't know what to say. I slide a hair tie from my wrist and whip my hair into a braid. I'm trying not to feel so overwhelmed. But I am. So overwhelmed. Because she's starting to vibrate at a higher frequency, this hum she makes whenever she asks about Bly. Like, *The Future's Bright!* I'm no academic superstar, but I think she's still hoping I'll magically become a doctor and have a perfect life. Better than now. The thing is, I'm not good at The Future and Bly is marching us toward it like little well-educated soldiers. We're supposed to be confident in our intellectual ability, and if that's not the case, at least backed by the larger army of family support. Scholarship kids have two choices. Sink or swim. I'm not a strong swimmer.

My dad died of lung cancer when I was six. I don't really know how to feel about it, which sounds weird, because sad seems obvious, but it's hard to miss someone you don't remember. When I was younger I used to look at this little dirt-colored leather album my mom made of pictures from his funeral and burial, but a glossy flower-covered coffin doesn't offer much. My dad's more like an empty room than someone I lost. Anyhow, for a little while after he died I told people I wanted to be a doctor, and I think my mom's still riding on the idea.

"How do the bends fit in with *Empire Building and American Optimism*?" she asks, reading over my shoulder from the rubric for my Investigation.

On a map of my mother's moods, this one would be hiding between the softest blankets in our linen closet, building up static, ready to give an unexpected shock.

"The workers on the Brooklyn Bridge," I sigh. "They got the bends digging under the river."

What my mom doesn't understand is that at Bly I'm a dim bulb in a marquee made of sparklers. My grades in science are mediocre at best, never mind that the thought of becoming more intimate with the human body and its unpredictable fragility makes me want to run as fast and far in the opposite direction as my legs will carry me. If your dad can start to cough at thirty-nine, then die two days after his fortieth birthday in the most agonizing way possible, the task of ending that nightmare should be left to people who actually like science.

My class is crazy competitive, in a school that's crazy competitive, in a city that's the same. No college is going to pick me out of the bunch, offer me the money I need to go.

"Jack hasn't been over in a while. Everything okay between you two?"

Another knife. There are so many in me now, the blades clink when I walk.

"Jack's been invaded." I try to make it funny, because if you have a black sense of humor, maybe it is. Evie makes a mess of everything. Loses all her friends. Ha ha ha ha ha ha.

"How so?

"Total love drone. Hormonal pod-person." I'm on a roll. "Colonized by Alice Weir."

"Alice Weir?" my mom says. "Isn't she the one with the lunatic mother? The one always in fur?"

I nod.

"Poor Alice," my mom laughs.

I try to laugh with her, but it's a choke at best.

"I always thought Jack liked you," she says with a yawn. "Is he doing the Brooklyn Bridge for Investigation as well?"

Frustration washes over me. I know she's trying to connect, but all these little questions are hitting me like grit on a windy day.

"We all are! It's part of the *Investigation*."

I hang so much scorn on the word it practically scrapes the floor.

My mom's eyes cloud a minute, and a little muscle near the side of her mouth twitches. She looks so tired.

"The upside is no school on Friday." I force a smile. I want to erase the last few seconds between us. I made her feel bad. I hate it when I do that.

"No school? Why's that?" she asks.

"We tour the Emily Roebling House. Over in Brooklyn, by the bridge? Then we're supposed to *make use of public resources to further our research*." I use air quotes, then shrug. "Teachers probably just want a long weekend."

My mom stands and yawns. "Are you okay if I skip dinner? I'm ready for bed. Tomorrow's another day."

Sometimes I picture my dad's death like this train that tore into the station of our family, heavy, metallic, an unstoppable force. My mom's still running alongside it, pounding on the windows, trying to get him back. Or ride off with him. No wonder she's tired.

I force another smile. "Sure, yeah. No problem. Long day."

She looks at me a minute longer, the skin between her brows drawn together, then kisses me on the top of my head.

"Sleep helps a lot." She floats down the hall toward her bedroom. "We'll feel so much better tomorrow."

the dog of me

BLY'S SMALL AND EVERYWHERE I GO I run into Emma. When she stepped through me again this morning on the front steps of the school, I almost tripped over Jack and Alice limb-locked in a human knot. In case that didn't make me feel crappy enough, Mandi Iyer asked in the loudest voice possible if I was okay, the implication being, could I possibly be okay now that I'm an empty specter?

When the lunch bell rings I'm the first one out, head down and rushing through the cool air toward Wharton Playground. We have off-campus lunch, and Wharton Playground's the one place I'm guessing Em won't be, because we only go there together. It's far enough from Bly no one else makes the trek.

While I hurry there my next map project takes shape. The city without Em. It'll be like a new pair of glasses. The world more crisp, a summary of how it is now. If a French lady can map love, I can map absence, and then at least I'll know where I am.

One of the first maps I made was like that, a rough grid of our neighborhood with all the things I'm supposed to remember about my dad on it—the deli by the subway where we got mango smoothies, Bruno's barbershop, with its stacks of hot towels and high spinning chairs. The condo where we lived as a family, right around the corner from Wharton Playground. We lost our condo when he died because money was so tight. I made the map so my mom would never know how much I've forgotten.

The playground is hopping, a hive of toddlers buzzing around in daffodil-colored safety vests. I press my forehead against the heavy black gate and watch them. If I go in without Em, the park's mine, a first landmark on my new map. The metal latch on the gate lifts up with a clank and I push in.

Our favorite spot's an old, gouged-up wood table near the back tucked under a mottled sycamore. I drop down at it and pull out my sketchbook. If I soften my focus I can picture Emma stretched out next to me on the tabletop like she does while I hunch and draw. I run my fingers under the edge where we scratched our initials.

Still there. Smoother now. I made the ampersand so huge Em said our little *e*'s look like cross-legged kids under a Christmas tree. I open my sketchbook, but I can't find the right place to begin. I draw the sycamore. Places in the splotchy bark look like faces, so I work on those, starting to imagine it full of people like me, so lost and lonely they ended up in the tree. This map's already weird. A cautionary tale. Don't end up in the tree. I'm shading a pair of haunted eyes when Emma climbs up onto the picnic table and looks down on what I'm doing.

I keep my eyes on my work and act casual while I blacken it out. It's private, and I have to protect my ghostly tree.

Em nudges my journal slightly with the toe of her boot.

This is officially worse than hearing her in the hall. Tears needle the edges of my eyes. Alice is probably behind me. Jack. With my luck, they've been here awhile, watching me try to draw my way out of myself. I wrap one arm around my middle while the other keeps at its task, swinging my pencil like a graphite scythe.

Emma clears her throat.

"Stalk much?" I lift my eyes from my journal, the sketch safely hidden under a bajillion sparkling arcs.

She looks weird, her mouth drawn tight. There's no sign of Alice. She came alone.

Em paces the length of the table, then back, until she's immense over me, gazing down, her hair loose around her face. She looks sad and I miss her so acutely it makes my throat ache.

She kicks the edge of my journal again, lightly, but still. Anger shoots through me. Maybe this is how a fight starts. People poking each other's softest spots until blows are thrown, hair torn out. I straighten up and let my pencil drop. For a second I think I'll get up and leave. Walk away from her. Out of the park. But that's more her style. I'm not that brave or that dramatic. I look down at my dark page instead. My anger melts to tears.

"This is the longest fight we've ever had," I say, trying to keep my voice from wavering. "And I don't even really understand it." I mean my role in it, why I did it, but I can't bring myself to say that.

She makes this little noise like a hiss-filled laugh.

We stare at each other.

"I don't know what to say, Evie," she says finally. "You got me in *so* much trouble."

There's something in her voice, the sound of it, the way her eyes look empty toward me. I hear her words like, *we're not friends anymore.*

"I'm sorry," I plead. "I screwed up, this *once,* but you're acting like you *hate* me or something, like you've been dying to get out of our friendship and you finally found your chance to slip loose."

She looks around wildly a second. Shakes her head. "You wouldn't understand."

"Try me!"

"All you had to do was cover for me!" she yells, her voice raspy. She pops her hip out and mimics me texting her dad. "Yeah, hey Mr. Sullivan! Em's here with me but she's in the bathroom. I'll have her call you in a bit." Her voice is sharp, bitchy, doesn't sound like her.

A toddler boy chasing a red ball stops in his tracks near the table and stares at us a minute before running off.

"I couldn't reach you. Your phone was off."

I want to say I was out of minutes, but my heart's beating so hard I feel like it's going to knock me backward off the bench. I hate fighting.

"So *what.* You *lie.* I had it in airplane mode. I didn't want my dad tracking me. I was out in Bushwick with Ryan and those guys."

Ryan. All I've gotten out of her is that he works in a bar in the East Village and is supposedly a student. She's vague on the details.

"And *those guys*," I say, flat, a challenge.

Emma stares right back at me. Says nothing.

"Seriously, Em, what do you know about them?" The knuckly gray branches above her look like dark cracks in a painted blue sky. "I waited for you outside Dos Toros for over an hour. In the *cold*. I didn't know where you were. When you'd show up."

"I was coming," she snaps. "I was just late!"

"The Hanovers—I had to babysit . . ." It's a hollow defense. Emma's always been better than I am at making her position sound legitimate. I'm always apologizing for mine. But I did need the money. I always need the money.

She crosses her ankles and sits next to my sketchbook with a sigh.

"Do you have *any idea* what it's been like in my house since that night? The *minute* I walked in the door, my dad started yelling."

Emma stands up again and hops off the picnic table, pacing near the end of it. A little girl rolling around on a scooter sees the look on her face and clears out.

"I'm sorry you got in trouble," I try. I don't know how many times she wants me to say it, but I want this to end.

"Trouble?" She's incredulous. "I'm not in *trouble.* It's so far beyond that." She laughs, a cynical sound. Then she looks at me wearily. "You're such a—" She thinks a second, then shakes her head. "God! I was having fun! You should have covered for me whether I was late to meet you or not. That's how it works. I don't know, Evie. It feels like you wanted me to get caught."

She might be right. In the tiniest way.

"I'm such a what?" I ask.

"Chicken."

I put my head down on the table. It's true. I get scared easily, overwhelmed, but I fight it with all my might, and she knows it. She knows it's the part of myself I can't stand because it makes me feel like I'm like my mom, and my life is going to be small and lonely too.

I take a deep breath and look at her again.

"What is *wrong* with you?" I demand, surprising myself.

She's so mad right now, it can't all be because of me. Emma doesn't get like this often, crackling, explosive, but when she does you either duck and wait it out or go down like a bystander in a drive-by. Not this time. Not after this whole dead-to-me thing. I slip my sketchbook back in my bag with shaking hands.

"Me?"

My stomach lurches. I'm out of here.

"Em," I say, struggling with the zipper on my bag. "You got high with those guys? I mean, who *are they*? Do you know anything about them?"

Emma's like that—if it exists, she tries it. We vowed not to drink after the night Patrick died. If we hadn't been drunk ourselves, maybe we could have stopped him from racing out of there. But I'm the only one who kept the promise. I stick close to Em when she does stuff at parties.

"I would have covered for you," she says, her eyes narrow lasers. "I would have had like a thousand lies at the ready. I would cover for you no matter what, because *I trust you* to do what you want in your life, a feeling which obviously is not mutual." Her voice is small and quiet. She lets out an exasperated blast. "It's bigger than this." She shakes her head, as if she's about to tell me something but decides against it. "You have no idea what's going on right now."

"What?" I ask, my heart in my throat. "Please, tell me."

"Forget it." She closes her eyes. "You *know* my parents, Evie."

The thing is, she's right. I didn't trust her. And I do know her parents, how they are, especially since Patrick. But I can't bring myself to tell her she's acting wilder and it scares me. Or that I'm afraid I'm so boringly boyfriend-less she needs to find a new best friend.

Before I can say anything at all, Emma turns and walks out of the park.

I watch her go.

I try not to cry in public. This city is big and packed with people and for the most part we mind our own business, a survival thing, a way to share the tiny miles that hold us. And at first people try not to look at me, extend me a little privacy, but pretty soon they stop pretending. When you walk down the street crying like someone just ran over your dog right in front of your eyes, people can't help themselves, they stare. And Emma totally ran over the dog of me.

missing

THE NEXT MORNING EMMA, Jack, and Alice are in a happy knot at the end of my subway car. The train's packed with Bly people making the trek from Manhattan to Brooklyn—Ben, Jay, Stella, Mandi, and Vanessa; even Roman and his crew, but neither he nor Em seem to register the other's presence.

I shrink into the opposite end of the car, where I'll be invisible and a barrel-chested man crowds me in even tighter. It's so awkward there's no chance I'll fall asleep standing up. I was awake most of the night trying to figure out what it is Emma can't tell me and why.

In the scratched and filthy window my reflection and I whip through the dark tunnel. I look like the kind of girl who would fall for her first-grade earthworm compost partner. Jack and I took turns stirring the red wigglers and spreading their earthy castings in the Bly Lower School Sunshine Garden. It was so easy back then. The three of us had Friday night sleepovers until Jack's voice changed. Em's mom pulled the plug on those. She was smart to end them too, because that's when Jack turned magic. He slouched in late to assembly on the first day of ninth grade all lean and cute, like he'd spent time at science camp whipping up a hormonal transformation. Bye-bye, baby fat. Hello, strange new grace. His voice was deeper, his shoulders wide, and new angles of muscle stretched across his chest.

And the first thing he did was fall for Ming Li.

Emma said, *Don't sweat it. Ming will break him in.* Like he was a puppy, which he kind of is. Only it lasted *forever.* I liked Ming, but it got harder and harder to hide how I felt about Jack. Then Ming's mom got a job in San Francisco and they moved away.

Jack was free and he noticed me.

The train lurches and Mr. Barrel Chest steps on my foot. He apologizes, then raises an arm above my head to brace himself on the train car ceiling.

From beneath his man-scented armpit I see Alice's hand

in Jack's hair, twisting two tufts into devil horns. Jack swats her away and smooths it down again with a bright grin. Emma's laugh travels the length of the car, cutting through the track noise and the morning murmur.

Emma hates me and I blew it with Jack. I chew a hangnail until it bleeds.

When Jack put his hand up on the cupboard in his kitchen—it wasn't like it was my first kiss. That one happened the night Emma's brother died. We were at a party on the beach and I barely knew the guy. Emma set it up. *It's no big deal,* she said. *It's just lips on lips. Jump in, let your body be your guide.*

The guy was the friend of some guy Emma liked and they brought us to this senior party out on Montauk. We drank foamy beer in the dunes, and even though he was kind of cute, when he leaned in his lips were like pushy worms, beer-cold and slick. I kept waiting for the sexy rush Em said I'd have, but his breath made me sick. No sexy rush. I need to like the guy first. When I tried to pull away, he gripped me tighter, pushing a hand up my shirt and his tongue down my throat.

Then Patrick and Mamie got into their huge fight, crashed their car, and nothing else really mattered. The relative importance of a miserable first kiss kind of shrinks when your friend's just lost her brother.

So when Jack leaned over me in his kitchen with that look in his eyes I laughed in his face—nerves, I guess. And now he's with Alice.

Barrel Man shifts again, leaving me exposed, but it doesn't matter. Emma's laughing about something and the rest of those guys are all talking to one another, not looking down here, anyway. To them no one's missing.

voorse means vhat?

I HANG BACK AT THE SUBWAY so I don't have to walk down the hill behind them all. It's strange to be down here. The last time we came to this part of Brooklyn we were with Patrick and Mamie because Mamie wanted pizza from Grimaldi's. We hit the Ice Cream Factory before walking back across the Brooklyn Bridge. Mamie took a lot of photos that day. I don't think I ever saw her without a camera. I'd love to see those pictures now, the ones of Em and me, of Patrick with the river behind him. Forever ago.

By the time I make it to the Roebling House gift shop the Bly School group is out the door. I rush to the ticket counter to try for a spot in the next tour.

The guy at the register signs me up, prints my pass, and points to another tour guide standing by the door in a pool of morning sun.

He has a black eye and a split lip and he's sort of cute.

No. Scratch that.

He's totally cute.

He looks like he might be about my age, but he's dressed like a visitor from the 1880s, so it's kind of hard to tell. He's wearing high-waisted dark pants with suspenders, a rough collarless shirt, and a wool cap pulled down over what appears to be a nice mess of straw-colored hair.

He scans through a list on an iPad, then checks a watch he pulls out of his pocket. Awesome anachronistic clash. He hasn't looked up at me but I get the feeling he's about to. I turn and wander the creaky floors of the gift shop, pretending to be interested in a bird's-eye map book. I could do one for that TeenART thing. Call it Bird's-eye View of Confusing Conflict and then sketch an aerial view of New York with tiny trash-can fires on random corners.

The bell on the door jingles and a big group of tourists fills the place with their language. German, maybe. I glance over at them, with their backpacks and travel books, and when I do, the guide rocks onto his toes and catches my eye. I look away, but not before a smile sneaks its way across my face. He announces the tour. I blush and walk over to hand him my ticket. He gives me a bright half smile. I'm about to turn away when he looks at me again, in that way people do when they're not trying to hide that they're checking you out. I've seen Emma get this look a thousand times. A thrill ripples through me until I realize this is probably just part of his routine. He holds the shop door open and we all file out into the cobbled street.

"Welcome to 1883. My name is Theo Gray," he says in a loud, clear, theatrical voice, "illegal pugilist and oldest son of Francis Gray and Hannah Nolan. I'm a typical Irish immigrant for my time. Since the death of my father on our crossing to America, I've worked on the bridge you see behind you and am the sole breadwinner for my family."

Emma would make fun of this, say, *Okaaay . . . the tour's conducted in character.* Or maybe not. With his looks, she'd be up by his elbow, blinking at him brightly, finding a way to meet up with him later.

His brogue is so convincing I decide that barring actual time travel, he's at least a recent Irish transplant. The Germans are studiously attentive. I wonder if they can understand his accent. We follow Theo Gray down to the Fulton Ferry Landing. He asks us to imagine it before the bridge was built.

"Brooklyn is hills and farms. Robert Fulton's steam ferry

transports thousands to Manhattan, weather permitting. But I'm here to build the future."

We follow him to a small wooden lean-to near the base of the bridge. He holds the door open while we take turns peering inside.

Work pants and shirts similar to his dangle like tired ghosts from hooks lining the walls. Long wooden benches run either side of the room, rows of rough-hewn leather work boots beneath them.

"The bridge changes everything. Dubbed the 'eighth wonder of the world' when it goes up, it's the tallest structure in the Western Hemisphere. It marks the beginning of what becomes the multiborough city of New York."

He closes the door to the hut and scrambles onto a huge block of sand-colored stone. The high morning sun highlights his profile. The bruise under his eye blooms brilliant blue and I spot another along his jawline. The light catches a thread on his split lip. Actual stitches. Not part of his act.

"The blocks of granite that form the towers and support the suspension span must be built on bedrock. Hundreds of us dig under the murk." He points to the dark river. "The caisson we work in is meant to be a pressurized, oxygen-filled, watertight chamber." He looks grave. "It is not. It's a hellish place with such poor pressurization we get earaches and pains in the head that are unbearable."

He pulls several plastic laminated images from his back pocket and passes them around. Pen-and-ink line drawings show bridge workers digging in a small dark space, swinging pickaxes and pushing wheelbarrows.

Theo raises his voice, startling me slightly, and claps his hands over his ears, his face twisted in a grimace. "Some of us tie roasted onions to our ears with rags to ease the pain. Others twist and drop, so contorted we can't straighten them out. We call this caisson sickness the bends." He pauses for effect, then lowers his voice. "Some find themselves paralyzed . . . or worse."

A German with a massive sandy mustache breaks the spell.

"And voorse means vhat?" Like he can't take the suspense.

I giggle. Impossible not to.

Theo flashes a quick wink in the direction of my giggles before turning a solemn face to his questioner. "Ah, well, they died, sir. *Sie starben*."

A laughing fit surges through me, an unstoppable wave. I turn away from the group and look out at the water while biting the inside of my cheek. Hard. The breeze off the East River smells good, like wet pennies. I'm glad I lost my class. I'm actually enjoying myself.

The sun is high and too hot for winter. I loosen my scarf,

senses on overdrive. Em calls it squirrel-jitters. She says it's how I act when I flirt, which is not, for obvious reasons, often. But right now the air has the crackle it gets when you like someone and have the feeling they like you back.

My hand floats up like it's got a mind of its own, then I pull it down when I realize I'm about to ask if he's one of the men who survives. I swallow another wave of giggles. Theo glances my way, but the Germans are full of questions. One guy wants to point out that the first engineer, Roebling's father, was a German immigrant himself. Another man steps up close to Theo and, squinting at him, asks if the black eye is real. Theo laughs and says with a grin, "Aye. More on that in a minute."

He turns back to the rest of us. "Any other questions?" he asks, shooting me this look for one more beat.

My pulse does a happy dance.

"Okay, then follow me back this way." He waves us in the direction of the Roebling House. "We'll have a look inside an average worker's apartment."

Right as we get to the door of the building, Emma, Jack, and Alice's group files out.

Jack's wound himself around Alice, his mouth near her neck, but when he spots me he comes up for air.

"Courage," he whispers as he passes by. "So, so boring."

exit from the gift shop

AFTER THE TOUR, THEO BRINGS US back to the gift shop. Jack and Ben are at the register buying candy. Em and Alice are in the middle of a Bly throng laughing at something *so* super funny. It sounds fake, but apparently that's the hallmark of this new best-friendship. I fight the urge to rush out. I'd have to pass them if I did, so I beeline for the back of the shop and squeeze behind a pyramid of books.

"Good morning, Veddy Most Sexy Lady." Mandi slinks an arm around my neck and purrs in my ear in a fake Russian accent.

I jump. She laughs.

"I didn't see you there," I whisper.

People are a little scared of her because in addition to being at the top of our class, she does stand-up at all-ages open mic nights, and no one's ever really sure if she's going to roast them in the hallway or not.

"Why are you whispering?" she loud-whispers back.

"Sore throat," I lie, like a freak. Time to bolt.

"Dude, bummer day to be sick!" Mandi says, kind of loud. "Did Em tell you? Everyone's gonna hang in the park after the library since it's so damn nice out."

I shake my head and move away from her.

"Feel better, Ramsey!"

I rush toward the exit.

Em and Alice have moved over to a rack of Brooklyn Bridge–inspired necklaces and earrings. Jack's outside on the sidewalk talking to Ben and Jay, but I can blow past him.

I'm contemplating Mandi's "everyone" and how, without Em, it doesn't seem to include me, when a woman with two sticky-looking kids in a double stroller pushes in through the shop doors, blocking my escape. I back up near some *1917 Votes for Women* letterpress posters to let her pass, but before she does, the kid in the front catches my eye, winds her arm back, and chucks her cup at me. Full-on hurls it. Like I'm a hoop and she's gonna sink it.

Any normal person would jump out of the way, but I lunge, try to catch it instead. The cup grazes my fingers and the kid's eyes get huge. She looks like she's about to cheer, like this is the event that's going to *make* her morning, make up for however long she's been stuck in that stroller, and for a second I think I've got it too, disaster averted, but then the waxy paper sides compress between my fingers and the lid pops off with a *smuck!* In slo-mo the cup collapses in my grip. A plume of cherry soda geysers from it, dousing me from my chin to my waist.

It's so, so cold.

I look down. The thin blouse I'm wearing is now transparent and glued to my bra, clinging to the blue lace underneath. The right sleeve of my coat is soaked and there's soda in my pocket too.

Before I can even react, the kid laughs. Hard. From the sound of it, this is the funniest thing in her life so far. Her mom's oblivious. The other beast in the back of the stroller is wailing, and she's bent over her, too busy to notice what the dastardly cackler in the front just did.

I stand there stupid another second and gape down at my wet chest.

Thanks to the din in the gift shop, the murmuring Germans, and the general clatter of more arrivals, the embarrassment of this disaster appears to be all mine. I could probably stand very, very still and drip-dry if I wanted. If Em and Alice weren't six people away with their backs to me.

"Holy shit!"

Theo comes climbing over the edge of the stroller, one long leg after the next until he's by my side. The woman glares at him and pushes her kids away from us.

"I saw that go down. Nice save. Thanks!" he says, with no trace of an accent. His eyes dart a millisecond to my chest, then quickly shift away.

Theo points over my shoulder. I glance behind me to the suffragist posters.

"Not a drop on 'em! We got those in last night. The last set sold out in two days."

He's right. They're unmarred. My chest, on the other hand, looks like I lost a paintball battle. I curve my shoulders forward to try to loosen the fabric's sticky cling.

Theo sizes me up with a slow grin. "So, I bet that feels awesome." He has a crooked eyetooth, and it sticks out a little over the next. "Your next tour is definitely free."

The way he's obviously avoiding looking at my chest makes me blush brighter. This is not happening. I glance over at Emma, but she and Alice are oblivious, half turned and huddled, laughing at something on one of their phones. I turn back to Theo.

"Um, yeah." He blinks at me a second. Clears his throat. "Okay. Uh, *sprechen Sie Deutsch*?"

One brow shoots up high, his eyes startlingly light.

He thinks I'm German.

"I don't know what that means?" I say, suddenly fighting back another laugh. This is all so absurd and so totally something that would happen to me that I'm scared if I start laughing, I might never stop. I roll my shoulders forward even more. I probably look demented, but my shirt's freezing cold and revealing much more of me than anyone's ever seen.

He laughs for me. A big open sound. "Sorry! You were so quiet I thought maybe you were German."

I shake my head and delicately pinch the wet fabric away from my skin, but there's this weird suction action, and when I pull it away in one place it clings more in another.

"C'mon," Theo says, wrapping a hand around my wrist. "You can't go out like that. I'll get you another shirt."

Theo weaves us through the crowd and over toward a door behind the ticket counter.

"Hey, Jeremy," he says to the guy at the register. "We need serious paper towels on the floor over by the posters. I'm running upstairs for a few. You got this?"

Jeremy nods.

"Excuse us, coming through," Theo repeats, and people shift to let us pass.

His fingers on my wrist. I must be blasting the place with pheromones. Em's eyes are on me now.

I meet them. I can't help it. It's a reflex.

Theo's hand is a distractingly hot circle around my wrist and I need her to see it too. I glance at it, then back to her face, widening my eyes at her with a slight smile, like, *What crazy happy thing is happening*?

And then, even though we're looking right at each other with no one between us, she acts like I'm not there. It makes her look blind, the light in her eyes gone out, like I'm nothing more than a minor disturbance, a mirage, a flicker in the clarity.

I try to shake it off, pretend that didn't just happen, focus on the heat in Theo's fingers, the angle of his shoulders in front of me as we pass through a door behind the register marked "Private."

other people's families

I FOLLOW THEO UP a narrow staircase. We rise into a sun-bright apartment. Unlike the narrow tenements on the other side of the building, this space is opened up wide, many of its windows facing the Brooklyn Bridge.

"This is your place?" I ask.

"Yeah." He smirks. "Brace yourself for Gray family chaos."

"Can you own a historical site?" I marvel at piles of rugby gear and tennis rackets and towers of books.

"The Roeblings' building no longer stands," he says. "When my mom started poking into the history of our building, she discovered it was here back then, so she decided to bring it back to life."

"Kind of like the Tenement Museum."

"Exactly."

The apartment's a colorful explosion of mismatched furniture. On the floor to my right, a battered marble bust lies on its shoulder next to a rickety upright piano. The piano keys are chipped, and I wonder who thundered across them until the bust shimmied over the edge. Before I can ask, a small boy slips out from a blanket tent under the dining table and bounds across the space to us. His hair's a straw nest on his head and his blue glasses are crooked.

"Theo! Guess what?"

He spots me and stops.

"Who are you?"

"Alo, manners." Another voice comes from the far side of the sunny space. A woman stands working at the kitchen counter. There's so much to see in here I didn't notice her at first. Her eyes land on me.

"Well, hello." Her face is wide and open like Theo's and framed with what is obviously the family hair.

"Hi," I say, tentative.

She pushes the bridge of a clunky pair of tortoiseshell glasses up her nose with a potato-covered knuckle and comes over to us, wiping her hands on a dish towel. She's baking something savory.

"I'm Margaret Gray. Theo, introduce us?"

"Yeah, sorry . . . Mom, this is . . ." He looks at me, furrows his brow. "I didn't catch your name." He turns back to his mother, "she's *not* German."

"Evie Ramsey," I laugh, plucking at my shirt to unstick it from my chest again before I step forward to shake her hand. There's a small bit of potato on the side of her nose.

"What happened to you?" Alo grimaces like I'm covered in blood.

"Shark attack," I say casually. It's the kind of thing that makes the Hanover twins crack up.

Alo's more circumspect. He raises his brows at his brother, then turns to me, skeptical.

"Are you Theo's friend-friend or are you a *Lindsay friend*?" he asks, hand on his chin like a mini professor.

"That's enough out of you, blockhead," Theo says, lightly ruffling his hair. Alo takes a swing at him, but Theo laughs and holds him off with a straight arm, palm flat against Alo's forehead, while the kid whirls his fists in a frenzy, just out of reach.

Margaret shakes her head at them both, then turns to me and takes in the full state of my shirt and coat.

"Don't freak out." Theo sidesteps Alo and leans against the piano. "A kid in a stroller threw a soda."

Margaret gives Theo a horrified look. "In the shop?"

"Nothing got wrecked," he says. "Evie caught most of it. She saved Jonathan's posters too. We need to mop down there, but otherwise all's cool."

"Well! I guess we owe you a thank-you!" Margaret says, looking at me like she's sizing me up. "I'm sure we have something here you can put on. Theo, run upstairs and find Evie a shirt and some kind of jacket, okay? Laundry goes out this afternoon. I'll add yours in with our order. I hope they can get that terrible red dye out of your beautiful coat!"

"Oh, really, that's not—"

"Nonsense! Your things will be ruined if someone doesn't get to them right away." She grabs a notepad and a crayon from the dinner table and hands them to me. "Write down your address and Theo will bring them to you when they're done."

"If that's cool with you." Theo looks kind of embarrassed.

If I give her my clothes I'll see Theo again.

I smile gratefully. "Yes, that would be great. Thank you so much!"

While I crayon out my address, Margaret Gray fingers the sticky wool on my arm, making a *tsk* sound. "I hope they can save this lovely coat. If they can't, we'll reimburse you, of course."

I look down at my sleeve. I hope they can save it too.

The coat's my mom's, and I only grabbed it this morning because the last time I borrowed it, Jack told me the blush-colored wool looked great with my hair.

She takes the paper with my address on it and hands it to Theo. "I'll lose this," she says. "Hang on to it for me." She turns and points to Alo. "You. Run to the bathroom and brush your teeth. The unschoolers will be here any second if they're not down there already. And you"—she turns back to Theo—"how was that tour? It wasn't too big? You're still feeling okay? No headaches or anything?" She leans toward her son and inspects the meaty-looking bruise near his eye.

"Jesus, Mom. Enough." He shrugs his head away from her, his face closing up, eyes gone distant.

"Okay, then, a few things."

Theo groans.

"Shush. It's not much. There's a new pile of dirt in the basement near the back chimneys. Sweep it before tonight? Film people are coming to look at the chairs down there and I want it clean before they come. Also, if you have time, check the roof. They're talking about using it."

She eyes me a second. Shakes her head. "We have to rent the place out. Getting Porter to pay for repairs is an impossible task!" She laughs, making this exasperated face like I know who Porter is or what the heck she's talking about. I laugh too, because it seems rude not to.

Theo looks at me a little surprised, and then I feel stupid.

Alo races out of the bathroom, a toothpaste ring around his mouth, and grabs his mother's hand. "Let's go!"

"Go wipe your mouth and let me get the shepherd's pie." She rushes back to the counter to retrieve a low dish with a golden crown and covers it with a linen towel.

"Hurry, hurry, hurry!" Alo bounces on his toes. "I wanna get down there!"

"And Theo," Margaret says, passing us, "I told your father to bring the rakes with him when he comes. He should pull in by three or four."

"Great. Thanks, Ma."

"Thank you, Mommy," a voice mimics in falsetto.

A sleepy-looking guy steps into the living room from the back stairs. He has insane hair and deep pillow lines on his face, but neither is as remarkable as the fact that he's shirtless and wearing only what appear to be a pair of seen-better-days navy boxers.

He freezes when he spots me, then scratches his head.

Theo bends over and explodes with laughter.

"Dude," he says, collapsing back against the piano, which emits a plinky complaint. "Roll in late last night?"

"Oh! For heaven's sake, Lazarus!" Theo's mom says, turning at the stairs. "Pants!"

"Pants, Lazzy!" Theo mimics his mom in a mocking tone.

Lazarus has the same wonky nose as Theo and solid jaw, but he looks older. His top lip dips in a sharp bow. Instead of hay-colored hair and light eyes, his are both dark, and his skin is olive brown. He runs a hand through his hair and blinks at me a second, as if I'm the startling vision and not him.

"Shit, Ma," he says, ignoring Theo's laugh. "No one prepped me for company."

I look at my feet, my face hot again.

"Welcome home, Spazzy," Theo laughs as Lazarus heads back up the stairs.

"Theo!" Margaret shouts on her way down. "Quit mocking your brother and get some clothes for Evie!"

"On it," he laughs. He steers me to a chair at the dining room table. "Back in a minute." His hand's warm on my shoulder.

like a dream I don't remember

I WOULD GIVE ANYTHING FOR EM to be here, to see Theo, his crazy family, this incredible apartment overlooking the bridge. But if Em were here, none of this would happen to me. He'd see her first and she'd be the one flirting.

Because Theo's cute. Empirical fact.

I touch a spiky tower atop a glue-and-toothpick model of a pretty out-there-looking building on the table near me. I'm trying to absorb as much as I can about other people's families so I'll know how to do it myself someday—make a noisy, bright one like this, like Em's used to be *BPD*—before Patrick died.

BPD, we were innocent. Even me, even though my dad died. The two deaths don't even compare. My dad's is like a dream I know I had but can't remember.

It feels like Patrick went missing. I imagine papering the city with posters of his face, I can still see him so clearly. He and Em have the same dark hair, and I don't know how to put this on a poster, but when he came in from soccer all wet and sweaty, he smelled like mud and onions. He taught me how to stand on my head by letting me kick my legs against his shoulders over and over again until he had bruises and I wasn't scared for him to step away.

Then he stepped away.

BPD, Mrs. Sullivan drove us up the Hudson to pick apples, go sledding, or poke around sleepy towns full of whispering trees and wooden houses big enough for families who fill all the seats around the table. Mrs. Sullivan is very can-do, the opposite of my mom. She's never gone to lie down in the middle of the day.

When Patrick got his license, he took us places. Mamie made a list of upstate swimming holes and we tested them all. The water was usually icy and I'm not much of a swimmer, but driving around with those guys, I felt free. We don't have a car. My mom grew up in the city. She says driving's one of those things she thought my dad would teach her. I'm going to have to teach myself.

Upstairs, a door opens, then closes with a bang. Low voices laugh. I pull out my sketchbook and sketch a few details. Piles of books, the lumpy couch and sagging armchairs.

"Casing the place?" Lazarus asks, startling me. He looks over my shoulder. "I can help you with the location of the valuables. There are none."

I blush and flip my book shut. Then I try to casually curl forward to loosen the front of my shirt. The fabric's starting to dry and stiffen.

He raises his hands. "You should see how red your face is right now," he laughs. "It matches your shirt. Theo's such a sucker for shy girls."

I shove my sketchbook into my bag and avoid his eyes. He's the one who came down in his underwear. My flush deepens.

He stretches, yawns, and heads for the kitchen. "Coffee?"

"No thanks."

A few seconds later, he lopes back holding a steaming mug. "So, how do you know Theophilus, boy genius?"

I'm not even entirely sure what he just said. I stare at him a second.

"Come again?"

He laughs.

"Lazarus, Theophilus, and Aloysius." He ticks their

names off on his fingers. "Gray kids develop a certain strength of character. In case you didn't notice, this family's super weird."

"Oh. Um, he led my tour," I say. "And then a kid tossed a soda at me."

He pulls out a chair and sits with his coffee. Stares at me a second. He's cute, even though I can't tell if he's nice or not. Emma is missing out.

"Well," he says, leaning back and taking a sip, "you look like a decent person, so here's a heads-up. Theo tests people. And he's a harsh judge. Most people fail."

I can't tell if he's teasing or not. I shrug. "I don't really know him. Boy genius?"

Laz laughs. "Ha, yeah, and that topic's off-limits. So are questions about our family, like why I'm brown when they're all so very white."

"Thanks for the intel," I say, feeling even more awkward. "As soon as he gives me a dry shirt, I'll belly-crawl out of here so I don't trip any wires."

This earns me a huge laugh. He changes his voice to sound like a carnival barker. "Home-school prodigy. Finished high school at thirteen. Polyglot."

He rocks back in his chair, looking smug.

"Polyglot," I say, trying to remember what the word means. "Okay . . ."

"I'm messin' with you. But he is a superfreak."

"You sound jealous."

Before he can answer that, Theo steps into the room, surprising us both.

"Fuck *you*, Laz," he says.

He tosses me some clothes, then glares silently at his brother, his hands clenched in fists.

"Bathroom's over there." He cocks his head to a door near the stairs.

I go to the bathroom, but not before I see Theo stride around the table and give his brother a fast, hard punch to the shoulder.

Laz winces, but it doesn't shake his smile.

I lock the bathroom door.

flight after flight

WHEN I STEP OUT OF THE BATHROOM, the apartment's empty.

It's probably for the best. This T-shirt's humongous. Almost like a dress. It says "Don't Believe Everything You Think" across the front in small, plain letters. I fold my sticky shirt and coat neatly on the far end of the table and grab my bag. The navy hoodie he gave me is only slightly smaller and lined with supersoft fuzzy cotton. I zip it up. Bold block letters across the back spell out "Gleason's Gym."

Someone bangs around overhead.

I walk to the base of the stairs.

"Um, bye!" I call up, trying to sound like someone cute,

or amused maybe, anything but the lonely-person feeling overtaking me. "Thanks!"

"One sec!" Theo calls back.

He thunders down less than a minute later dressed like a person from this century, in a sweatshirt, track pants, and high-tops. A heavy-looking gym bag is slung across his body. I smile at him. I can't help it. He's indisputably hot, and some of my loneliness burns off me like morning fog.

He smiles back, but it's not like before. Something's changed. It's a regular smile. Not at all flirty. Maybe I imagined it earlier—I'm no Emma. The loneliness storms back. I try to hide how embarrassed I am.

"A or the F?" he asks, rushing past me, pulling a set of keys from a bowl on top of one of the many bookshelves, and grabbing a skateboard leaning behind a pile of shoes.

"Huh?"

"The subway. Are you taking the A or the F?"

"Um, I was thinking of walking back, across the bridge?"

As soon as I say it, I feel stupid. What am I doing, trying to impress him, like I'm talking to Theo the Irish bridge-builder guy, the one who winked at me? That was acting. I always fall for the story.

The real Theo pats his back pocket for his wallet, makes a face, and swears under his breath while he starts digging in the pockets of the coats hanging on the hooks by the stairs. He pulls out a MetroCard.

"But it'll probably take too long," I prattle on. "Um, so the A, I guess?"

The vibe has totally changed. Theo's so hurried it's obvious I'm outstaying my welcome. The vast gap between what I imagined could happen and the reality of how it's actually going is so big I am lost in it. Stupid imagination.

"Too bad," he says, his back to me. "I have to go toward the F."

He thunders down the narrow steps and we cut through the crowded shop—out of the dream and back into the real world.

Before I have time to worry about whether or not Em's still here, I spot her outside, leaning against the plate-glass window. She's staring at something on her phone with this lost expression. Her long hair has worked itself loose from its twist and wisps of it flutter around her neck in the light breeze.

Theo flings open the door, nearly jingling the bells off their springs, only pausing long enough to hold it for me.

Em straightens and turns, this look on her face like she's been waiting for me, like she wants to tell me something, but when she sees me with Theo, her expression brightens. He rushes out, but before he gets past her, she playfully pops out an elbow and catches him in the side.

"Hey," she laughs, her voice high and thin, "you work here, right? I just wanted to say this place is so great." She's using flirt voice.

He looks back and without breaking his stride, beams at her, bright as a stage light. Even for people in a breakneck hurry, there's time to flirt with Emma.

She's trying to hurt me. She saw me with him in the shop before, I know she did, but still, I slow a second, because her expression doesn't match her words. The pale skin around her eyes is all pink and blotchy, like she's been crying.

I glance around for Alice, but she's nowhere. Maybe they fought? I allow myself a millisecond of happiness at the thought. But Alice is probably in the bathroom and Em's out here waiting for her. The other Bly people are gone. I feel bad for her, even though the way she's making a play for Theo makes me fall down flight after flight of stairs inside myself.

I turn and follow Theo. He heads up the block, walking so fast I almost trip trying to keep up. Once we're near the corner and hopefully out of Emma's line of sight, I slow down. He's not acting the least bit interested, and what am I doing? Chasing him?

Theo notices, turns to see why I'm not there. "Sorry, I'm kind of late." He stops and drops his skateboard to the ground and puts a foot on it. Shakes his head. "Also, my brother's a total dick."

I shift my bag to my other shoulder. A double-decker tour bus wheezes past, wrapping us in a hot cloud of exhaust.

"I thought he was cool." I shrug.

Theo flashes that smile again, brilliant, vacant. "Yeah, well. Thanks for saving those posters. Sorry about the hassle."

"I liked you better with your Irish accent," I say, surprising myself. It's the kind of thing Emma would get away with. I'm not sure I can. Whatever. I rake my fingers through my hair and tie it into a bun. Game over. I concede defeat to the stingy gods of romance. Or to Emma and her flirty voice, or to the other girls Theo's brother says he's a sucker for. Spoils to the victors. I'd rather keep my dignity.

But Theo's not rushing anymore. He keeps his eyes on me.

I ignore the shaky thrill building in my stomach, and to break the tension I dig in my bag for my glasses and a book to read on the train.

Theo's still inspecting me, so I look up. I can't help it. His face breaks into a smile. Eye-crinkles at the corners and everything. A real one. Is it possible to fall in love over a smile?

"Nice glasses." He reaches behind my ear and wiggles

the back of my glasses so they jump up and down on my face.

I pull my head back and laugh, feeling strangely weak after his palm brushes my cheek.

He leans toward me. "Forget that stupid shit my brother said."

"Yes, sir," I say in a mocking tone, straightening my glasses.

"Whatcha got there?" He turns over the book I'm holding.

"*The Great Bridge*." I read the title, suddenly super glad this is the book I brought. Emma has pointed out more than once how super dorky my obsession with Madeleine L'Engle's *The Moon by Night* is, but she also doesn't know how much time I've spent imagining Vicky Austin's family was mine. It's pretty dog-eared.

"Oh, of course," Theo says, scanning the cover. "You were here for that school project."

I nod.

"So, Bly, then?"

I nod again.

Theo keeps staring at me, bouncing a little on his toes, so I straighten my shoulders and stare right back, fanning the pages of the huge book with a nervous thumb.

"Well then, see you later," he says, smile fading. He tips

his head toward the intersection. "I turn here. The A's up the hill. Thanks again for saving the day."

"Yep."

Before I can think of a brilliant line or even manage a decent smile, he gives the board a kick and sails off down the block, away from me.

Evie Ramsey, world's biggest flirt flop.

I skip the train and hike up to the bridge after all. I could use a long walk. For a second I hope Emma's behind me, that she saw us talk. But I don't turn to look. She made it clear in the shop. I'm dead to her.

something else

IT TAKES ME AN HOUR AND A HALF, but I walk all the way to Emma's block. She didn't look like she was up for the park, and I have to know what's really going on, the thing she wouldn't tell me yesterday, what she was maybe ready to say today. But no one's home. I look down the block. Emma doesn't keep stuff to herself. If anyone knows what's going on with her now, it's probably Alice.

I stand on the sidewalk a full five minutes before I can make myself ring the bell. I don't know why I'm scared. She's probably out with Jack. Besides, coming to her is not defeat. It's being a true best friend, stepping up to end this fight, to find out what's making Em so upset, if anything, beyond what I did.

I climb up the stoop and ring the bell. It's one of the old ones, a time-worn creamy button in the middle of a golden circle. An actual bell warbles somewhere deep inside.

I straighten up, toss my shoulders back. I'm sweating this for nothing. Alice is probably at the library like a good cabbage, or at the park with Jack and everyone else.

A hand parts the lace curtains on the glass door. Alice opens up. She looks as surprised to see me as I am to be standing here.

"Evie. Hi?"

Her face is flushed and my stomach sinks. Jack's in there. She's all pink in the face because I'm interrupting . . . something.

I close my eyes a second and try not to laugh. I'm so naïve.

Yesterday Jack did this huge stretch in Holmes's overheated seminar room, his shirt lifting up, and I saw his stomach, the delicious plane of it, flat and pale. It took me like ten minutes to pay attention to anything else.

"What's up? Do you need something?" Alice asks.

I force myself to speak despite the scene replaying in my head.

"Emma."

"She's not here." Her expression changes. Alice eyes me like she knows why I've come, fidgets with a button near the bottom of her sweater. "Um, didn't she find you? She was waiting for you at the Roebling House."

"I know," I say. Tears prick the corners of my eyes. I take a deep breath. "What's going on with her?" I demand. Before she can answer I add, "I mean, obviously she's super pissed, but it can't be only because . . ." I swallow, shift my bag to my other shoulder. "You know. I know you do. Did something else happen?"

"You didn't talk to her?"

Standing in the doorway at the top of her elegant stoop, Alice has the upper hand. She could totally drag this out, lord it over me, enjoy it. The house is dark behind her, but I've been in there. She's an only like me, but their place isn't sad like mine so much as it's cluttered, in the way rich people's houses can be, full of art, shabby beauty, inherited furniture, and all the weird stuff Alice's mom likes, including a seven-foot-tall stuffed bear her grandfather shot. Kind of crazy, actually. I couldn't live with that poor bear standing there, but it doesn't stop me from feeling inadequate right now, like I don't really have a right to be here, like I'm a pauper begging at her door, *please, Miss, a scrap of information?*

Desperate times. I'm locked out from Em and Alice has the key.

But she doesn't seem to sense any of this. Instead, she shifts her weight to her other foot and chews the corner of her lip, still looking surprised to see me. Finally she utters one word.

"Mamie."

Not what I was expecting.

I take a quick step back and almost fall down the stoop.

"Mamie?" I repeat, dumbfounded.

Mamie Wells. Patrick's girlfriend. The person in the car with him when he died. We idolized her. I wanted to be her sister. She took me to lunch once, just the two of us, no Emma, no Patrick. We were alike, she said, both alone with single moms. She told me people with siblings don't get it, and we could stick together. I wanted to *be* her. She and Patrick were my blueprint for what it's supposed to be like when you go out with someone. They were a master class in cool, and when I was around them I thought it might rub off on me, whatever magic they had, how cute they were together, their connection. It's super hard to hate her, but we do, because Emma says it's her fault, that night, everything, it's Mamie's fault her brother died.

"Mamie." I say her name again, still stunned.

"Yep." Alice nods, solemn.

"She's back?" Mamie moved away after the accident. No one saw her again, not even at the funeral.

"I guess."

"What about her?"

Alice shakes her head and takes a step back.

"That you'll have to ask Em."

Then she closes the door, the lock clicking like punctuation.

arctic fox

WHAT ABOUT MAMIE? And why can't Emma tell me?

I'm facedown on the couch, Marcel wheezing next to me, nearly pushing me off the edge. I'm trying to get it together, to figure out how to go over there and ask Emma what's going on.

I tell myself I'm not my mom. This is simple. I need to find her, make her talk to me. I don't move. Maybe it's from thinking about the night Patrick died, but I'm immobile. Inert. Maybe inertia's what's got my mom too. Before that thought sinks in, the door buzzer grinds to life and Marcel startles, executing his parquet-floor leap, skid, and scramble.

Theo Gray is the last person I expect to see when I stick my head out of the elevator and look across the narrow lobby of our building, but there he is, squinting at the panel, pressing our number again.

I freeze. My face has an imprint from the couch upholstery on it and I'm wearing my dad's ratty Yale Law sweatshirt. It makes me look like an apple on legs, but I swear it still smells like him. Ghosts might manifest as scents, you never know.

Theo must hear the elevator, because he looks up, his face breaking into a smile. His hair's an even wilder mess than it was this morning.

He's seen me. It was so much easier when Mr. Gutierrez still worked here. He was more than a doorman, he was our door grandpa. According to my mom he spent forty years of his life in this small mirrored lobby, captain of the ship, walking Mrs. Cohen's dog, Dominic, for her in the snow, reminding me to wear hats in the cold. Then the building changed hands, Mr. G. retired, and we got buzzers. Ours sounds like an electric shock, and the intercom is worthless. Mom says we'll grow old waiting for them to fix it.

I slide forward in thick socks and unlock the flimsy glass door between us.

"Um, hi?" I say, a little confused by his sudden appearance.

"Hi . . ." He thrusts a warm, cloth-wrapped bundle at me.

"What's this?" I ask, taking it.

"Colcannon," he says. "My mom was going to send a shepherd's pie, but she wasn't sure if you guys ate meat, so she sent this instead."

I lift a corner of the cloth and a little steam escapes. Buttery mashed potatoes with what looks like leeks. My mouth waters.

"And that's one of the dish towels we sell in the store—it's for you—you can keep it."

"Wow, thanks," I say. For some reason I'm always embarrassed when people give me stuff. I feel like I should have something to offer in return. "How'd you know where I live?"

"I'm good at finding people," he laughs. When I don't laugh with him, he clears his throat. "Wow. Sorry. That sounded super stalkery." He laughs again, scratches his head. "No, you gave my mom your address. For your clothes?"

I must still not look convinced. He looks at his feet a second.

"She made me come. After she saw the mess in the shop she felt like she hadn't properly thanked you for saving those posters. She says to tell you to come by anytime and pick one, if you want."

"Cool, thanks," I say, embarrassed again.

I catch our reflection in the mirrored wall. He looks

cute, if a little nervous, and I'm a total disaster. Lying on the couch did my face no favors. I shift the dish to one hand and pull the wide neck of the sweatshirt back up on my shoulder.

Someone lays on a car horn outside.

Theo's head whips toward the door. A beat-up VW van edges into sight with a round, very white-haired man at the wheel. Dwarfing him in the passenger seat is a massive, drooling Great Dane.

"Yeah . . . so that's my dad," Theo says with an embarrassed laugh. "And showing up at your building with an old guy in a beat-up van probably totally ups the stalker quotient, but I assure you, we're both harmless."

The dog barks then, a great baritone *woof*.

"Chester, on the other hand . . ." Theo tilts his head toward the dog. "That dude's a total perv."

I laugh. "Well, thanks for coming by."

"I had an errand to run over here anyway."

Theo turns toward the door, then stops and squints at me. His irises are so pale it's like being caught in the gaze of an arctic fox.

"You look kind of weird."

"Thanks." On reflex, I reach up to my hair. It's twisted in the world's messiest topknot.

"Everything cool?"

"Yeah, I guess." I shrug.

Mr. Gray lays on the horn again.

Theo makes a face, then checks his watch.

"Uh, you wanna go for a coffee or something? I mean, do you have time? Like, now?"

He can't be asking me out. Not when I look like this. I don't get to answer, though, because Theo's dad hits the horn again, then taps his watch, waving impatiently for Theo to come.

Theo sighs. "Gimme a sec," he says, stepping out.

I stand awkwardly in the doorway, holding the warm colcannon, while Theo talks to his dad. People's dads make me nervous.

Theo leans his whole upper body in through the passenger window and pulls out a sweatshirt and a set of keys on a thick string. The dog sticks its head out the window over Theo's back and barks another juicy *woof.*

Theo slips out from under him, says something, then pats the roof of the van. His dad nods and pulls away, gunning it down our block.

"Wait! Hang on a sec!" Theo shouts, sprinting after him. I step out a little more to watch. As he runs, he pulls the gray sweatshirt on inside out.

His dad brakes, midblock, and lets Theo catch up. He leans in the window another second. Then the Westfalia tears off again and Theo sprints back to my door, his wallet in hand.

"Total menace," he pants, rolling his eyes. "He's the world's *worst* driver. It doesn't help that the cut-rate mechanic he uses to keep that thing going has the idle set at like forty miles per hour. He's going to kill someone one of these days."

He stops himself a second. Takes a breath, then grins at me kind of sheepishly.

"Uh, I hope you're going to say yes," he laughs. "I probably should have waited for that."

Emma called me a chicken, but a chicken wouldn't go out with this strange, cute stalker guy.

I look him right in the eye. "Gimme ten minutes."

the first hold

I'M DOWN IN TEN LOOKING PRESENTABLE—considering the circumstances—in a nubbly oversize sweater my mom gave me for Christmas and a scarf Emma says makes my eyes look extra gray.

Theo's cross-legged on the upper ledge of the planter box outside the door, eating a granola bar.

"Wasn't sure if you were coming back or not." He hops down, popping the last bite in his mouth and shoving the wrapper in a pocket.

"Hey," he says, turning on the smile, the one that caught me first thing this morning and made me forget all the chatter in my head. "Wanna go someplace kind of cool?"

"Where?"

He grins at me sideways, flashing the edge of that crooked tooth.

"Very mysterious . . . ," I say.

"Yes or no?"

"Sure." I shrug, trying to act totally cool, and not like this is the most exciting thing I've done in a long time. I send a quick text to my mom so she won't wonder where I am when she gets home.

"You were at the gym?" I gesture to his clothes as we head down the block.

"Boxing," he says, walking fast.

I try to keep up. Earlier I thought he was trying to ditch me, but maybe this is just his speed.

"Wow, for real? Hitting people?" I mime like I'm a fighter, make a fist and send it out toward an imaginary jaw.

"For real." He eyes my fist with a smirk.

"What?" I pretend to be offended. "I know nothing about sports. Are you trying to tell me my form's no good?" I smirk back.

"Could use work."

"Is it for your act—for the tour?"

He scoffs. "Boxing? Hardly."

His answers are so terse it occurs to me that boxing

might be one of those secret tests his brother was talking about.

I give up trotting like a Chihuahua and drop back.

He notices and slows a little.

"Why?" I say.

"Why what?"

"Why box?"

Theo turns like he's assessing me or something before he answers.

"I like it," he says finally.

"Illuminating, thanks." If this is a secret test, I failed.

We wait at a light in awkward silence. Theo is kind of like those swimming holes, full of unexpected cold spots. I look away from him. What's left of the sun is lazy and pink, slumping lower and lower. I wrap my scarf a little tighter.

He pulls his sleeves down over his hands. Clears his throat. "Sorry. I just had a giant fight with my parents about it. They want me to stop boxing, among other things."

"Will you?"

"No way." His voice is clipped, tight.

The light changes and we cross, heading west toward the Hudson.

"Wow." I'm mystified. "You like it that much."

"Yeah. Makes me feel better."

"Violence makes you feel better. Interesting. Do you

always need stitches?"

He shakes his head, like what I've said is a disappointment.

"Boxing and violence. Not the same thing."

"Your face begs to differ." I point to his lip.

"This was something else—after the gym."

I wait for him to explain, but he doesn't. Another mystery.

The wind picks up and blows Theo's hair down into his eyes. He pushes it back, revealing his forehead. It makes him look younger.

I try to make light. "So, getting pounded makes you feel better?"

Theo laughs and looks at me, eyes twinkling.

"Ah, but you have it backward. *I* do the pounding." He pulls a knit hat from the pocket of his sweatshirt and yanks it down over all that hair.

"I can't imagine it. . . ." I hunch my shoulders and curl my hands in front of my face, trying to see it. "Someone's fist flying at me?" I shudder involuntarily. "I'd turn and run out of there so fast."

This earns me another laugh. But it's true, I'm scared of conflict, physical or otherwise.

Theo keeps walking, eyes down, like he's thinking. His smile's faded and I can't read his mood.

"So . . . what, then?" I try. "Why do people box? I don't

get it. Why do you? Are you some kind of angry person?"

His head whips up.

"Not when I'm boxing . . ."

"I don't like anger," I say.

He pauses a beat, then his eyes meet mine. "If you don't like anger, then you don't like a part of yourself."

I focus on the sky. Thready pink clouds trail over us like the sun's fading wake. I may have misread this—Theo, the day, everything. It wouldn't be the first time. What I took for flirting was something else, some other frequency coming off this mood-wild blond boy.

"No one likes it." I forge on, my heart adding a few extra beats. "Anger's poison."

When I say it, Theo's eyes flash so pale and sharp I nearly flinch.

"Anger's only poison if you deny it, keep it in." His voice is tight.

A man walking in front of us lights up a cigarette. A gray cloud envelops us.

"And that's literal poison," Theo says, taking my arm and cutting over to the other side of the street. "Sorry," he says. "Asthma. But let me ask you this . . . what did you do this afternoon?" He stops a second and brushes the top of my cheek, just below my eye, with the tip of his finger. My heart minnows. "You had a rough day?"

I swallow, hard. Sometimes when people speak the plain truth it makes me cry.

"It wasn't the soda," I say, so he won't feel responsible. "It was something else."

He nods. "A little sparring might have done you some good. You should try it."

I picture it, me in those huge gloves, lips bulged out over a mouth guard. I'd look so badass. The image makes me smile. In my mind I start mapping a ring. A perfect square. Dotted lines crisscrossing it like ferry routes or steps for a ballroom dance, arrowing this way, then that. In one corner, Evie's prefight optimism, in the other . . . blank.

"Could my opponent wear an effigy mask?" I ask.

"That's an awesomely weird question." He eyes me from a new angle. "Whose face?"

I was picturing my own, or Alice's, but I open my mouth and *Emma* comes out.

I try to swallow it back. Fail. Theo raises his eyebrows but doesn't ask.

I'm mad at Emma. The revelation's so big I almost step off the curb against the light, but Theo catches me by the elbow. I squint at him. He read me. Pegged it. I spent the afternoon feeling bad for failing her when she's dealing with some Mamie situation, but I think I might actually be pissed. I mean, Mamie? And why'd she tell Alice whatever's going on instead of me?

There's a gap between us now, a widening crack that wasn't there before. I've been telling myself it's because of Patrick, but it started earlier than that. I felt it when Emma started doing stuff with guys. She acted like she outgrew me. Maybe it's not two-way between us now, maybe she doesn't need me anymore. A pained *oh!* slips out.

Theo looks at me, but I keep my eyes straight ahead.

Why didn't I go find her after Alice's instead of slouching home to lie like a lump on the couch?

I sigh, huge. I can't help it.

"That bad, huh?" Theo checks me lightly with his shoulder.

I say nothing.

We turn down a block flanked by a high brick wall.

"Here we are," he says, stopping midblock.

"Huh?" There's nothing on this side of the street other than this wall.

"Ready?"

"For what?"

He turns my shoulders so I'm facing the bricks and pats them with his hand. "This. How are you at climbing?"

The wall is high, ten feet easy, and runs the length of the block. All I can see on the other side are the tops of tall trees and spires of a churchy-looking building down at the far end.

"Ha ha."

"No joke," he says, face straight.

"You brought me to a cemetery and it's not a joke? No thanks."

He cocks a brow and laughs. "Scared of cemeteries?"

"Not really. That's where my dad is."

It's mean of me to drop it on him like that, but he's trying to make me scale a wall. Desperate times.

Theo looks surprised.

"Oh, sorry. I didn't know. Shit. But it's not a . . . it's a garden. Come over here."

He grabs my hand and brings me to a section of the wall where some bricks protrude and others have crumbled away or are missing. The year 1820 is chiseled in a cornerstone.

"See? These are your footholds. It's like climbing a ladder." He smiles at me.

I stare back at him.

"Are you insane? You're not kidding. You seriously want me to scale this wall? People lock stuff in New York on purpose. To keep us *out.*"

He kicks his head back a bit and looks at me. "So you follow all the rules?"

I say nothing.

"Come on." He pats the wall. "Don't be scared. Live a little. It's fun."

"I'm not scared!" I protest, but I am. Terrified. I'm no climber.

Theo presses himself flat to the bricks and, gripping the top of one that juts out, he scrambles up a few feet, makes it look easy, the toes of his sneakers wedged into a crevice here, stepping on a broken brick there. He climbs to the top, then jumps back down next to me.

"See? I'll stay here in case you need a boost, but you won't. The first few holds are the trickiest, but once you're up, grab the top and swing your leg over. It's worth it, I promise. There's this iron pergola thing on the other side. Use that to climb down. I'll be right behind you."

I touch the rough wall. "I'm going to fall and break my neck."

"No you won't, and you won't regret it. It's beautiful in there."

"It's winter."

"Even in winter."

The more cautious parts of my brain are strongly urging

me to get out of here. For all I know, once I'm trapped in there he's going to strangle me or worse.

He looks at me all innocent. The downward-sinking sun shines through a curl below his ear and adds to the angelic impression.

I chew the inside of my cheek.

"You're nuts if you think I'm doing that."

"You should see your face," he laughs. "Relax. You look so freaked out. It's not like I'm asking you to suction-cup your way up the side of the Empire State. It's a fence around a Jesuit churchyard."

"A wall."

"A wall." He confirms.

He follows my eyes to the top. It's very high. I look back at him.

"Take a risk," he says. "I'm right here to catch you."

What is it with people trying to get me to take risks, do things I don't want to do? I must come off as really uptight. I shake my arms out and look at the crumbling brick, then back at him. The rosy light around the edge of his face seals the deal. He bumps me with his shoulder.

"Might even be better than boxing," he teases.

This is me refusing to be a chicken. I blow on my hands to warm them, then press my fingers tight around the first hold.

no map of lack

I FALL BACK AGAINST THEO THREE times before I make it high enough to hook my arm over the wide top of the wall. I hang there a second, muscles twitching and shaking, then I hoist myself on wobbly arms until I can swing my legs over.

He wasn't kidding. It's a secret garden. Old rosebushes wear a few winter-battered blooms like gems on gnarled knuckles. A marble bench rings around a dry fountain. Limbs of giant oaks sway and whisper through rusty leaves. I shimmy down the pergola onto another marble bench. It's quiet enough in here to be another dimension.

Above me, Theo crests the top of the wall. He grins, then springs down like a parkour superstar, swinging from the pergola into the air, arms overhead, sweatshirt hiked up, showing his stomach. He lands light on his feet in front of me.

"Pretty cool in here, right?"

"Now that I'm on the ground again, yeah."

"Are you afraid of heights?" He nudges the toe of my shoe.

"Only ones I fall from."

He laughs.

"Props to you, Ramsey. Few girls would agree to scale a wall like that." He takes off his hat and pulls on his hair so it stands up all sweat-salty and crazy.

"Oh. Is this one of your tests? What's the average length of time it takes for a new girl to say yes to scaling walls with you?"

"Huh?" Theo wrinkles his brow, looking genuinely confused.

"Your brother told me you give people secret tests."

Theo's mouth forms a small O, but he says nothing. His eyes darken. He turns and walks the perimeter of the garden.

Great. I offended him.

At the other end of the yard, he picks up a rake from a

haphazard pile of yard tools and starts to loosen the top of a hill of mulch. The metal tines of the rake skip and jangle over the cold mound.

Theo's mad and I'm stuck in here with him. I look around, suddenly aware that we're trespassing. At the far end of the garden, an old brick building overlooks the yard.

His rake is noisy.

"Um, you sure you can do that? Won't someone hear?"

He looks up and grins. "Worry much?"

A flash of embarrassment.

"Someone has to."

"Worry?" He sounds skeptical, keeps raking. A chocolaty smell wafts over.

I close my eyes and inhale. "Why does that smell like a candy bar?"

"Cocoa mulch," he says, his voice closer than I expect. I open my eyes to find him standing in front of me. He drops a few brown husks into my hand.

I lift them to my face and inhale.

"Tell me this," he says. "Has worrying ever saved anyone from anything? Ever?"

I shrug, ashamed to be having this conversation.

"I'm not trying to make you feel bad. I just think people spend more time worrying than they do actually living."

"A kid I knew died," I start.

"And worry could have saved him?"

"Well . . . caution."

"Ah, not the same, though, worry and caution."

"I guess not," I concede, feeling super stupid. "But maybe for some people it's hard to stop."

He stares at me a minute, bouncing the rake off its tines from one hand to the other. "I'm not saying it's easy, especially if your brain's tuned that way, but isn't that all the more reason to resist? I mean, worrying kind of makes the thing come true. You know? In your head, whether it happens for real or not, you're living it either way. What's the quote? You're paying interest on a debt you may never owe?"

He goes back to work, the rake tines jingle-singing next to me.

"I make maps." I don't know why I'm telling him this. Partly to change the subject but partly because he's making me say things I don't normally say. Some kind of magnetic fox power or something.

"Maps?"

"Yeah."

"That's cool. Like with software or something?"

No, maps for art, I think, embarrassed. I shake my head and play with the ends of my scarf. I hate having to talk about it. Explain myself. This is what it will be like if I apply to TeenART. A private world made public. My face heats up. I'm a citizen of Embarrassment. Their senior ambassador.

"Pencil. Paint sometimes. Whatever's on hand. They're not . . . literal. I mean, I make them for myself. It's weird to try to explain!" I'm stammering. "It used to be something I did kind of for fun, but now they're changing. They feel more important or something, like they're . . ."

I don't know what they are.

"Tools of resistance," Theo says. He's so right I'm quiet a minute. "Show me one sometime?"

He shovels mulch onto a large plastic tarp, then gathers the corners and drags it over to another rosebush, where he starts to spread it.

"And I'm in this fight with my best friend—I've been thinking about another map—the city without Em."

"So, a moving-on kind of thing?" He cocks his head toward me.

I shake my head because I don't know what it is, but the thought of losing Em, moving past her, makes me feel sick.

"She's not speaking to me," I say, my throat tight.

Theo stops and leans on the rake, squints at me through the mulchy dust.

I fidget under the inspection.

"What?" I ask, really blushing now. Glad for the fading daylight.

"Maybe I didn't understand what you meant," he says. "The city without Em sounds more like a map of lack than a tool of resistance."

A map of lack.

My face must show how close I am to coming apart, because Theo sets his rake down, sprints to the other end of the yard, and pulls a second rake from under a bench. He brings it over to me and we work in silence until we're both sweaty.

When we're done, we lean the rakes against the wall near a heavy wooden door at the other end of the garden.

Theo gives me a sly smile and produces a dark skeleton key from a cord around his neck. Waggles it in front of my face, then slips it in the old lock.

I hit him on the arm. "You had a key."

"You thought they made me hop the wall every time I come to work?" He grins, dodging my second blow.

"You work here?"

"I wasn't spreading mulch out of the goodness of my heart," he laughs. "Although I probably would. I love yard work, and you don't get much of that in the city."

"God, I feel so stupid!" I'm kind of giddy from the manual labor, my limbs full of blood and twitching. Drawing maps doesn't really count as exercise. "You made me do that impossible climb for nothing!"

He clutches at his chest like I've shot an arrow into his heart.

"For *nothing*? Excuse me, but was I wrong? I believe I promised you something cool?"

"No, yes." I shake my head. "You did."

"The first time I came here, I was kinda . . . I don't know . . . anyway, that's how I got in," he says.

"Over the wall."

"Yep." He wiggles the key a few times until it engages, and the door swings in, heavy on its hinges.

"That's mysterious."

"After you." He extends his arm with a flourish and I step out. While he coaxes the old lock shut again, I bend and grab a rock. Theo's right. Who needs a map of lack? Chalk would work better, and I make a mental note to pick up some, but an artist makes use of the tools at hand. I scratch a pair of rakes crisscrossed like swords onto the soft surface of one of the bricks. I'll map where I've been found.

Theo smiles at me, ready to go.

I glance at my tiny rakes. I'll map it right on the city itself.

souvenir

IT'S DARKER ON THE STREET SOMEHOW, like we left our lighter selves in there and slipped back out into the city as shadows. We walk toward my place in silence, Theo with his long-legged gait, and me trotting next to him, trying to match his stride.

"Sorry," he says, noticing my scurry. "I walk super fast." His face has darkened, or maybe it's just how the bluish streetlight hits it, but he looks like he's working something out.

"So how did you find that place?" I ask. "Are you like one of those Hidden New York people going around sneaking into locked places?"

"I was hiding out."

Not what I was expecting. I look up at him, but his face is unreadable. I slip my phone out of my pocket and check for texts. It's a reflex. My phone's on airplane mode until my month rolls over.

"Hiding out?" I ask, eyes on the screen.

He doesn't answer.

I look up.

"I hate phones." He says it evenly, but his tone is cool again.

"Okay . . . ?"

Maybe he's crazy. This doesn't feel like my life. There has to be a catch here, somewhere. I slip my phone back in my pocket.

"So, don't expect me to have one," he says, like that explains the random conversational turn. "I can't stand them. Everyone walks around half here, dim-lit by screens."

He touches my arm and I flinch. I can't help it. He looks at me, startled, like I'm the one acting weird.

"When I told you to climb up that wall, you looked at me like I was insane, but you were looking me in the eye. You know? People on phones never look at each other. My mom and dad text when they're in the same room. It's so messed up."

I stop caring about whether or not he's nuts, because now he's grinning at me, his hand on my arm, shaking it a little like he's trying to wake me up. For a second I see myself reflected in his eyes, smaller and perfect, like I'm not just me, but half of something else, a him-n-me.

"Why were you hiding out?"

Theo's face closes up. Another cold spot. He drops my arm and keeps his eyes on the sidewalk.

One sidewalk square silent.

Then two.

Then three.

If I had chalk in my pocket I'd drop to the ground and outline myself. *Place where Evie murdered her own chances.* So much for the tools of resistance.

Another endless minute, then Theo clears his throat.

"I needed a place to stay."

"You needed a place to stay?"

He nods. "I was in there three nights before they noticed me."

Okay. He is crazy, and you're not supposed to taunt crazy people, but tell that to my mouth, which is already open wide and tripping over its disbelief.

"*Three nights?*" I forge ahead, incredulous. "You slept in there? Outside? Like a homeless person?"

A lot of people are nuts. Statistically speaking some of

them must be cute. I squint at him peripherally, like I'm not conducting a sanity inspection, but he's not blind.

"Oh yeah. Now you're really freaked out," Theo says, sounding somewhat satisfied. He makes a weirdo sideways face at me. Cackles.

"So, like, um, was it some kind of religious retreat?"

Theo laughs. "I'm totally scaring you!"

I smile, but still shove my hand in my pocket, wrap it around my phone. "Because my friend Emma's Catholic, and they—"

"I'm not religious."

He wrenches my arm, pulling me to one side. This is it, he's going to murder me. Of course he is. No one this cute pays attention to me. I let out a small scream and kind of skip to catch my balance. Why don't I ever trust my instincts?

"Wow, jumpy! You were about to step in dog poop." Theo points to a smeary mess on the sidewalk and steadies me with a hand at my back.

"Oh! Ha!" I try to recover. "Sorry! I mean, thanks." I'm jittery. "Did they call the cops when they found you?"

"No cops."

"Why—"

He shakes his head, cutting me off. "Nah, that's a story for another time. It's how I met Father Joe, though, and he got me into boxing."

"A priest got you into boxing?"

"Excellent, right?" he says with a half smile. "Sparred with him this afternoon."

I point to his lip. "Did he give you that?"

"Mr. Play-by-the-rules? Ha, no," he laughs, touching his stitches. "That would totally destroy him. This was something else. Unrelated."

We round a corner close to my place and there they are, Alice and Jack, lounging in the deepening chill on the stoop of Alice's redbrick town house looking all couply and cute, Alice bundled in a plaid wool blanket, with Jack wrapped around her from behind, a step above.

My stomach rolls over.

"Eves!" Jack spots us before I can change course. He raises an arm to wave as we approach, but his hand stops midair, hovers there a minute while he squints to see who I'm with. "Where'd you go this afternoon . . . ?" he says slowly, like he's trying to assess the situation.

The tables have turned. Even though Jack's sitting there wrapped around Alice, I've thrown him for a loop by being out with Theo.

"Where you headed?" he tries again.

Emma's always reminding me that just because someone asks a question, I don't have to answer it.

I step ever-so-slightly closer to Theo.

"Hey, Jack, hey, Alice." I try to keep my voice flat, like I'm totally underwhelmed to see them. Then I turn back toward Theo like he was in the middle of telling me the most interesting thing ever.

If I'd been paying attention to anything other than the electric shiver in the air around Theo and me I would have avoided this block, with Emma's and Alice's houses, one on either end. I've walked it a billion times. Broke my wrist practically on this very spot when Emma braked sharp on her bike and shot me off her handlebars.

"Evie," Alice's voice rings out. "Did you talk to Em?"

I narrow my eyes in the dark to see if Em's out too, sitting with them on the stoop, but she's not. It used to be the three of *us* on Em's stoop—Emma, Jack, and me—warm on the self-heating stadium cushions Mrs. Sullivan keeps in the cupboard in the foyer. How neatly I've been swapped out for Alice Weir.

"Been busy." I quicken my pace. Theo slows and catches me by the shoulder. For a second I worry he's going to echo Alice's question, ask me why I haven't talked to Em yet, but he reaches to untangle something from my hair.

"Souvenir?" He grins, his face so close to mine our foreheads nearly touch. He lifts his palm to show me a cocoa hull. "Did you want that there? Something to remember me by?"

Before I can answer, Jack stands and starts down Alice's stoop.

"Dude. Is that Theo Gray?" He squints at us, surprised.

"Hey, man." Theo nods, throwing his shoulders back and straightening up.

I roll the cocoa hull between my thumb and forefinger and we pass them by, walking the rest of the block, each of us lost in our own silence.

between thrill and disaster

HE SQUEEZED MY HAND GOOD-BYE.

That's it.

I stand in the hallway by our door a minute. What does that mean? A hand squeeze. When I let myself in, my mom has Mrs. Gray's colcannon on the table, and she's humming something cheerful. I sit across from her ready to be mildly peppered with questions about where I was and who I was with, but she's weirdly preoccupied, checking her phone. She only half listens when I tell her where the food came from, and asks me nothing about my tour. Must have been something good at work. She looks happier than she has in a while.

I push the food around my plate and replay our good-bye. Theo's lean-in-over-me, breath-on-my-face almost-kiss . . . then the awkward hand squeeze. I cup my hand over my mouth to smell my breath. Smells like colcannon. Thanks to the mirrors in our lobby the weirdness was infinite—endless Theos squeezing endless Evies' hands.

Agony.

Blindfolded on a fire escape. That's what this feels like. Treacherously high. Teetering at the point between thrill and disaster. A hand squeeze!

Not as bad as what I did to Jack . . . but still.

"Oh," my mom says, as if we've been talking to each other and not eating in silence.

"Yeah?" I take a bite. Theo's mom's dish is fluffy and buttery and tastes like heaven.

"I thought I saw Emma near our door when I came around the corner," she says, taking a sip of water. "I waved at her, but after I looked in my bag for my keys, she was gone."

"Em?"

My mom nods.

"She came by?"

"Well, I thought it was Emma," my mom says with a little shrug. "But I don't know where she went."

I reach across the table for my phone. No messages. Weirdest day ever. Some kind of portal's obviously open between my normal life and Unpredictable Otherness. May as well keep stepping through.

I shove a few more bites in my mouth, then stand to clear my plate. I can't keep wondering. Emma was here. She wants to talk to me too, face-to-face. Time to go see her.

wild eyes wide

THE WHOLE WALK OVER I TRY to plan what I'll say, but when I get there words are beside the point. The noise of a fight pours through the front doors. I peer in. The windows into the foyer are only slightly obscured by lace curtains. I can see the three of them almost as clearly as if I'd been invited inside. Emma's dad is shouting, and beneath his cacophony, Mrs. Sullivan murmurs like a mourning dove. The dogs, Grizzle and Sam, are running nervous barking circles around Em, who's closest to the door, arms crossed over her chest. Her dad kind of spooks me when he's like this.

I doubt my dad would have yelled. Mr. Sullivan can really lose it.

My heart starts skipping around inside me like it's already decided we should get out of here. I didn't count on this.

I'm just starting to back down the steps when their front door flies open. Emma bursts onto the stoop, wild eyes wide. She stops when she sees me.

"Why are you here?" she demands.

Not the warmest welcome.

Before I can answer, their door swings open again and her dad barrels out, nearly crashing into where she stands frozen on the top of the stoop.

"You will not leave!" he bellows, clamping a hand on her shoulder. Then he spots me.

"Evie." He stops short, composes himself. He looks just like Patrick when he does it, this suppressed fury face he made when he'd had it with us bugging him. Patrick was at his nicest when Mamie was around.

Mr. S. wraps his mouth into a straight line that's probably meant to be a smile.

"Well then."

We stand there a minute, the three of us, in stunned silence.

The front door opens again and Mrs. Sullivan steps out,

her hand at the collar of her blouse.

"Ah, Evie," she says in her super-calm voice. "I saw you through the window. At least it's family at the door and not someone else. How wonderful!"

Emma hates it when she talks like this. She says her mom acts like anything other than *nice* is a sin. I've never seen her yell. When they fight Emma's the one making all the noise. I can't remember Mrs. Sullivan ever reprimanding us for anything. She's more likely to offer a gentle suggestion, a reminder to rethink. Emma told me just once she wanted to see her mom go nuts and totally lose it. I said but then the world would end, there'd be too much disturbance in the natural order. Emma doesn't know what she's asking for. Her mom has it *together*.

Mrs. Sullivan sweeps us all inside like we're a manageable mess, her eyes wide, that calm smile. "Come in out of the cold. Evie, if you can stay I'll make tea for you girls. I'll bring it and the rest of the ginger cake up to Emma's room."

About fifty expressions flash across Emma's face rapid-fire, like she's a sped-up time-lapse, reliving every look she's ever reserved for her parents, until she settles on a death glare, keeping her back to her mother and her fists clenched at her sides.

Still. It's not a rejection.

I follow her in.

an act of love

I TOUCH MY FINGERS LIGHTLY ON Patrick's bedroom door when we pass it on our way to Em's room. It's been closed since he died. I do it every time I walk by, but never if Em's looking.

I follow her into her room.

"What about *trust*?" Emma shouts. She slams the door so hard on *trust* her chalkboard falls to the floor and the walls issue a gritty, crumbling-plaster shush. Grizzle snuffle-whines outside her door. He was Patrick's but sticks close to Em now. I crack the door and let him in.

She looks at me in disbelief. "I was *barely* late today, but when I come in, they're both up here like cops on a bust, Mr. High-n-Mighty digging through my stuff!"

She sweeps her arm wide around her room like an incredulous tour guide. Emma's parents have rules, and they're strict, but this is new. They have always made a big deal out of mutual trust and respect. But her room's ransacked, dresser drawers out, the closet door open wide, and her stuff in piles on the floor. Probably because of the other night, because of me.

Emma shakes her head. "They're all, *We have faith in you. . . .*" She sucks in a huge breath and yells, "*Hypocrites!*" She stomps her foot hard on the floor and I catch my reflection vibrating in the sticker-covered mirror on the wall behind her.

I bite my lip, not sure what to say. Sometimes it's best to sit it out, let the storm pass.

Emma looks around her room like she might spot something that will make sense to her.

"*Forgiveness is an act of love,*" she says in the voice she reserves for imitating her mother. She uses air quotes, her hands like claws. "*Healing's a process.* It's such bullshit."

She turns to me, her chin jutting out the way it used to when she and Patrick got into it. "All that holier-than-thou crap. They're trying to guilt me. All they care about is how they look to their friends at church."

I hover near her door while she drops to her knees and starts shoving things back in her drawers. The healing stuff has to be about Mamie, but I'm afraid to ask questions because things have never been this bad between us before.

"Mamie?" I choke out.

Emma stops what she's doing, looks up at me, nodding, then deflates.

"Don't—I can't—"

"Why?" It comes out desperate, like a plea.

We stare at each other a minute, then I walk over to the cushion in her window. My usual perch. I drop down on it and pull my knees up tight to my chest, fight the urge to walk out of here before she says things that hurt.

Emma looks like she's thinking.

I brace myself to hear she doesn't need me anymore, she's outgrown us, there are too many things I just don't get.

She says nothing.

I try again.

"Why can you tell Alice and not me?"

"Because you still *worship* her."

A wave of embarrassment hits me, hot shame, because it's true. Emma doesn't get it. She's always been herself, charging forward, all the time, but I'm not like her. The only thing that ever really dented her confidence was the extra few months they made her wear her braces. I'm lucky if I can spot myself in the mirror. I used to joke with her that sometimes I forget what I look like, and it's kind of true. But it's not about looks. It's bigger than that. I'm a blank. I need an example, someone to look up to, someone to tell me how to be. I've always needed to see how other people do it, check out the possible options before I can decide for myself. Mamie did that for me. She made no apologies for taking pictures, for loving what she did, for doing what she needed to do. She seemed like she had something essential figured out, and when I was around her I felt like I might figure it out too.

But then Patrick died and Mamie disappeared.

I hug my knees tighter, look up at Em. Her eyes are narrowed, accusing. We can't have a Mamie gap between us. This is something I have to fix.

"I don't! Not anymore, I promise! I did . . . before, you're right, but that's over, you can talk to me about her, you can tell me anything."

She sits back on her heels and exhales. "My parents are talking to her. It's obnoxious. She's doing some stupid art project, something about Patrick. And they're okay with it!" Before I can ask what kind of project, she adds, "Do you know the one thing that girl really, really *needs* to do?"

I shake my head.

Emma's voice rises. "She needs to shut up about my brother and leave us alone! She has her stupid life. She should stay out of mine."

She drops the clothes she's holding and stands up, hands loose at her sides. She looks at me like nothing makes sense anymore. It's this dazed face she wore a lot after Patrick died, emptied-out, like she's been suspended or something, her spirit crushed by the whim of random absurdity. She sits heavily on her dove-gray puff of a bed, flops on her side, and pulls a pillow over her face.

Tears.

After that May when he died, she was like this a lot, sudden cloudburst, the sky torn open, an ocean of loss.

I don't care if she hates me, I wrap myself around her on her bed.

"She took a year off, then started art school," Em says after a bit, voice muffled.

Mamie went to art school. The information gives me a momentary thrill. I'm not in the art-kid group at Bly, but neither was she.

Emma lifts the pillow and turns her face to mine, eyes swollen. I stop thinking about Mamie.

"Patrick didn't get to start anything. I can't deal with how *unfair* that is. And she changed her name! Like now she's just gonna be someone new. Must be nice to step away from the ugly parts of yourself so completely. My mom, God, Evie, you should have *heard my mom,* she was a regular Mother Teresa, all about forgiveness and love."

I imagine talking to Mamie again, calling her maybe, asking if she could back off a little, for Em's sake.

I picture the phone call, catching up, maybe we'd meet for lunch—God—Em's right. I worship her.

There's a light knock on the door.

"What." Emma's tone shifts, hard. She pushes the pillow away and sits up.

"Open up? My hands are full. I'm bringing tea," her mom says through the door like it's any old school night and we're in here studying, all peaches.

I hop up and get the door for her.

"Thank you, honey." She steps in, her white tray like a flag of surrender. She eyes the chalkboard on the floor and avoids looking at her daughter. There's a plate with two slices of warm ginger cake and mugs of steaming chamomile tea with lemon. It smells so good, for a second I'm just relieved to be back over at Emma's again, even in the middle of whatever this is. I could almost cry or hug Mrs. Sullivan. Instead, I clear a spot on Em's makeup-cluttered desk for her to set the tray. After giving me a quick pat on the arm and a grateful smile, she slips out, closing the door softly behind her.

"Em." I sit, tucking a leg under me on the end of her bed. "I think you have to tell your parents how you feel."

She shakes her head. "I could hardly tell *you*." She wipes her eyes with her sleeves. "I don't get why everyone loves her so much. Besides, you know how they are. They can't deal. They won't. They'll tell me to talk to God."

I sigh because she's probably right. My mom's not a lot of things, but she'll listen when I talk, and I'm allowed to feel bad. She's soft, like rain. Not a problem-solver. More of a hand-wringer, only she never wants me to see that part. But I hear her sometimes crying quietly in the bath or wake up to find her asleep in weird places around the apartment, because some nights she has to wander until she can't stay awake anymore.

"Em, I really am sorry about the other night."

"I know you are," she says, her voice starting to wobble again. "I'm sorry too. Things are just so . . . I don't know, everything's changing, and Mamie's only thinking about herself. You know? This is totally another way for her to feel okay about what happened, what *she* did. Why does she get to feel okay?"

Emma blames Mamie for the accident. She's never really clear on how she thinks it's Mamie's fault, but she does.

She leans against her headboard and pulls a pillow to her chest. "Patrick was a great driver. There's no way he rolled that car like that."

My mom told me the police report said Patrick's blood alcohol level was sky high. There is every way he could have rolled the car like that.

Em starts to cry again, her outrage spent, and in its place is a curled-up hurt person. I scoot closer to her.

It makes me sick to imagine what it would be like to be Mamie and have to live with what happened, to face the Sullivans and all their loss.

But then I feel guilty. I'm thinking about Mamie again. Who cares how she feels? She's hurting my friend, and it has to stop.

sumo sushi

WHEN I LEFT FOR SCHOOL ON Monday, Em was waiting in my foyer looking bright and fresh, the way the world does after a huge storm. On our way in I told her about Theo, that whole confusing day, right up to the almost-kiss, awkward hand squeeze. She eyed me, sly, and said, *That's my girl!* like there's hope for me, then grabbed my hands and danced me around on the sidewalk, cheering so loud at seven forty-five a.m. I thought one of the neighbors was going throw something out a window at us or call the cops.

In advisory when Dr. Holmes got to my two favorite topics, college applications and the Junior Spain trip, Emma distracted me with anagrams of *Theo Gray* along the edge of my planner. *Hearty Go, Gather Yo, Get Hoary, Heat Orgy.* We cracked up on that last one, which earned us a withering scowl from Dr. Holmes.

The whole time, Alice sat across from us looking smug and diplomatic, like she'd brokered a major peace deal, like they'd already debriefed on the Evie situation. Whatever. Jealousy's crap. I came to the library happy anyway, ready to make a dent in my Investigation.

When Jack's head pops over the edge of my carrel, his headphones grate against the edge of the wood. He drops a small paper animal onto my desk. I brush it aside and try not to look. He hasn't made me one of these in a long time. They're part origami, part pictures and glue. I have an impressive menagerie.

"All good with Em?" he says, forgetting to whisper. "You guys looked pretty cozy in advisory."

The librarian clears his throat.

"Guess so," I whisper back, tilting my head toward my work.

"What?" Jack nudges the Yoda-looking creature across my desktop with a nail-bitten fingertip. I keep my eyes on my screen. "No love for this little guy? Guess what he is."

"Go away," I hiss. "I'm actually getting work done."

"A tarsier!" He ignores me. "Nocturnal. A carnivorous

primate. Small enough to hold in your hand, yet he can jump up to fifteen feet. Awesome, right?"

Jack's enthusiasm always gets me. I grin and pick up his weird paper creature. He's scrawled "IHYB" on the back, something Em and I text each other.

I have your back.

I raise a brow in his direction and he nods at me, solemnly. It appears this tarsier's a peace offering. I'm reading between the lines here, but I guess we'll forget about the almost-kiss and not talk about Alice, and then we can go back to how we were. Jack's folded the tarsier's legs in such a way that when I flick his tail, he jumps.

"Luuunnncchhhh . . . ," Jack zombie-whispers, waggling his arms over the side of my carrel, messing my hair, and flipping my laptop lid shut.

"*Death* if you just made me lose my Investigation," I hiss. My laptop's on its last leg. Jack smiles like a devil and grabs for my phone, but I'm faster.

I check it before I hide it away. No texts. After attendance in advisory, Em took a "mental health day," which means she's somewhere on the Lower East Side with Ryan, probably at his apartment. She promised she'd sneak a picture and send it, but there's nothing yet.

"C'mon, let's hustle." Jack wiggles the edge of the carrel.

"Not hungry," I say, even though I am. I have a peanut

butter and graham cracker sandwich in my bag and not much cash.

Jack circles around behind me so close I can feel a heat-shaped version of him. He leans his head in, mouth to my ear.

"Come *onnnnn,*" he moans like the undead, which weirdly makes me shiver. "Eat with me. My treat."

The librarian clears his throat again. "*Mister* Darling," he says, crisp on the *Mister.*

Jack Darling. That's seriously his name. People don't make fun of it, though, because pretty much everyone has a Darling Mill blanket in their home. Darling Mill is part of New England history. It's a regular destination for lower school field trips, busloads of kids heading up to see the old shuttle looms in action, their clacking rhythm, the vivid fibers spinning off the spools. My blanket was on my bed until I saw him with Alice. It's on the floor of my closet now.

Jack wiggles the back of my chair. I blush. How does he have this effect on me? He used to be so round Emma called him Snack. I had no idea he'd turn out like this, supercute and luring me, hovering so close I can smell his laundry soap.

"No Alice?" I don't even try to hide how happy it makes me.

"I'm Alice-less," he says, picking up my braid and flipping the ends of my hair against my cheek.

This is the problem with Jack. He's a terminal flirt. Even being with Alice doesn't stop him from doing this with me.

The librarian shakes his head in our direction and pushes back from his desk with a certain resignation.

"Sorry!" I mouth, and quickly pack up.

We run down all three flights laughing, then dash past Ms. Vax near the office, who calls out, "Evie, come see me! We need to talk TeenART! Deadline's approaching!"

We hop around Mandi, Ben, and Stella on the steps with their lunches and spill out onto the street.

"So . . . Theo Gray?"

And here's the real reason for lunch. Disappointed, I ignore the question.

"Wait. Where are we going? I have forty minutes, then I have to meet with Dr. Holmes about my Investigation. He gave me a yellow light on my outline."

"How are you already behind on this project, Eves?"

I shake my head. Shrug.

He looks at me like he's my hero. "Tomorrow. After school. We'll get together to work and eat the cookies you'll bake me?"

I eye him. He's trying so hard to make everything seem normal.

"Fine. Whatever," I concede. If Jack comes over I'll get more done, even counting the time it takes me to bake cookies. The gods are a moody bunch if my life can swing from no friends, no boys, back to this in a single day.

"You met at the Roebling House? Alice saw him leading a tour."

He's still going on about Theo. Hard not to smile. Jack's jealous.

"Theo?" I act like I'm not sure who he's talking about.

"Let's hit Sumo," he says, sounding kind of annoyed. "It's closest."

Jack slips his hand under my hair at the base of my neck and steers me left, around the corner and down the next block. This is an old habit. He says he likes to "drive" because I'm always wandering off to look at stuff—like I even do that. Em says he just wants to have his hand in my hair. I tilt my head back into the warmth of his palm.

We get our food and snag the last open table in the pen-like backyard Sumo Sushi calls a garden. Despite the delusional description, the concrete terrace is packed. This weird winter warmth has everyone confused. Jack unzips his hoodie and shoves up his sleeves, ready for serious eating. After stealing my pickled ginger, he stirs the full mound of wasabi into his soy sauce and digs in.

I crack my chopsticks apart and lift a piece of my roll.

Asparagus, avocado, and cucumber. Same one every time. We focus on eating, but from the way Jack's looking at me between bites, I'm pretty sure whatever he's going to say is something I don't want to hear. There's a vibe coming off him that was there last night. Alarm. It kind of makes my heart sink. I'm afraid Jack knows something bad about Theo. I think I sensed it myself. Theo's too good to be true.

Jack pulls a shrimp tail from his mouth.

"So. You and Gray."

I pop another bite in my mouth, but the seaweed's clammy in my throat. I chew fast, then down some water.

"Yeah?"

"Why were you with him?" Jack surveys the box for his next big bite.

I meet his question with a blank stare. Shrug. "Hanging out."

Jack pops two major pieces of broccoli tempura in his mouth and eyes me while he chews, both cheeks bulging. What is wrong with me that I even find this cute? Then, as if he's reached some important gastric baseline and can now speak, he downs half his soda, wipes his mouth, and sits back. Locks me in with those green-brown eyes. They go pond or leaf depending on what he's wearing. Today they're dark algae.

I don't blink.

"It's just . . . I know that dude," he says finally, tilting his chair back.

"So?"

He curls the paper sleeve from my chopsticks into a little snail. Tosses it at me. I let it hit the ground.

I pick up another piece of sushi and dip it, defiant, in his flavor-destroying, sinus-clearing wasabi-spiked soy sauce, but it falls in, splashing me instead.

Jack grins and pops it in his mouth. "Gray was on my dorm hall my first summer at SciTech," he says, one eyelid shuddering shut at the super-seasoned roll.

"So he's a science freak. You are too."

Jack raises a finger and downs the rest of his soda. "Not the same. No one liked him."

"Criminal." I set my chopsticks down. "Besides. I can relate." I want more than anything to be able to control this conversation, to steer it away from where Jack tells me something I don't want to hear.

"Shut up. People like you."

"Yeah, that's why no one told me to come to the park after the Roebling House." I cross my eyes at him.

"I told you!"

"Did not. I heard from Mandi. In passing."

"Whatever, you heard. Anyway, dude's a psycho, Eves."

"You're jealous!" I tease, trying to act like I feel anything other than panic that Jack's about to ruin Theo for me, then happily head back to Alice himself.

"Not likely." Jack scoffs.

A black hole swirls in my stomach.

"Your first summer at SciTech was ages ago. People change."

"Eves, listen to me, will you? Theo Gray's the guy they talk about after he charges in somewhere and shoots up the place. The one they all say was quiet."

"Quiet?" My turn to scoff. "He was quiet? That's what you've got on him? So what?"

Jack looks at me like I've issued a challenge.

"He left camp in the middle of the night. Anger rolls off that guy. Seriously, you can't tell me you didn't pick up on it. And what was with his face? Alice said he was beat up. Eves, come on. Do not get involved with that dude."

"Why?"

"I just told you!" Jack leans way back in his chair and runs his hands through his hair like he can't believe I'm not listening to him.

"Hardly. But, I mean, why'd he leave camp in the middle of the night?"

Jack rocks his chair forward again with an exasperated bang. "Who cares?" His eye does this little twitching thing at the corner when he's nervous. "He acted superior the whole time, like he knew more than the rest of us." He peels the corner of the label on his soda bottle.

"Well, maybe he did," I say, remembering what Lazarus said. It comes out snottier than I mean it to.

Jack squints at me, critically. "God, what's your problem? I'm not Em, you don't have to act all bitchy with me. I'm trying to have your back here."

"I don't know what you're trying to do, but I like him and you can't wreck it for me," I snap. "And Em was pissed at me, not the other way around."

I clamp my mouth shut and look at the concrete slab under my feet. What a perfect place for him to take a mallet to my heart. Jack's always been good at winning arguments by getting me on the defensive.

This is payback for the kiss. It's not like we're going to talk about it, but he's obviously mad or hurt or both. I would be. I look at him again, his brows up like he's waiting to see if he got through to me.

"Whatever. Thanks for lunch." I stand and grab my backpack.

Jack's face falls.

I walk out. I can feel his surprise at my back, his open mouth. I panic a second when I actually hit the street.

First Em, now Jack?

What am I doing, fighting with everyone?

string lights

I'M IN THE BODEGA NEAR SCHOOL, picking up a little box of chalk for my pocket, when Em texts me from Ryan's begging me to cover for her after school. There's nothing like a second chance. I walk home from Bly rehearsing possible lies to use if her parents come looking.

Our apartment's dark and cold when I let myself in. Jack says it feels sad in here, and today it totally does. My mom's not big on organization, and the randomness of our hodgepodge looks more abandoned than homey. I dart around clicking on all the lamps, then head to the kitchen to make popovers. Salad and popovers is her favorite dinner, and the oven will heat up the place.

I sit on the kitchen floor in thick socks and my dad's sweatshirt and stare through the cloudy glass on the oven door like it's a window to someplace better. Emma was right. I totally worshipped Mamie. Still do. Easier to focus on that than it is to think about what happened at lunch with Jack.

Instead of working on my Investigation, or looking at the TeenART application link Ms. Vax keeps sending, I lie back and stare at the cracks in the ceiling until it comes to me.

It wasn't a crazy idea to call her. Mamie liked me too. I'll just do it, ask her to stop. I'll tell her the project is hurting Emma. She'll listen.

Recharged, I look for her online. It's not like I can call Em for her number. Googling her feels weird. I kind of used to stalk her a lot. Like she was some ideal. A window into a possible future. Mamie and Patrick were friends *and* hot for each other. They were doing everything right, and still, look how that turned out. I haven't seen her since the party that night. She left town after the accident. Emma said she went into hiding because it was her fault and she knew it. Jack's brother said he heard she cracked up, stopped talking, and skipped college. People will say anything. She left, and I felt deserted, even though I'm sure she only thought of me as Patrick's little sister's friend.

If she thought of me at all.

The few results that come up for Mamie Wells are old. Patrick's obituary, articles about the accident, human interest pieces about drinking and driving. That spring was a bad one for teens in cars on Long Island.

I click on Mamie's page. Looks untouched, her profile photo still the one of the two of them, grinning cheek to cheek in a photo booth.

I close my computer and take a deep breath. Doing this brings up memories, makes me feel kind of sick. Patrick's face mute and pasty at his wake was pretty much the most incomprehensible sight ever. He looked like a weird school-photo version of himself. Retouched. The wrong color. Even though it was the end of May, I couldn't stop shivering. When we got home my mom wrapped me in blankets and hung string lights above my bed so I could sleep.

I don't remember my dad's funeral, but I'm pretty sure I didn't see him all laid out in his casket. Death felt more conceptual before I saw Patrick like that, there but not there. His waxy face. A gray suit, like he was going to some kind of luncheon instead of ceasing to exist for the rest of time. That's when I really understood. Death is part of the deal. For all of us.

I open my computer again and stare at Mamie's timeline.

More like a time capsule, her last update was two days before Patrick died. Not that it stopped everyone else from posting. It's an endless scrolling memorial, an electronic spool of insincerity, people one-upping each other. Do they really think she'll read it? Each comment tries to outdo the ones before: sappy condolences, clichés about angels and heaven, weird messages directly to Patrick himself, as if he's lounging bored on a cloud somewhere, checking in from the afterlife, and not totally flying around using X-ray vision and listening in to people's thoughts, like any self-respecting ghost would do if they had the chance.

I lie back on our cushy kitchen rag rug and stare at the collection of flies trapped in the ceiling fixture. Then I pull my laptop onto my stomach. The last photo she posted of them together has over 150 comments, more comments than there are upperclassmen at Bly, every one of them angling for a claim on the doomed pair, grabbing a little disaster for themselves. People are so clueless. No wonder Mamie ditched her page.

My popover timer dings and I almost toss my laptop. I laugh at myself. Spooked by a friendly ghost. I pull the pan out. The popovers are golden, full of promise. I wish I still felt hungry. Twenty minutes until Mom comes home, and I should make salad, but tragedy-trawling killed my appetite. I shoulder through the kitchen door and down the narrow hall to my room.

Up in my loft bed I look at Mamie's page one more minute, then close my computer and lie back. I won't find her there. Total waste of time, especially considering how much work I have for school. I squeeze my eyes shut and press on my lids until I see stars.

Possible new map: Evie's inner galaxy. Dark matter.

Then I remember something.

I sit up.

Emma said she changed her name.

I stare out the window at the gray and darkening sky and try to remember if she said what the new name was. I roll on my side and reach for my phone.

Changed her name to what?

We're on the same wavelength. Em's reply's instant.

Wren.

Then, before I can reach for my laptop, another text from her.

Why?

Gonna get her to stop the project.

. . .

I hold my breath and wait. Maybe it's a mistake, even mentioning Mamie.

Her texting dots disappear. I'm about to set my phone down when this comes through:

Almost home, late again but had FUN! Stopping for some mouthwash! :o !

I send **XO** back.

"Wren Wells" doesn't bring up much, but I find a photo account with a profile picture of a rocky coast. I click Follow before I see the account's private.

Her name also shows up on a list of student shows at RISD, but there are only a few low-res images of blurry paintings, and I can't even tell if they're hers.

I search everywhere, using every name combination I can think of, but she has no footprint. She's a ghost.

"Evie? You home?" My mom's voice floats down the hallway. She sticks her head in my bedroom doorway. Her cheeks are rosy. It must be getting colder outside again. "Sorry I'm so late tonight! Something smells terrific. Tell me you made popovers."

"I made popovers."

"Aaah, best kid, ever! What did I do to deserve you?" She climbs up my ladder a few rungs to plant a kiss on me, her face tired but happy. "Whole bunch of college mail on the table by the door."

"Mm-kay," I say, noncommittal. I know what's there. I'm the one who brought it in.

Her eyes linger on my face another second, but she lets it go.

"You working on homework?"

"Yeah," I lie.

"All right. I'll change and get started on the salad. Good day?"

"Good day." I smile back at her. "Emma and I walked in together this morning. Fight's over. Tell you more at the table."

She leaves and I close my laptop. It was a good day. Even counting my lunch with Jack. Emma and I are back on track. That's really all that matters.

I text Em.

IHYB.

She sends a heart back.

I'll find a way to get Mamie to leave her alone. I'll think of something. I have to.

brilliant, contagious

5:20 A.M. MY PHONE BUZZES ON the shelf overhead.

I squint at it, then fumble for my glasses.

Be on ur corner in 10.

It's Em. My stomach shimmies.

U ok? I text back.

HURRY.

I sit up so fast I get a head rush, then nearly miss a rung on my ladder. I land on the side of my foot funny and limp around my room, groping for a pair of jeans. I tuck my sleep tee in and pull on my dad's sweatshirt. While the weird cousins of excitement and dread slap me awake, I brush my teeth and pull my fingers through my hair. I'm on my corner in under ten.

Emma's nowhere and it's cold out.

I pull my sweatshirt in tight around my still sleep-warm body and look for her, up and down the block. I should have pulled on a jacket. Winter's back. I'm ready to head toward her place when a yellow Mini Cooper zooms up alongside me.

"Hop in!" Emma says, leaning out a back window and smiling like she won the lottery or she's about to tell me I did. She throws open the door.

"What's with the car service?" I slide in next to her.

"Nice 'do," she says, patting my sleep-challenged hair. Emma's one of those people who washes their hair before bed because sleep just makes it prettier. Mine looks like I've fallen down a steep ravine and wrestled something dangerous at the bottom.

"Drink." She hands me hot coffee in one of her mom's big mugs. It's the perfect color, sandy brown, made with heavy cream, exactly how I like it.

I sip it carefully and watch her from the corner of my eye. Her face is all joy, like someone's taken a photo and cranked up the luminosity, brightened her until she became her own glow. Her hair's in two fat, tousled braids and her lips are cherry red, an old favorite, a color I haven't seen her wear in a while. Emma looks completely reborn. I won't ask, because I don't want details, but she obviously did have fun at Ryan's yesterday.

"Um, where are we headed?" I ask as the car pulls onto Eighth and starts cruising uptown. I regret how it sounds the minute it's out of my mouth. Ever the buzzkill. But Emma's not fazed.

"You'll see." She smiles mysteriously.

While I sip my coffee and watch the city stir, she pats me on the leg and laces her skinny white fingers through my other hand. She's bitten her nails super low, but painted them a pale and sparkly silver. My heart does another happy skip.

I have no idea what's going on or how it happened, but this is more like it. Emma's back from crazyland. Or maybe still in it a little, but she's leaning against me, smelling like her perfume, steering us out on a zany errand—this is the Emma I know. A sliver of rising sunlight angles in low across her face until she's blinding to look at, brilliant, contagious. I close my eyes, sink back into the seat, and finish the coffee she brought, trying not to laugh.

whisper

THE CAR LETS US OUT AT Grand Central.

I hesitate a second, worried now about what she has planned.

"Wait, where? I don't—" I start, then stop. "I'm not dressed for a trip!" I try to make it sound like I'm game for anything. I mean, I've got my phone. I'm not going to wreck this, whatever it is. Not yet. Not until I find out what she's got in mind.

Em's at the door already, but when she sees me hesitating on the curb, she rushes back to me, takes her mom's mug from my hand and chucks it in a trash bin, then wraps her fingers through mine.

"Got the jimjams?" She laughs in my shocked face.

"What?"

She pulls me across the sidewalk and toward the station.

"SAT word of the day, Dummy. On Dr. Foley's door? Means worried. *Jimjams.* Isn't it great? Perfect for you!" She laughs, then shuffles us both into one triangle wedge of the revolving door.

She's not trying to hurt my feelings, but she does, a little.

"Come on." She tugs me along, her grip tight. We cut across the marble floors under the zodiac ceiling, darting through the still-mostly-unpeopled place, until she brings me to a domed intersection on a lower part of the terminal.

I follow her, laughing. Impossible not to, she's practically dragging me. We dash through the space like maniacs, Em pulling my arm like she's going to free it from its socket.

"Stand here." She squares my shoulders and pushes me into a corner. Shoves me right in so my nose is nearly touching the place where the stone walls come together, like I'm a kid in trouble made to stand in the corner of the classroom.

"Kinda bossy this morning," I say to the wall.

"Shush! Now stay right there," she says, a teasing laugh in her voice. "Don't move. Stay just like that. Okay? Trust me!"

I turn to look at her while she darts off. She stops, hands

on her hips. "Evie. Face the wall. Come on. Haven't you ever done this?"

I have no idea what she's talking about, but I turn back and wait.

"Spain," she says, standing right behind me again. Just the one word. I whirl around to face her, but she's not there.

She's on the opposite side of the gallery, facing a corner herself.

"How'd you do that?" I call across to her.

I heard her as clearly as if she whispered it over my shoulder.

Her laugh rings out. "Turn around!"

I do and I swear I can even hear her breathing.

"Patrick and I tried this once when we were younger. Then I saw it again on that Mysterious New York TV show last night. It's so cool. The arches in here are nearly perfect. They carry the sound."

"Why Spain?" I ask the corner, still stunned that this even works.

"We're going, baby. Together. You and me."

My stomach drops. I've been doing everything in my power to pretend this trip's not even happening. I lean into the cool stone corner. It's supposed to be our cultural betterment trip, full of art and architecture, like the Casa Milà, the Sagrada Familia, and the Picasso Museum, in Barcelona. It ends on Ibiza, a World Heritage Site, which is really, according to the people who've gone before, a giant party place with midnight dinners and dancing in clubs and nightly evasions of the super-lax chaperones. And I won't be there.

"Stop it, Eeyore! I can hear your despair from there!" she laughs. "We're going. I'm taking you. It's my treat." Emma's voice floats to my ears from nowhere, startling me again with its clarity. "My parents were so glad to see you the other night, you know? Start working on your Spanish, because we're on our way, *chica*!"

I whirl around to face her again. People are passing between us now and she looks farther away, popping in and out of my sight as morning commuters hustle through.

She leaves her side and darts through the morning travelers to join me.

"*¡Hola, chiquita!* Tapas! Midnight dinners! Hello! Who's going to Europe? We are!" she singsongs as she comes close.

I turn toward my corner again. This conversation would be easier if she'd keep to her post. She rests her chin on my shoulder. Digs it in a little to make me relax, but I feel really weird now.

"I can't let your parents do that," I say, keeping my voice low.

Em and I don't really talk about money, mostly because it makes me feel unequal. Uncomfortable. They have more than we do. But she knows, she gets how I feel. How hard it is sometimes. I'm convinced that some of the clothes she buys, then decides look better on me, are things she's really just buying for me.

She slips to my side and wedges her face in so I have to look at her. She's beaming at me, willing me to catch her mood. This Em is night and day from the person I sat next to on her bed the other night.

"We're going." Her voice sharpens, almost betraying her smile. "We deserve this, Evie. After eleven long years at Bly? Think of the maps you can make over there! I'm not going to Spain without you."

I turn and lean back in the corner a second and let myself imagine it. Spain. Totally more my speed than snorkeling anyway. Europe. A dream trip. Em and me together. And let's face it, no matter what she says, no school that takes Em is going to take me too. And even if it did, we couldn't afford it.

"Anhedonia, they destroy ya." She sings it like the Kinks.

Now Em's the one staring at me, waiting for me to be happy. Weird how fast the tables turn.

"Oh my God, I'm going to Spain!" I laugh.

She dances around me singing, "Silly girl, ya self-destroyer!"

The nightmare of our recent fight recedes like muddy floodwater, and in its place comes a dream of a sunny somewhere else, with centuries of history, small delicious plates of food, and cathedrals that look like they're alive or melting or both. Feels too good to be true.

"Oh!" I say as it starts to sink in. "I have to get a passport!"

Emma squeals and hugs me.

If I'd thought to pocket some chalk on my way out this morning I'd have marked that corner with a pair of suitcases. Or a mouth to an ear. Tools of resistance. Place where the world opened up.

something new

MY MOM AND I INTERSECT NEAR the door when I rush in to get ready for school. She looks worried when she sees me. I'm usually heading out right around the time she's staggering down the hall for a cup of coffee. Morning in the candy office starts later than it does at Bly.

I give her the rundown of the whispering gallery but omit the Spain trip. For now. Her brows are already knit together. She'll object to the impossible generosity, just like I did, but she won't have Emma dancing around all bright and happy to convince her it's okay. Besides, this kind of thing isn't unprecedented. The Sullivans sent me to camp for two weeks with Em one summer, even if it didn't go well. Everyone already knew each other and I didn't fit in. I was miserable and never went back.

"I'm glad you and Em are happy with each other again," she says, looking around for something. "But honey, hurry up. You're going to be late! Have you seen my other boot?" She hobbles down the hall to her bedroom, lopsided, to look for it.

"Em went in ahead of me," I call after her, scanning the living room for the missing boot. "She'll tell Dr. H I forgot something. It's cool. Found it!"

I bend and pull my mom's other boot from under the corner of the ratty velvet armchair by the radiator.

She grabs it from me, zips into it, and clop-clops in her heels to the door, kissing me on the top of the head as she goes.

"Mom, you look cute today," I say before she steps out. "You should try to meet somebody."

My mom hesitates by the door, and for a second I think I've hit a nerve. But then she smiles. I expect her to say what she always does, which is *I've already lived my great love*, but instead she says, "I don't have time to talk to you about this now, but have a great day, okay?"

She digs in her bag for her MetroCard, then blows me a kiss.

"I might be late again this afternoon, implementing something new."

"Woo-hoo." I wave a weak fist in the air. "Innovation at the candy company!"

"Don't knock it," she says, smiling back at me. "I'll take what I can get."

Could be our family motto.

house arrest

"NICE ONE!" EMMA SAYS. "Do it again."

She opens her mouth and I pluck another grape off the cluster her mom left us. We're cross-legged at opposite ends of the long marble island in the center of her kitchen. Em's on "house arrest" after coming home late for dinner again last night. She said we were together, but it didn't matter. She was already in trouble. Sneaking out early this morning didn't help either. Rules are rules. No more wiggle room.

I inspect the grape. "This one's a little squishy."

"Come on," she groans without closing her mouth.

"Hey, it's all about the aerodynamics."

I aim. Toss. The grape arcs high and lands right in her mouth. It's a useless talent, but I'm pretty good at it.

"Fourteen!" I shout, arms in the air. "A new record!"

Emma throws one my way. It hits me in the forehead.

"Pride cometh before the fall," she laughs. "Shut up or you'll jinx it."

"Think he'll ever call?" I moan, plucking another one, ready for lucky fifteen.

"Well, he has your clothes, right?"

"Yeah."

"That no-phone thing is seriously inconvenient, but in your case it's for the best."

"Meaning what?" I demand.

"Meaning it's harder for you to blow it by doing something stupid."

"Thanks."

"I'm serious, Evie. You can't be eager."

"I'm not eager."

She raises one brow. "Repeat after me: I do not care whether Theo Gray ever crosses my path again."

"What? No way. I'm not going to say that."

I hop down off my end of the island and go to the sink for a glass of water. It's like she wants me to end up alone. I can't be like my mom. Love scares the hell out of me, but I still want it, the kind where you don't feel lonely, where you have someone to talk to, even if neither of you knows what to say. Where that would be okay. But I can't say that to Em. She'd mock me. Tell me to play it cool. She doesn't need that. She acts like she's complete or contained or something. Guys to Em are like extras in a movie—they walk on, deliver a few lines, then she forgets them. She's the star, the hero of her story.

"Say it, Eves. You don't have to *believe* it, you just have to put it out there. Come on . . . I do not care—"

I turn to face her. "And this incantation is going to somehow travel to Brooklyn and work its way into his mind?"

"I don't know how it works, but it does. Trust me. Guys are simple. If they think they can't have you, they want you more."

"A gross generalization! Besides, what about love?"

"Love shmove," she scoffs, then flashes the tiniest look of pity my way. "This is a game you're playing—and I'm speaking from experience—if you put out even the *tiniest* whiff of desperation, members of their species—"

"Species?"

She adjusts the poppy-colored strap of her bra and lowers her voice knowingly. "*Species*, trust me, one whiff and they're like animals before a storm. They go all quiet and start plotting their escape."

I turn and look out the sliding glass doors onto their

back garden. I hate it when she takes this tone, like she's in possession of womanly wisdom and I'm some child she has to guide. As soon as Emma had sex, she started acting like we weren't equal anymore, like she went up a step.

"I've been there, that's all." Emma grabs the rest of the grapes and crosses by me to flop on the L-shaped sofa they have facing the yard. "Trust me. Every time I'm impatient or go after a guy before he comes to me, it's ended badly."

I grab my bag and park it on the other end of the couch. I open my laptop on a pillow in my lap.

"No homework, please," she moans, throwing a grape at me, giggling when it lands in the V of my sweater. I dig it out and eat it.

"My mom's volunteering until four thirty. Can't we just hang out?" She scoots down so she's stretched out most of the length of the couch and reaches with her toes for my pillow, closing my laptop.

I slip it out from under her feet and tuck it back in my bag.

Emma wraps a throw around her shoulders and gives a huge sigh. With her long, dark braids, and wide, sad eyes, she looks like a peasant girl from another century or one of those sad seventies paintings.

"It's like a freakin' gulag around here," she says, cementing the impression. "I can only see you and Alice, and on top of having to come straight home every day after school, they've reinstated meetings with Father George."

Meetings with Father George is the closest Em's family comes to psychology. He's a priest but also some kind of counselor. Em had weekly sessions with him in middle school, when teachers at Bly started grumbling about her inability to sit still. He defended her, said her classroom antics weren't the character flaw her father thought. More likely something closer to ADD. Mrs. Sullivan took her to some doctor who put her on Ritalin, then Adderall. When Patrick died, they sent her to see him again. I think he met with all three of them for a while.

"They're trying to act all chill about it, as if my"—she deepens her voice to sound like her dad—"*recent outburst of defiant behavior* is something we can pray away."

She laughs, but it's a hard sound, like cracking glass.

"You don't get how lucky you are, Evie. You're *normal*."

I shift on the couch. She's weighted the word to make it sound like I'm dull or something. Like I don't have feelings the way she does. Or they don't matter as much. I cross my legs and face the garden. Maybe I'm reading into it. Feeling defensive because Emma has to see Father George again, and it's kind of my fault. If I'd run interference for her that night, her parents wouldn't be all over her case like this.

"Em, I'm so sorry."

"Whatever." She shrugs and blows a wisp of hair off her forehead. "I don't care if he's a counselor, he's a priest first, and let me tell you, until you've been given a talking to on your *inappropriate sexual behavior* by a priest, you've had it easy."

I don't know what to say. She mistakes my silence as reason to continue.

"Alice gets it."

Alice's name thuds into me, dull as a cannonball.

"She sees someone too?"

Em nods. "Not a priest, but, you know, her mom's nuts, and her dad's gone—Alice knows what it's like not to feel so freaking perfect all the time."

That hurts. I don't feel perfect, ever. I would love to be able to go talk with a counselor sometime, ask if it's normal to have a mom who sleeps in weird places and cries in the night, or if I'm supposed to feel scared like this, so afraid of the future. I can't imagine talking about how worried I am we'll lose our apartment or that the only way to dig my mom and me out of the hole we're in now will be to dig an even bigger hole with student loans, and where will that leave us? No matter how wild she is, Emma's parents look out for her. I feel like I'm barely holding my mom up. Who catches me if I fall?

I glance around this perfect bright room until I can

control my expression, then I look back at Em. This is an old struggle. I straighten up and pull the pillow close, a huge wave of sadness washing over me. No matter what's going on in my life, Emma thinks she has it worse, always has, long before Patrick died.

"I don't feel perfect," I manage.

She eyes me closely, then shakes her head, exasperated. "Whatever. Semantics. You know what I mean. Alice's dad *left* her. He's not gone like yours. He just doesn't care. And you're, like . . . this rock, Evie. You're not all over the place all the time like I am."

I freeze my expression while another riot of feeling guts me. What am I supposed to say? I'll never be over my dad being gone? Invent words for the indescribable lack? Is there some kind of rule regulating appropriate sadness levels about missing fathers and broken-down mothers that I'm violating? I can hardly look at it myself, much less explain it to anyone else.

Emma eyes my frozen face, then shakes her head. "Sorry, dude, don't get all worked up. I'm stressed *out*. First session with the *padre* in an hour, and my parents are coming along. Should be fun." She checks her phone, keeps her eyes down. "Family therapy with *Patricia* and *Frank*." She rolls their names out, sarcastic. "Jesus, sometimes I'm so pissed at Patrick for not being here."

When she says his name, some of the noise inside me dies down. Problems can't be compared. No one really knows how anyone else feels, and it's how we feel that matters.

I clear my throat. "Maybe you can bring up Mamie's project? With Father G? How hard it is for you?"

Emma stands and goes back to the kitchen. She looks narrow in the echoing space. BPD, this room was alive, all of us in here after school—Patrick and Mamie; Patrick's friends, Luca, Malcolm, Meredith, and Henry; Emma, Jack, and me. Now it's like one of those huge clamshells on the beach. White, wide, and empty.

"Cookies?" she asks, at the cupboard, her back to me.

"No thanks."

She climbs over the back of the couch and sits down again. For a second I think she might cry, but she tears into a box of Vanilla Newman-O's and pops one in her mouth.

"I'm not telling them how I feel," she says finally. "My dad's all *my way or the highway.* Why bother?" She sighs dramatically and sends out a little cloud of crumbs, which makes us both laugh.

"Seriously," she says, brushing them off her shirt and onto the floor, "I almost don't care anymore. I've been trying too hard not to be a total fuckup since Patrick died, but you know what?" She pulls out another cookie. "Their perfect kid died. He just did."

She pulls the cookie apart and tosses me the dry side. We have our favorites.

"I mean, there's no undoing that one! Right?" she laughs. "They're stuck with me! And if they want to let this terrible person use us for *art* and then act like it's some sacramental forgiveness—whatever. I mean it. WHATEVER. I don't really care. I will never understand them, and really, it doesn't matter either way. It's not like it's bringing Patrick back."

Her voice has gone thin and high, like she's trying to convince herself.

The urge to protect her is overwhelming. Even if I looked up to Mamie, no matter how much I thought she was cool, Emma's right here, a half-eaten cookie on her leg, squeezing her eyes shut and pressing on her temples.

"Your idea got me thinking . . . ," she says, her voice low.

"My idea?"

"Yeah." She opens her eyes. "The other night. You said we'd get her to stop. But what if we don't? What if it . . . somehow got wrecked instead?" She has her eyes wide on me now, something flickering in them.

"Wrecked?" I'm not hearing her right.

"Yeah, I mean . . . what if something happened? Somehow we take it down?" She sits straighter. The idea's giving her strength.

A million nos are smashing around inside me like particles in a collider, but I don't let a single one out, because . . . her face. She's bright with purpose.

Emma stares at me, watches me think about it, then shakes her head, her eyes dark again. "You hate the idea."

"No," I say slowly, "but what is it going up that, um, gets wrecked, exactly? Is it photos?"

Emma shakes her head, weary again. The liveliness was like a struck match. Brilliant, then out.

"Don't look like that," I say. "I'm just trying to figure out what you're talking about."

"Not photos," she sighs. "A bunch of shitty paintings. My mom's been sending images of them to me via email, but I refuse to look."

"Paintings."

Mamie wasn't a painter.

Em nods. "She's going to show them. In public. Some gallery connection through her dad. Like Patrick's life's hers, he's her story to tell."

"Paintings of Patrick?" I picture some of the super-sappy, hyperrealistic portraits up right now in the art room, and the thought makes me kind of sick. Em's right. Mamie needs to stop. I feel stupid for looking up to her.

Emma shrugs. Takes the half-eaten cookie off her leg and sets it on the coffee table, flicking crumbs from her fingers.

"She gets to take my family's disaster and turn it into something else, and we can't stop her. She always did exactly what she wanted. Mamie gets her way." She sighs, then straightens up again. Starts wiggling her foot. "What if we went in there right before it opened and pulled the fire alarm? They couldn't open. They'd have to evacuate!"

I shake my head and sit up straighter. "You're kidding, right? We can't do that."

Emma sags again.

"I've been looking for her online."

Emma's silent.

"And you'll do what when you find her?" Em smiles at me, but it's obvious that she has no faith in my ability.

"I'll tell her to stop." I hate how stupid it sounds. I try to be more forceful. "I'll tell her to leave you alone." An idea takes shape. "Or . . ."

"Or . . . ?"

"We go. When she shows her paintings. We'll be there. Make her face us. We'll challenge her. Show people who she really is. What she's doing to you."

Tears fill Emma's eyes.

"You're the best," she says. "I love you so, so much."

Mrs. Sullivan's key squeaks in the door. Emma pulls the throw over her face a second and reemerges, eyes dry.

I stand and hug her fast before her mom comes in.

anywhereelsebuthere

I'M SPRINTING DOWN EM'S STOOP RIGHT as Jack and Alice round the corner.

"What gives?" Jack calls out, spotting me. "You stood me up!"

"What?" I try to breeze past them, twisting my scarf around my neck.

He grabs me by the elbow, swiveling so he's following me. "I was going to come by today, remember? Work on our Investigations?"

"Oh." I shake my arm free and keep walking. "I forgot. I'm sorry."

I'm still pissed at him, but Alice doesn't need to know.

"I looked up TeenART. Did you apply yet? That thing looks perfect for you."

"What? Shut up. Mind your own business."

"Where you goin' now?" Jack sticks obnoxiously close.

"Home."

Jeez. Emma's right about ignoring boys. I've been side-stepping Jack since lunch at Sumo, and it's clearly driving him crazy.

"We're going for bubble tea in Chinatown. Wanna come? My treat."

I glance back at Alice. She hesitates a sec, looking pained, like going for bubble tea is news to her. She tucks a strand of hair behind her ear and avoids my eyes.

"No thanks."

Jack positions himself between us, flinging one arm around my shoulders, the other around Alice's. He hugs us in so close I swear I can smell Alice's citrus perfume. Poor cabbage. Her boyfriend is not treating her well.

As if he heard my thought and wants to cover it up, Jack starts whistling like some old guy, a happy geezer. He's a freakishly good whistler. Another one of the nerd skillz that doomed him before he was cute, along with memorizing a good chunk of pi and winning robotics awards three years in a row. I lean away, annoyed, but that only makes him squeeze me tighter. He tugs my ponytail.

"Ouch." I smack his hand out of my hair.

I don't look at Alice for her reaction, but if I were her I would be seriously annoyed with all the extrarelational flirtation.

Jack presses his body so close to mine our hips touch.

"Dudes, I'm so happy. You know why?"

Deafening silence. Alice looks straight ahead.

I lean away. I hate this Jack. This was his routine when he first got skinny and cute. My mom said it meant he was still insecure and I should wait it out, but I'm tired of waiting for boys to catch up.

"Because I'm with my two favorite girls." He fake pouts.

My cartoon self spews a never-ending arc of rainbow-colored vomit. Makes me smile. I slip a piece of chalk from my pocket and stoop to sketch a monochrome rainbow on the sidewalk. Who says maps can't contain inside jokes? Place where Evie shook it off.

"What's that?" Jack looks down.

"Never mind." I pocket the chalk, feeling better.

He tries to fling his arm over my shoulder again, but I dodge him and walk faster.

"Wait up, crabby pants." He slides his arm from Alice's

shoulder. "I know just what you need." He darts into the deli at the corner.

I look back.

Alice eyes me, surprised.

"Don't look at me. I never know what he's up to."

I keep walking without saying bye or anything. I'd rather be anywhere else but here. It's not like I'm going to chill with Alice on the sidewalk while she waits like a dog outside the deli for Jack.

I stop at the newsstand by the subway corner to grab a bottle of water. The owner's out front, restocking his cooler. I'm handing him my dollar when I hear feet slapping the pavement fast and hard behind me.

"You know . . . *what* is your problem?" Alice rushes up, her voice incredulous, cold, and suddenly very close.

I turn to face her. Her face is vivid with color, conviction.

"I'm so sick of it. Why do you hate me so much?"

I open my mouth, but no words come out. This is the last thing I expected from the cabbage.

"Girls, girls," says the newsstand guy, his hands patting the air in front of us like we're a wildfire springing up that he can still tamp down.

Alice juts her chin forward, gets in my face. Behind her the sun's covered by clouds, the sky a murky pearl.

"I don't know what kind of hold you have over Jack, but

you had your chance already."

She shoves me, hands wide on my shoulders.

I trip backward, away from her and into a rack of magazines. Time slows, and I feel like I could fight. Is this what Theo likes? This urge to push her back, to smack her face, shove her body hard and fast away from my own?

"What the hell?" I yell right back at her instead. "Are you crazy? I mean, I know it runs in your family."

The second it leaves my mouth I regret that last part, but there's no taking it back. Alice's mom is notorious for the night she drove her ancient rusted Mercedes onto the sidewalk outside Bly, nearly taking out a crowd of kids and parents spilling from the school after an awards ceremony.

Alice narrows her eyes, steps forward, and raises her hand like she's going to smack me, hard.

"What did I ever do to you?"

"Make nice, make nice," the newsstand man says, catching her wrist.

I have this weird sideways feeling I'm having a crazy dream. The kind where everyone's terrified because there's a psycho on the loose, and you're cowering too, only then you jolt awake, because the psycho's you.

Jack runs up.

"What the hell?" he asks, looking back and forth between us.

"Ask her," I choke, my heart beating a thousand times a second.

I stare at Alice. Her head is tossed back, nostrils flared. This is the most alive I've ever seen her.

"All you've *ever done* is act like I'm dirt on your shoe, and try every stupid, obvious trick in the book to get away from me," she says.

"Wow. Okay . . ." Jack waggles the king-size candy bar between us. "Who wants some Reese's?"

"You know what?" Alice yanks her wrist free from the newsstand guy. "I don't care. I really don't. I thought you were more, but you're a *bitch*, Evie. And I try not to say stuff like that about people, you know?"

Alice keeps her eyes on me, but the raging fire's dying down.

"Alice, I—"

"Save it. I'm done. This was stupid. You're not worth it." She straightens her posture, grows taller before my eyes. "One more year at Bly, then I'll forget about all of you."

The look on her face shifts into something pure, a clarity I've never seen there before. A prickle of jealousy creeps across my skin. Alice looks confident. Free.

Jack stares at us a second, his thumb sinking into a peanut butter cup, not sure what he's supposed to do.

"I was in that deli for, like, three minutes!"

Just then a familiar straw-colored head sprints up the subway steps next to us, a dry-cleaning bag fluttering like a cape on his back.

Theo's face lights up when he sees me standing here.

"Hey!" he says, starting up the second set of steps. "Perfect timing! You're the person I'm coming to see."

Theo appearing at this moment is a miracle of untold magnificence. I look at his cute face and feel fall-on-my-knees grateful.

He comes around toward me, loops his arm through mine.

I take as large a step away from Jack and Alice as humanly possible.

secret foxes

"HI," THEO SAYS AFTER WE ROUND the corner away from them. His voice is a little softer than it was before, like he's greeting me now for real.

"Hi," I say back, so happy to see him I almost laugh. I can't tell if the rushing gallop my heart's doing is left over from the Alice insanity or because I'm standing next to this very cute boy who came to see me.

"Did I walk into something?" he asks.

"You could say that." I'm still shaking.

"You okay?" He eyes me closely.

"Yeah . . ."

I'm not going to tell him what just happened. I don't even know what happened yet, and really, I am all right, because Theo's standing here like some kind of mystical force making me forget everything else. I'll figure the rest out later.

"I have your clothes." He lifts the bag on his back.

"I see that, thanks." I reach out to take them, but he shakes his head.

"I'll deliver them right to your door," he says with a grin.

He's wearing jeans today, and high-tops and a wool coat. I sneak another peek at him, and he still has his eyes on me, bright, happy.

"My mom says to remind you to come into the shop and pick out a thank-you gift," he says as we walk down the block to my building. "And the dye all came out. Your clothes look as good as they did on you before you took a cherry soda for the team."

I pull open the door to our building, not sure what I'm supposed to do. While I hesitate, a damp crosstown gust whips us from behind, sends my ponytail whipping forward into his face.

He sputters, laughs, and takes a step back.

Oh, to be as spontaneous as the wind.

"Coming up?" I ask, catching my hair, like I'm that casual, that easy with boys.

"Sure, yeah." He slips his old watch out of his pocket. "I've got a few minutes."

"That really works?"

He holds it up to my ear so I hear the ticking. His wrist is warm against my face.

"I mean, you use it? I thought it was a prop."

He pretends to be offended, then breathes on the glass, shines it on his shirt. He hands it to me. "Look at this thing. Beautiful inside and out. It didn't work when I got it. Took some fixing up."

I hand back the watch so I can unlock the foyer door.

"Was it expensive to fix?" I ask, looking back at him.

"I did it myself."

"Yourself?"

"Yup." He looks proud. "My dad and I used to go to all these estate sales. It was during my taking-things-apart phase. For like a week I thought I'd become a watchmaker. Hilarious, right? No one wears watches. Theo the watch-maker. Ha."

"Taking-things-apart phase?" I press the elevator button.

The better elevator comes.

"Yeah, haven't you ever done that?" He steps aside so I can enter first. "Wondered how a lock works or looked at what's inside your microwave?"

I shake my head and push the button for our floor. "Not

enough to break it, which is exactly what would happen if I tried to take it apart. Besides, aren't microwaves all manned by teams of tiny nuclear physicists?"

Theo laughs. We step out on my floor and he follows me down the hall with a wry half smile. His smile's making everything look and feel different, the dim hall shrugging off its air of neglect, taking on a kind of weary, historical charm.

"How do you know what things are like if you can't look inside them? I need to take stuff apart, check it out."

"Good question." I unlock our door casually, like having boys I barely know come over is something I do. "If only that worked with people," I say, thinking of Emma. "Like a human snow globe, or glass girl."

Theo makes a face. "Sounds like a nightmare," he says, stepping in behind me. "No mystery. Too transparent."

"Yeah, I didn't really think that through." I laugh, awkward, while I kick off my shoes. Framed there in my doorway, blond hair wind-wild, he's so cute my heart stutters on a beat. "There'd be no secrets, no places to hide. I'd be frantically mapping all the places people could hide."

"Okay. You have to show me one of these maps."

Theo strides in and lays my dry cleaning over the back of one of the dining room chairs. He looks around, like I'm going to have them hanging on the walls.

"Nah, no. I don't know. Maybe? Sometime." I'm tripping over my tongue. I'm not ready to show him a map yet.

Theo laughs. Marcel leaves his spot on the couch to sniff Theo. Gives him a lick of approval.

"I tried to map worry once, like a visual of the electric tangle in my head would make it easier to navigate?" I don't know why I'm telling him this. I laugh, nervous, blunder on. "But I ended up in an edgy pencil trance, filling a page with tiny circles tucked in tiny squares, so many the paper looked cancerous."

"That one I have to see."

"I threw it out."

Theo walks over to the bookcases and inspects our pictures.

"She looks familiar . . . ?" He picks up one of Emma and me on the water taxi last summer.

I sigh. I can't help it. Even on the periphery, Emma makes an impression. I move closer to look.

"That's Em."

"The fight girl?" He holds the picture up for better light, then smiles. We were playing tourist in matching green plastic Lady Liberty sunglasses.

"Well, she's more than that, but yeah, we made up."

"What's going on here?"

I laugh. "That's a home trip. It's a thing we do. Like,

go to the top of the Empire State, or eat popcorn on the Staten Island Ferry. Sometimes we pick a set of tourists and mimic them—not to be mean, or obvious, or anything, we just let them dictate our day. We take lots of pictures, buy the same cheesy trinkets. Our next trip is on one of those double-decker buses, but Em says we have to wait for *really* bad weather so we can sit up top and get soaked in those light-blue plastic bags they sell to wear over your clothes."

Theo laughs, sets the photo back on the shelf.

"We're going to Spain," I say. "In May. We'll finally be *actual* tourists." A shiver of joy lifts the hair on my arms.

"Cool," he says.

"She talked to you," I say. "The day of the tour."

"Saw your friend Jack that day too. You all go to Bly?"

I climb over the back of the couch and sit down. Theo walks around and joins me. Suddenly I'm all body, shifting uncomfortably, like having Theo here made me forget how a person's supposed to sit on a couch. I wedge myself into the corner and wrap my arms around my knees.

"Yeah, and we're all doing this project. It's so stupid. Juniors at Bly have to conduct this *investigation*. It's part of a yearlong curriculum. American Empire Builders." I roll my eyes. "It gets woven in with junior seminar. It's a ton of student-led work. They're basically making us teach ourselves."

He raises a hand. "Can we talk about *anything* else? Slivers under thumbnails? Eye surgery?"

I close my mouth, embarrassed.

"Sorry," he says. "It's not you. Alternative education is one of my parents' obsessions."

He scoots a little closer to me on the couch, stretches his legs out long. I can feel the heat coming off his body. I take a deep breath. He's so close I can see the little white flecks in his irises that make his eyes so light.

"So this is where you live," he says, looking around.

"Me and my mom." I nod, embarrassed.

The lowering sun filters in the window and catches the side of his face, highlighting blond stubble along his jaw and what's becoming a narrow scar on his lip where the stitches were.

"Hey, your stitches are out."

"Dissolved." He smiles, reaching up to touch his lip.

"What happened, if it wasn't boxing?"

But Theo just looks at me, lips pressed together in a small straight smile. "Not important," he says.

I press my back against the corner of the couch, an unsettled feeling sneaking over me. What if Jack's right about Theo?

"Want something to drink?" I ask, standing. "Or eat?" I'm nervous, and I sound like it.

He blinks back at me a second, as if he's appraising this change in my behavior.

"No, thanks," he says. "I have to get back. It's not easy being a member of Margaret Gray's eclectic empire. A location scout wants to use the unrenovated part of the building for a television show."

"Cool! Any show I know? Emma's family let TV people use the outside of their house once."

He shrugs. "I don't watch TV. Insurance is making us do some stuff before the film people come in, but my mom's paying me a third of what she gets if I take care of it. I'm saving every cent I can at the moment."

"Your mom's so cool," I say, sitting again.

He looks at me, skeptical, eyebrow arched over an arctic eye. "Yeah, I guess, for a benevolent dictator. Neither of my parents really dwell in reality."

I laugh like he's joking, but he doesn't laugh with me.

"I could use a job," I sigh. Suddenly it's hard to swallow. I don't know why I'm telling him this. "I'm pretty sure I have to pay for college, and babysitting the Hanover twins isn't exactly helping me *reach for the stars*."

Theo makes a face at the cheesy sentiment.

"Sorry, that's a Bly counseling office positivity message."

"Private-school kid," Theo teases.

I laugh.

He shifts like he's going to leave, but he doesn't. He turns those bright eyes on me instead. "So, um," he says after a second. "Talking about jobs isn't really why I'm here. Do you wanna come to Dumbo tomorrow night and hang out? Meet up at my house? There's all this development going on by the waterfront and there are some new places to walk around. We could get a slice or something?"

He's asking me out.

I say nothing. I can't make myself speak.

He looks down, then up at me, running a hand through his hair. "No? Okay, don't worry about it, I thought I'd ask, but—"

"No, yes, that'd be great." I cut him off before he takes it back. "What time?"

He grins, wide.

"I'm at the gym with Joe until six. Meet by the bridge at seven?"

I picture him in a helmet and mouth guard, swinging his fists at a priest.

Once I tried to do a map of soul location. I made a small accordion book, a catalog of things. On each little panel I painted an object or place a soul might hide. I put it away when I realized I had nothing for myself, but Emma's was easy, a night-blue sky full of fireworks, the cascading kind, silver and gold. My mom's was a desk, an old oak one like in the basement of the library, drawers full of my dad's stuff, everything she doesn't want to forget. I could pull it out, add a boxing ring for Theo.

He mistakes my silence for second thoughts. "Sorry. This is weird. It's okay if you're not—you don't want to—I just thought . . ."

"Seven's great," I laugh, and he lifts his brows like he wasn't aware he was making a joke. He studies my face a second.

"Gotta go serve the dictator," he says, knocking his knee lightly into mine.

His warm knee, my caught breath.

Instead of standing, though, he leans forward, elbows on his knees, then back again, turning to me kind of suddenly, his face so close I can feel his breath on my lips. Is this what happens before a kiss? A real one, not that rushed, groping thing I had on the beach?

But he clears his throat instead. "I don't have a phone. If you're there, you're there. Okay?"

"You like being unreachable." I draw my knees back to my chest. Jack's words ring in my ears. *Dude's a psycho.*

Theo picks at a hole in the knee of his jeans. His fingers look kind of swollen, the knuckles bruised and cut. His lip twitches a little at the corner.

"Being unreachable is the new black." He stands and

checks his watch. "Gotta fly."

I'm super confused. I thought he was going to kiss me, and now it seems like he can't get out of here fast enough.

I follow him to the door. "Thanks for bringing my clothes."

Theo pulls a hat out of the back of his bag and pulls it down low on his head.

"Sure, no problem," he says.

I flip the lock on the door and he reaches past me to pull it open. He smells good. He hesitates a second in the doorway and I wonder if he's smelling me too. I glance up at his eyes and picture us like a pair of foxes. Then I imagine a map of hidden city foxes, mistaking themselves for teenagers, sniffing each other in doorways.

Just before he steps out, he turns back like he's going to say something, but then he just looks at me a minute and gives me a small smile.

"Yeah?" I ask, trying to blink past the raging flames crackling off my cheeks.

"Nah, nothing," he says, shaking his head.

"See you tomorrow," I say, because I can't shut up, can't stand here in silence for the two seconds it takes for him to walk out the door.

"Yep."

He straightens his posture slightly, looking a little

flushed himself, and takes a small step backward, like he needs to look at me from a different angle or something. Then he goes.

I watch him lope down the hall. Sometimes the secret foxes find each other. He glances at me just before he steps in the elevator, and this time we both grin. Toothy, huge, and stupid.

fern code for soul location

MY PHONE'S HOT IN MY BAG, Jack's sent me so many texts.

You there?

Call me.

Can I come up?

Hello?

Evelicious . . .

They devolve into *call me, call me, call me* times a thousand, like he copied and pasted it into infinity. Jack doesn't have to worry about burning through his data plan. Alice is probably standing next to him seething while he sends endless texts.

Whatever. They can have each other.

I toss my phone onto my bag and head to the kitchen for a snack. I meant to make a new tray of granola last night but watched *Simpsons* on my laptop instead.

My phone buzzes again.

I'm on my way up.

Before I can text back, I hear Jack's voice.

"Eves!" He bangs on the door with the flat of his hand.

"Jack?" I head back out to the door.

"Followed your neighbor in." His voice is lower than normal, brusque, gruff.

I flip the lock and fling open the door.

"Sorry I'm late." He pushes past me, talking super loud and walking with a weird un-Jack-like swagger.

"Late for what?" I look down the hall to see who he's putting the show on for.

He stops near the kitchen and looks down the hall, then he turns to me again.

"Gray's not here?" he whispers.

"What is your problem?"

"Is he here?"

"He's gone," I stage-whisper back, then turn to close the door, possibly a little harder and louder than I need to.

Jack's shoulders drop and he looks kind of relieved.

"Why are you acting like such a weirdo?" I snap.

"Me? Hmm, that's interesting . . . let's examine which one of us was just in a screaming fight with someone else, shall we?"

Alice. I was trying to forget that.

He drops his bag, kicks off his shoes, then flops on our couch, just like he's done a million other times. He hasn't been here in so long, his sudden presence feels like a loss.

"Were you fighting over me?" he asks with a grin. "Alice and I had just been talking about you."

I wonder who initiated that conversation. No. I don't. I close my eyes a second.

"Where'd she go? Ditch you in Chinatown?"

He lifts his head to fluff the pillow beneath it and narrows his eyes at me. "We didn't go. Since when do you and Alice hate each other?"

I shake my head. Embarrassment settles on me, heavy. Alice called me out. Thinking about it makes me feel sick.

"Snack?" I ask, popping in to the kitchen for Cheez Doodles.

Jack opens the bag with a dusty orange pop.

"Why are you here?" I grab a handful and sit at the far end of the couch. "I don't want to talk about Alice *or* work on my Investigation." I'm itching to draw.

"Can't a guy drop by?"

"You haven't dropped by in ages."

I hate him for it, and after whatever that was with Alice, I want him to leave, but here he is, still cute, stretched out there at the end of my couch, licking orange crumbs from his fingers.

"I wanted to make sure you were okay," he says, sounding sincere.

"Yep! Fine." I'm defensive.

"Did Gray come up?"

I say nothing.

Jack deflates.

I stand and take two clementines from the bowl on the dinner table.

"So, you guys . . . ?" He sounds slightly choked.

"What's it to you?"

"You hurt me, girl." He makes it a joke, frowning like a clown, pressing his hand to his heart.

I drop back onto the couch.

Some days are no-man's-land.

Alice screamed at me, but before I could think about that, Theo was in my house, and nearly kissed me, then didn't. Now this, with Jack.

Everything feels off, even our apartment, with its cracked plaster and tired furniture, like things are sucking up all the light, not giving any back. I'd have to map someplace really small and weird, like the inside of the toothpaste cap or the toe of a shoe at the bottom of my closet, in order to get at how precisely tiny, wrong, and lost I feel.

"Wow," Jack says, staring at me. "I'd hate to be inside your head right now."

My cheeks flush. Hell is spending time with people who know you too well. I try to make my face expressionless and toss him a clementine, which he snatches from the air with a grace that never fails to impress. Tell me to catch something and it'll hit me in the head. Every time.

Jack peels the fruit and keeps staring. Mom's out-of-control hanging fern spins on a draft through the window behind him. My mom is good with plants. They're quiet observers, like her. The fern droops one frond finger down in an arc over his head, bobbing on the slight breeze, as if it's pointing to his center. A living map. *Here. Right here.* Plant signal, fern code for soul location.

I forget to keep my face blank.

"What?" Jack follows my eyes and reaches up but misses the fern. He's vain now that he's cute. "Something in my hair?"

"No." I close my eyes.

Theo was flirting with me. I'm sure of it. I've watched enough guys work their way toward Emma over the last year or two to know it when I see it. So what went wrong?

"Eves."

Jack's coiled peel lands in my lap like a springy snake. I toss it back. His face is opaque.

"Please. Really. Don't hang out with that dude."

Of course he knows I'm thinking about Theo. Jack walks in to the most private parts of my heart because the door's wide open. It's been open to him for years.

"Not this again." I slide my thumbnail into the bright-orange flesh of my own clementine. An oily burst of citrus sprays my cheeks.

"He's bad news." Jack bounces his knee. The parquet squeaks staccato under his foot like a panicked mouse. *E-e-e, e-e-e.*

"You know, this day has been weird, and I have stuff to do." I stand up.

"Wait. I didn't tell you the whole story." He looks serious.

I sit again. My heart clops heavy. Jack's eyes are dark. Here's where he tells me Theo's a pervy weirdo with a closet full of wedding dolls or a fingernail clipping collection.

"I know why Theo left camp. It was screwed up."

"You said you didn't." I pull my knees into my chest.

"Well, I do."

"So you lied."

He lets out an exasperated blast. "Why can't you trust me? *No one* liked him. He was an arrogant asshole. Jeb and

Chase couldn't stand him. Kareem tried to get to know the dude, but even he gave up. And Kareem's a saint."

Once Jack grew out of his baby fat, the kinds of people who ignored him before were suddenly his friends. Popular guys like Jeb and Chase and Kareem.

"I need water." He grabs the half-eaten bag of Cheez Doodles and his peel and heads to the kitchen.

The sticky knob on the sink squeaks on. Jack's washing his hands. He acts like a regular slob, but he's a closet clean freak, picky neat.

I finish my fruit and write "LIAR" on my leg in strips of bitter pith. I'm not sure who I'm accusing, but it resembles an intelligent coral formation.

Jack comes out, so I wipe the word away, roll the pith into a tight ball.

"I don't see how Kareem, Jeb, and Chase deciding Theo wasn't cool makes Theo a freak. Seems more like an indictment of those guys." I hesitate for a second, Alice's face flashing before me, a fierce mirror. Then I go on. "You just want to make me feel bad about Theo."

Jack's chin pulls back. "Evie, the guy almost killed Jeb."

"What!?" I laugh. "That's insane."

"That's why he left."

I'm torn between wanting to know everything and telling Jack to leave and never come back.

"Shut up," I say. "You're jealous of Theo."

Jack's face freezes a second.

"Wasps," he says, leaning back like that explains it. "Guy's a sinister mastermind. We wake up one morning and he's gone, right? Cleared out. So we all go out to the lab, but when Jeb opens his lockbox, it's *full* of wasps. They did not just set up in there overnight. He planted them."

I laugh again. It's so stupid, I can't help myself.

"Wait." Jack shakes his head. "Theo did it! He poured soda on Jeb's stuff, and like a million wasps or bees or something came and were crawling all over everything. When Jeb opened his box he got stung like sixty times. It was insane. His face was all lumpy and disgusting. He went into anaphylactic shock."

"Wait. So he was allergic? And Theo knew?"

"It doesn't matter. When you get stung that many times—he's allergic *now*," Jack says, exasperated. "The EMTs barely got there in time. Jeb's tongue was so swollen he couldn't breathe. His whole face was puffed up." Jack shudders. "Anyhow, he has to carry this EpiPen thing around with him everywhere now. If he gets stung again, he could die."

"Seriously, Jack, you think Theo is some kind of bee whisperer? You were there with him? You saw him pour the soda? Or did he do some kind of trick to lure the bees in?" I shake my head. "You're insane. He probably left to get away from your asshole friends."

"Ooh. You never swear," Jack says. "You must really be into him. Look. I don't know how he did it, but the dude is a ball of rage. Look at his face! He probably beat the crap out of someone. I'm telling you, Eves, this is the quiet *before*—Theo Gray's an angry, friendless loser, and he's going to fuck with your head or worse. Besides, where has he been since then? I've been asking around and no one knows anything about him. He's probably been in juvie or something."

"Juvie." I laugh, but it comes out bitter. "Like you'd know anything about juvie."

"This isn't like you, hanging out with some random guy."

Jack looks at me, serious at first, then kind of pleading and cute.

"Time to go," I say, tilting my head toward the door and relishing this new feeling of power.

"Don't go out with this guy."

Jack holds my gaze another second, then stands to leave.

I stare back at him, but for a second my heart's in two places.

What if he's right? Theo's too easy, unreal. This kind of thing doesn't happen to me. I'm no Emma. I don't meet random cute guys and get swept off my feet. But then again . . . Theo.

I try for a deep breath, but it catches.

"Eves?" He senses my wavering.

"I heard you," I say, shaking my head.

Jack doesn't want me to see Theo.

Any other day, this would be the best news ever. But I'm already counting the minutes until I see Theo again.

black hole

I CAN'T SLEEP. TOO MANY SCENES on the insides of my eyelids.

InSANE day, I text Em. **How'd it go w/Fr. G?**

Nothing comes back. I send her a GIF of a puppy jumping.

Hope you're okay.

Still nothing.

I roll onto my stomach and tuck my head under my pillow. Why is it so hard to shut your mind off?

I flop onto my back again, grab my glasses and my

phone. Em's probably already asleep. I'll send the highlights. I number them like a list.

1. Alice attacked me.

2. !?!

3. Theo came over & asked me out . . .

4. Then Jack showed up.

5. Claims Theo's some kind of maniac.

What is the DEAL with this day? Hope, hope, hope you're okay.

I add a thousand kisses and hugs, then put my phone away.

I'm just starting to relax into the pillow when my phone vibrates on the ledge.

She's sick of you hating her.

All the air leaves me. I'm compressing like a black hole, swallowing light at my center.

Maybe that's what I am, made of darkness. It would explain a lot.

In defensive reflex, I text, **she bugs you too!** but delete it.

Emma used to be annoyed by Alice's presence, she was the first one to mock her lack of flair. She called her Lump for a while—not to her face, but still.

Only now I'm the one keeping it going. I feel deeply, darkly stupid, lemmingly mindless.

Alice nailed it. Nailed me, her accusation landing in my softest spot. She totally threatens me. Has done since the very first second Emma laid eyes on her. And now they're friends, bonding, banding together against me, and really it's all my fault.

I start to cry. I don't want to lose Em. Can't.

As if she senses my despair, Em sends another text. Cheerier, chatty. Excited about my date. Makes fun of Father George and her parents.

I can barely read her words. Today was hard for both of us, but apparently we're not going to talk about it.

I answer in emoji.

Laughing face, one tear.

Endless hearts.

A few dogs, then finally some *z*'s.

docent at the cloud cemetery

"MAYBE I WON'T GO," I say to Em at lunch.

We're at Wharton Playground, lying side by side on the picnic table, trying to stay warm in the weak sun. Neither of us has said another word about my run-in with Alice. I'm pretending it didn't happen.

"What? Of course you'll go," she scoffs. "Don't be a freak."

"I miss my dad," I say without thinking. I don't even know where that came from. It's not at all what I planned to say.

She lifts her head to look at me, the red tassels on her

hat dropping down behind her ears. Her new eyeliner is all smudgy and dark blue and against her pale skin makes her eyes look like ice ponds in the middle of a snowstorm.

I shove my hands in my pockets. I need to say this to her, but I'm not sure why. "It's not like Patrick, I know that, 'cause I mean, what exactly am I missing? It's not like I know. Pretty much all my memories of my dad are from pictures. At this point he's kind of nobody, someone who makes my mom cry, but I keep thinking if he were still around, like if I'd grown up with him, I wouldn't be wigging out about tonight or worry about love so much—I'd be less of a freak. And who would my mom be? I can't even picture that."

I don't tell her that I woke up in the middle of the night last night to find my mom asleep on the floor outside my bedroom door for the second time. I can't say that part out loud. Compared to a mom like Mrs. Sullivan—it's too weird. Embarrassing. Scary. I climbed over my mom's curled form, went to get water from the bathroom, then went back to bed. I didn't want to wake her up in case she couldn't get back to sleep again. When my alarm went off for school, it was like something I dreamed. She was in the shower and acting like everything was normal.

Emma sniffs. Scoffs.

"You think you'd talk to your dad about love?"

I shrug, my shoulder moving against hers.

She laughs without sounding happy. "Trust me, if he were here you probably wouldn't be talking to him about anything. For sure not stuff like that. He'd be like every other dad, controlling you and telling you all his stupid rules and requirements are in your best interest."

I sigh.

Emma puts her head back down next to mine and looks at the sky a minute, quiet.

Then she points up at the clouds.

"Okay. So, that's the cemetery," she says with a sweep of her arm, like she's some kind of graveyard docent.

"What?"

"See all those big headstones?" she insists.

I go along with it.

"Those"—and here she adopts a British accent, her voice suddenly old, proper, and warbly—"mark some of our most prestigious patrons."

"Patrons?" I laugh.

"Sleepers, call them what you will." She laughs, sounding like herself, then clears her throat to return to proper. "That one over there was commissioned to resemble angels' wings."

I follow her arm, squinting into the low sky and its gathering of cement-colored lumps.

No angels. Not even with the best imagination. Maybe I shouldn't have said anything. Emma won't even visit the cemetery where they buried Patrick.

She rolls her head toward mine to see if I'm looking.

"Do you see?" she points again, sounding like herself.

I nod and play along.

"Yeah."

"One of them's his."

"Which one?" I ask, and for a second I actually scan the sky, in case I'm missing something, in case he's up there, waiting for me to notice.

"Your choice," she says expansively.

I blink up at the blank overhead. The sun's entirely hidden and the clouds are turning the color of milky tea.

"Evie," Em says, in a suddenly and comically much lower voice. It's the one she uses when she imitates her dad or any other man.

She's joking again, but I roll with it.

"Evie," she says again, sounding somber.

"Yeah?"

"This is your dad."

"Shut up," I say, but I'm listening.

"I'm sorry I died and made you grow up to be a freak

about love and so you feel like you have to overthink everything all the time." Her voice gets so low it breaks on the last word and she coughs.

I flap my scarf across her face, and she sputters, picking wool fuzz off her lips. She rolls onto her side to look at me.

"I'm not kidding," she says in her own voice again. "We should do it. Let's go up there. You wanna? Go see it?"

"What?" I ask. "Where?"

"Upstate. Your dad's grave. When it gets warmer out again. We'll take the train, make a picnic."

My dad's buried in a small town along the Hudson where my grandparents used to live. He's in a tiny churchyard in a family plot. The town's cute. We drove through it once with Mamie and Patrick. I told Emma he was buried there only after we got home.

"Serious?" I blink at her.

"Dead," she says.

places the sun hides

I LOOK IN THE MIRROR and smooth a wrinkle in the short navy skirt I'm wearing. It was my mom's when she was in high school. Em picked my outfit. I'm wearing the vintage skirt with a fitted and faded red V-neck T-shirt we dug out of a bin in a thrift shop, knit tights, and black high-tops. I feel kind of Technicolor, but I think it works. Give me anything worn-in and I'm happy. We trade jackets, because Emma's is better cut, shorter, and highlights the whole skirt/tights/kicks combo.

"Show up late," she says when I check the time.

"No."

"If you don't you'll look eager."

"Maybe I am," I grin.

While she *tsk-tsks* me, I check my reflection a last time, then head for the door.

"That short skirt shows off your legs!"

Even though we're almost the same height, my legs are longer than hers, and, she loves reminding me, one of my assets.

Despite her warning not to get there on time, I use those legs to sprint up the subway steps near his place just shy of seven. The cloudy sky is dragging its dark early over everything, dense and low like a foam ceiling, and people shuffle hunched beneath it. Scrubby patches of exhaust-colored snow hang around the corners like addled icebergs. I feel like I'm startling my fellow citizens with my nervous smile and bright-colored clothes.

Just as I'm about to pass by the still-busy gift shop of the Roebling House, Theo steps out the door to the right of it, his face breaking into a smile the minute he sees me.

Could be a new map. Places the sun hides.

"Hey!" he says, sounding glad. "Perfect timing!"

"Hey yourself," I say back. Voices filter through the open door. Shouting. His mother, maybe.

"Major drama in there," Theo says, pulling the door shut and locking it up. "Can't wait to get out of here." He bends in the doorway to tie his shoe.

"Nice kicks," he says, lining his foot up to mine. Our high-tops match.

He pulls a red knit hat from his pocket and yanks it down over his hair, then bounds in front of me on the sidewalk like a gift. A ball of something bright, reflecting in the puddles.

"You look great," he says.

"Thanks." I blush. I'm so nervous I can hardly speak. I try to slow my internal engine from murder-fast down closer to his easy idle. I drift a second out-of-body until I'm looking down on us, two kids on the sidewalk, Theo next to me like the best surprise ever, giving me that twinkle-eyed grin, the one that makes me think he's maybe gonna kiss me. The one that makes me hope so. I wind myself back in like a kite.

"Can you still go out?" I ask, stupidly, tilting my head toward their windows.

"I'm not going back in there," he says. "A chunk of plaster came down in the kitchen and another one in my mom's office. It's marital theater, my mom whirling fury, my dad shambling around the apartment in his robe, a book in front of his face like a shield, pretending it's no big deal. He's been ignoring a bigger crack in the back wall forever. We need to leave before you find yourself caught in a full-on

Gray family skirmish."

I gape at him, unsure if he's teasing or not.

He laughs. "Nothing like that at your place, eh?"

My quiet apartment. My mom wasn't even home from work when I left. She's been working late a lot. I haven't asked her about it because I'm worried she's finally started to look at my grades rather than trusting me to do my best and has come to understand there will be no merit money for college.

A window squeaks open overhead.

"Theo!" Alo bellows, leaning out over us. "You have to come back up! Mom says you need to get Chester out of here. He's howling and he won't stop."

Theo groans and looks up at his brother.

"Hey, Evie, are you here to babysit?" Alo notices me, looks hopeful. "I heard Mom asking Theo if you would ever be free to babysit."

Theo shakes his head at his brother. "No way, lunkhead. She's here to see me, and I'm not here. Got it? Tell Mom it's too late, you couldn't catch me. I'm already gone."

"But . . . Chester!"

"That one's on you, little man. Take him for a walk yourself. Get out of there. Mom lets you circle the block; they won't even notice you're gone."

Alo stares down at his brother a minute, then sticks his

tongue out at us and pulls his head back in. The window falls down with a bang.

Theo laces his fingers through mine and everything inside me hums like I'm holding a ray of the sun. "Come on," he says. "Wanna walk?"

He stands there a second, like he's thinking about where we should go. I'll follow him anywhere. All I can think about is the feeling of his fingers woven warm through mine. The pulse between us.

The window squeaks open again.

"Let's get out of here," he says, dropping my hand and grabbing my arm to steer me instead. "I need to shake off the bullshit. I want to be well out of earshot, before I end up having to take Chester instead of hanging out with you."

Theo takes off running, pulling me along. I'm clumsy and strange next to him, not sure where we're going or, really, what I've gotten myself into, but he's easy in his body, so I loosen up. We pound down the cobblestones away from his place, toward the mist-heavy river.

flying free in the blue-dark

ONCE WE'RE OUT OF SIGHT, Theo drops my arm and we slow to a mellower pace, a rhythm of quiet footfalls, and it could even be nice, except I'm doing what I do when I'm nervous, filling the air with words. The mystery of whether he'll kiss me or not is an irrepressible itch. I'm scared to even use words that end in *s* in case I accidentally say "kiss" instead. I want it so badly I chatter at Theo like a demented bird, tell him everything I never say out loud, how scared I am about college, about Em acting erratic, Mamie's project that I want to stop.

He looks skeptical when I talk about Em. It makes me feel like I have to defend her.

"But I'm only telling you the bad stuff." I pull my phone out of my pocket and wiggle it at him. "I know you hate them but she gave me this iPhone. It used to be hers. I had a crappy flip phone before." He doesn't look impressed, but I don't care. I smile at him. "You'd love her. She's beautiful and funny and crazy and kind."

I'm seized with an involuntary shudder that contradicts my words.

"What was that?" Theo laughs, addressing the shudder. The way he's looking at me, I can tell I'm blowing this. I'm acting too nervous and weird. I'm all over the place.

I try to calm down, laugh, embarrassed. "I don't know, I guess I kind of have this feeling like an end's coming? And it's not going to be a good one."

My face is flushed. I can feel it. I press a cold palm to the far side of my face.

"Intense," Theo says, looking at me funny. "So you go around all wound up like this all the time, dreading some ending?"

I shake my head, try to be more specific, but find I can't. I open my mouth, then close it. We walk another minute.

"It's just a feeling," I backpedal. Laugh, nervous. "Emma's brother died. I mean, that was an *ending*. You can't plan for stuff like that." My voice climbs, breathy. I don't even sound like myself.

This is my first date, and I'm wrecking it.

Theo stops and squints at me like he's trying to decide whether to say something.

I look down, blink at our matching feet. Theo's sneakers are wet, the rubber peeling away from the sides. Mine look overly neat, sturdy, stupid.

"Is this what you do? Worry all the time, even about other people's problems?" he asks.

"You have to take care of people." I say, defensive.

"Why's that?" Theo asks.

"Because that's what friends do," I say, thinking about looking at the clouds with Em at lunch. *Because you never know when you're about to lose someone.*

We stop on a cobbled street just past the Manhattan Bridge, the East River a dark ribbon beside us. Theo looks over at it, face unreadable.

"I hurt your feelings," he states, shoving his hands in his pockets. He starts to walk again.

"No," I start, but it's true, so I shut up and follow him along the dark street.

"It's just, you should hear yourself." He looks over his shoulder at me. "It's like this girl is some brilliant torch or something. Did you ever consider that maybe that glow you think you see coming from your pal Emma is coming from you, instead? You're the one making it all up?"

"Making it up?" Jack was right. Theo's weird, and he's making me feel bad. I should leave. "I don't lie."

"That's not what I mean," Theo says, exasperated. "More like you're the projector and Emma's the movie you're showing, but Evie, all that light is coming from you."

He stops and looks back at me.

"I look at you and see this beautiful girl—" Closes his eyes a minute. Opens them again. Shakes his head. "I wasn't planning on, uh, going out with anybody. I just ended something. With someone—Lindsay. A month ago."

Theo sits on a big block of concrete with metal rods sticking up from the back of it like antennae. Pats a spot next to him. I sit too.

"I didn't mean to meet you." He looks at my mouth. "That sounds weird. I wasn't planning on meeting anyone for a while."

I bounce my heel off the edge of the concrete block.

Theo runs his fingers over a frayed part of the thigh of his jeans. His hands are a weird combination of beat-up and elegant. "Linds and I had too many problems. Her parents were splitting up, and it was like I was supposed to—" He looks at me. "I mean, I know that's hard, but I couldn't breathe. It was like she expected me to save her."

The concrete's cold under my thighs and I try not to shiver.

Theo looks up at the cloudy sky, then back down at me.

"I guess I'm saying it shouldn't be complicated," he says. "Not yet. And don't sweat college. You're either going to go or you're not. Nothing bad is going to happen either way."

I open my mouth, then close it again. He doesn't get it. I wrap my arms around myself, tight.

Theo sees me shivering, takes off his hat, and pulls it down over my head. He smiles at me so sweetly for a second I forget to feel bad about anything else.

"You know?"

I nod without conviction.

"I'm just saying there's no deadline. Maybe Bly acts like it, but they're wrong. Go to college if you want. When you want."

I start to protest, to bring up money, grades, competition, but he stops me midstream.

"No scholarship? So find a way to pay for it. That's what people do. But no matter what you do, you'll still be who you are now, you'll still have all your own things to work through, figure out."

My heart sinks. Why can't I just go out and have fun

with a guy like Emma does? Why does it have to be messy and complicated and awkward?

Theo takes my silence for doubt.

"Trust me," he says. "I've been there."

"You went to *college*," I say, sarcastic.

Theo stands and starts walking. Across the river, city lights twinkle on, make Manhattan's tiara. We walk toward a massive waterfront power plant, its metal twists and coils dove-gray against the darkening sky.

"I went when I was fourteen. My parents made me."

"No way." I laugh, despite myself, despite how serious he looks. "College? You're kidding."

"Wish I were." Then he flings an arm over my shoulders like touching each other is what we do.

"Your brother wasn't messing with me? You're really one of those prodigy kids?" My voice is weirdly breathy. For some reason this thrills me.

"Guess so. Wanna see my membership card?" he says, stopping and pretending to fumble for his wallet.

"Where?"

Oblivious to my shivery joy, Theo shakes his head, jaw muscle twitching.

"Irrelevant."

"Irrelevant?" I laugh, incredulous. "Come on, where?"

He's silent a minute.

"University of Chicago."

"Whoa." I stop, put my hand on his chest. "You *are* a genius."

"Shut up." He smiles and covers my hand with his.

"Seriously!"

He closes his eyes and shakes his head.

"I'm good at math, physics, and languages. Basically, abstract formal systems. But please, please don't be one of those people who make this into a huge deal, okay? I only brought it up because if you're freaking out about stupid stuff like college, you need to know that you don't have to go, if you're not ready. It's not complicated."

"Wait. Fourteen? So, after camp with Jack?" I'm having trouble tracking our conversation because I'm so aware of every millimeter where his body's touching mine.

Theo's head snaps up, eyes meeting mine with a cool spark of interest.

"Ah. Your pal Jack finally confess?"

"Confess?"

Theo breaks away from me and jumps from the edge of the curb to avoid a massive gritty puddle. I walk around it. He eyes me sideways, waiting.

"Let's just say Jack's not a fan," I admit carefully.

"What?" He looks surprised.

He opens his mouth to speak, then shakes his head like he's pissed off.

"So, how smart are you?" I change the subject. "Did you graduate in, like, two years?"

He smiles. "I dropped out."

I raise my brows.

"It wasn't my dream," he says. "In case you haven't noticed, my parents are intense. Like they know how we're supposed to be, *who* we're supposed to be. As if it's even up to them."

He opens his coat.

I shift a little closer, to the heat coming off his chest.

"Laz's mom, my dad's first wife, was a lawyer for the Native American Sovereignty Fund. She died of breast cancer when Laz was two. My dad married again within the year and what did they do? Groom Laz for law, of course. From day one. Who does that to a kid? Like it's his freaking duty or something."

"He hates it?"

Theo shakes his head, mystified. "No. I don't know. Who knows? Laz plays it close to the vest. He does not make waves with them."

He kicks a paper cup someone's left in the street.

"And you?"

"I took matters into my own hands."

I must look shocked, because he grins and bumps my shoulder with his.

"Relax. I quit. Walked away. And you know what? That was probably the best thing I ever did. Walking taught me who I really am."

"Which is . . . ?"

"A person who makes his own decisions," he says. "The walk was long. Gave me time to think about what matters."

I stop.

"Wait. You walked *home*? From Chicago? Isn't that like a thousand miles?"

"More or less. A little less." His jaw is set hard, proud.

Wind whips across the river. An empty bag follows us down the street with a plastic whisper.

"If I go back it'll be because I want to, because I'm ready."

"You *walked*?" I'm stuck on the impossibility of it. "The whole way?"

He laughs at the look on my face. "I read Whitman, Thoreau, Ginsberg, the usual suspects," he says, like that explains it.

"Where'd you sleep?"

"I picked up a tent. This country's so beautiful."

"You *walked* back to New York City." I say it with a laugh, like it's not the most absurd thing ever. "How long did it take?

"A little under six weeks."

I stop a second to take it in. Picture Theo small against the side of the road. Cars whipping past.

"I could never do that."

"Haven't you ever wanted to do something that scared you? Push yourself? Really be out of control? I kept lying in bed in my dorm picturing all that openness. I had to do it. See if I could rely on myself."

"And your parents were cool with the plan?"

"Wasn't up to them."

I picture him smaller, more like Alo, blond head and a backpack, bobbing along the edge of some endless highway, trucks flying by, covering all those miles alone.

"They weren't going to say yes. I made a decision and I left."

"If I did something like that, it would *kill* my mom."

He's quiet a second, like he's choosing his words carefully. "When people find out learning comes easily to you, they kind of flip out. It was worse in Chicago. My mom was this unschool celeb blogging everywhere about her 'success.'"

"Meaning you."

He nods. "I was a poster boy, and I wasn't the only one at

Chicago—this other kid was in med school, younger than me—isn't that crazy?—but we never saw each other. There was no way to blend in. Fourteen looks fourteen. I was the story people couldn't wait to tell, even my professors. I was a total aberration to everyone, all the time."

He takes a deep breath, straightens out of his slouch.

"So you ran away."

"I left. Not the same. I was going home."

I gape at him.

Theo laughs. Bends to pick up the plastic bag that's still following us. He ties it into a small knot and pockets it.

"I met Joe, learned to box. Got a job in the churchyard. You know?"

I'm mulling this over when something he said earlier hits me.

"Wait," I say. "Earlier. You said *confess*, about Jack?"

He walks a little faster. "Forget it. Doesn't matter."

My heart picks up a beat. Something about the tone of his voice.

"He told me about the wasps."

"Wasps?" Confusion crosses Theo's face, and for a second he looks younger. "Never mind," he says, shaking it off. "It's not worth it. You want coffee?"

He stops on the corner across from the John Street Roasting Company.

"Hang on," I say, grabbing his arm. "You didn't attack Jeb with wasps?" As I say it, I hear how stupid it sounds.

Theo pulls his arm free and laughs, but it sounds full of disappointment.

We stand there a second, staring at each other. He leans over me, pulls me close.

"You are really very pretty," he whispers, his breath on my face.

I blink back into those fox eyes, pull away the tiniest bit, instinct, or fear or something, a retreat anyone would make under that gaze. He lifts my chin and closes the space between us. Theo kisses me so true the sky falls down around us, scattering stars at our feet.

Kissing him is like losing myself in a map, only better.

"All good?" he whispers into my lips.

"All good," I whisper back. Then I press my mouth against his, lick the small scar on his lip.

Before I follow Theo into the coffee shop, I slip chalk from my pocket and draw stars on the curb.

Place where I found what I wanted.

I don't know why I thought there were rules, why I've been dreading an ending. Obviously we're making it up with each other as we go. Because right now I'm weightless, wild, flying free through blue-dark space.

need you

MY PHONE BUZZES ON THE LEDGE next to me. It's Em. At seven a.m.

"Hey," I answer, happy despite the time. She's calling to hear how it went, and finally it's my turn to have a night to report on. Every perfect detail—Theo walking me across the bridge, then all the way home. Sitting out front, shivering and kissing, until almost one in the morning.

"I was going to call you in a bit. What are you doing up?" I rub the sleep out of my eyes and double-check the time.

"Can you come?" Her voice is scratchy and raw, like she's

been up all night screaming lyrics into a mic and smoking hundreds of cigarettes.

"What's wrong?" I do a whole-body stretch that's so thorough my feet twitch and wake Marcel at the end of my bed. He's so fat he's hard to hoist up here every night, but if I don't he whimpers on the floor beneath me.

"Nothing. Can you just come?"

I kick off the covers and sit up.

"I need you."

I scramble down with Marcel and start looking for clothes.

"Sure, I'll be right over," I say, ready to hang up.

"Wait!" she says. "I'm not home."

"Where are you?"

"Tompkins Square Park."

When I hustle out of my room and into the hall, there's a noise in the kitchen, like my mom's already up. Maybe she never slept. Between my mom and Em, this is a bizarre Saturday. I hesitate by the kitchen door but don't let her know I'm awake. She'll be all questions if I do. I leave a note on my bed instead.

Ran out to meet Em. She needs me.

lookout

SHE'S ON A BENCH, EYES CLOSED, scarf wrapped high around her face.

"Thank *God*," she says when I run up to where she's sitting. "Did you bring water?"

"Was I supposed to?"

She moans.

"We can grab a bottle. Are you hungover?"

She gives me a half smile and presses her hands to her temples. "I've been trying Alice, but her phone's off or something."

Alice's name hits me low and heavy.

Emma's wearing tons of eyeliner, most of it smudged, and her hair's wound around the top of her head in an elaborate braid. What's left of some really dark lipstick makes her face more pallid than ever. She draws her knees up into the big jacket she's wearing. It's someone else's, a dark red plaid thing with a grubby-looking fleece lining.

I shrug off the Alice gut-punch and drop to sit next to her on the bench.

"What's going on?"

She puts her head on my shoulder. "Oh my God, I just really, really need to sleep. Can you sneak me into your house somehow? I'll sleep in your closet if I have to. I was with Ryan. My parents think I'm at Alice's."

I pull away from her a second to get a better look at her. I can't bring her home. It's obvious she's been partying all night. She smells sour, like beer and cigarettes.

"You were at Ryan's place?"

She gives me a slow smile, like she's still living last night. Considering she hasn't slept yet, I guess she kind of is.

"He asked me to meet him when he got off work. Oh my God, Evie, it was insane. We went to this crazy basement music venue, Candy's Dandy? All these bands were playing, then we met up with some people Ryan knows and followed them out to Bushwick to this party. But it was lame, so we left and walked everywhere, along the East River, for ages, until Ryan heard from this other friend, and we went to some weird empty office space downtown. There were all these cool people there—it was like being in the middle of some punk hacker dream or something. It was like this corporate construction site, a build-out in the middle of being built out? We snuck up to this really high floor that was just open! No walls or windows, just a layer of thin plastic whipping around in the wind."

She waves her arm like a wing and I can see the wide open space, the frightening edge. I open my mouth to say something, but she goes on.

"I love this guy so much and I have tons to tell you, but I haven't slept, and my temples feel like a zoo of caged dragons." She lays her head on my shoulder. "I really, really need to go somewhere and sleep."

The whole way here I pictured telling her about kissing Theo. I sit there a minute and wait for her to remember, to ask me how my night went.

But she doesn't. She breathes heavily instead, like she might have drifted off.

I turn my face away, disappointed. Sometimes I get this old/young feeling with Em. Compared to her wild night, my walk with Theo seems embarrassingly innocent. Immature. But at the same time, with her skinny shivering body against mine, her stinky head on my shoulder, I feel like I'm really old, weary from a thousand years of responsibility, from trying to steer Em clear of disasters in her path.

"I can't sneak you in," I say, breaking the silence.

"What? Why not?" Emma straightens up to look at me. "I was already dreaming about your closet."

"My mom's up early."

"Your mom's never up early."

"Well, she is today."

Emma eyes me to see if I'm making it up. Punishing her for her night out.

"It's the truth," I say. "And she's going to freak if she goes in my room and sees I'm gone."

Emma frowns. Pouts a second. Then, as if she's only now remembering, she gets this sly smile on her face and says, "Oh my God! How was it? Last night, with Theo?"

I hesitate a second to savor it, figure out what to tell her first, and I'm so happy she came through, but before I can answer, she moans, bending forward on the bench, burping and holding her head. "Wait," she says, resting her head on her knees. "Don't tell me now. Don't tell me anything unless it's where I can go sleep this shit off."

"Why didn't you go back to Ryan's?" I ask, trying to hide how hurt I feel.

She sits up again, her hands in front of her for balance, eyes closed.

"Hang on." She takes a shaky breath. "I might be sick." She kind of pants a second, then shakes her head and burps again. "Ugh, sorry." She smiles. "Guess not. We didn't go back to Ryan's because his roommate is super studious and not at all fun and doesn't like it when he brings people home." She laughs, wobbly. "I told him he totally needs to move, find a better situation." Her eyes light up. "I'd go apartment hunting with him. Can you imagine?" she says, squeezing my arm. "I could help him pick some incredible place and then I'd hang out over there all the time."

Her pocket dings, a different sound than her texts usually make.

"That's Alice," she says, whipping out her phone. She stands and shakes it in front of me. "C'mon," she says with a sigh of relief. "She says come over. Will you go with me? Be lookout? Make sure my parents aren't out on the block?"

My stomach flips. Maybe I'm the one who's going to be sick.

Emma slips out of the jacket she's wearing. "Can you believe this?" she says, shaking her head and looking at it with disgust. "I left my coat somewhere last night."

"Your coat?"

"Oh shit!" She widens her eyes at me, laughing. "*Your coat!* Oh my God. I'm sorry. I lost your coat last night! Good thing mine looks so great on you."

I liked my coat but don't say anything. It's done.

She turns and walks out of the park, tossing the janky plaid jacket in a trash bin on her way.

I follow her. That's me, Emma's lookout.

special affection

ADVISORY'S AN UNENDING BLUR OF INFO about test prep, mid-marking-period exams, and other deadlines. I'm looking up past recipients of TeenART on my phone under the table. I click on animated drawings by someone named Pippi Blackwood. The screen flickers, fills with a girl's face, eyes closed. Her eyelids flutter up and birds fly out. It's eerie and feels like a projection of a dream. I glance at Dr. Holmes every few seconds so I look like I'm paying attention. In her statement, Blackwood calls drawing "a manifestation of sight." My heart sinks. Pippi Blackwood and her manifestations—my name's not cool enough, and

I don't have words for what I do. Not like that.

Emma whacks her knee into mine and I darken my phone.

"Okay, people," Dr. Holmes drones. "For those of you planning to go to Spain, the time has come to hand in your forms." He checks a packet of information on the table in front of him, one old, wavering finger running down the page. "And your deposits are due today as well." He taps the sheaf, a husky, dry sound.

The room fills with rustling as people start digging through their bags, pulling out permission slips and doctor's letters and, most important, envelopes with deposit checks in them. I sit still in my seat, rigid with embarrassment. I've completed all the forms, my mom's signature's easy to forge, and I'm not telling her about the trip until my deposit's in and there's no turning back, but Holmes is collecting them now, and I have no check.

The radiators wheeze and fill the room with the heat of three suns. Or maybe it's my face doing that.

Eighteen hundred dollars per student, due today, the second eighteen hundred due four weeks before we leave.

I raise a hand to my burning cheek. I can't bring myself to look at Em. I knew this was coming, the deposit due date, but I haven't been able to make myself ask her about it. Feels beggarly.

Emma leans away from me and toward Alice to pull out her paperwork. She makes a big show of digging in her bag, pulling everything out in a giant pile on the table in front of her. Then she raises her hand.

"Um, Dr. H?" she asks sweetly. No one else gets away with starting a sentence like that, much less abbreviating his name, but Holmes has special affection for Em.

"Yes?" He surveys the mess on the table before her.

"I don't have my papers today. I forgot them at home. I'll bring them in next week? I promise?"

Dr. Holmes holds her steady in his gaze, blinking his watery fish-colored eyes from behind his enormously magnifying glasses.

I hold my breath.

He nods, once, solemn.

"Very well, Miss Sullivan," he says, straightening his vest. "See that you get them in first thing next week, or you may find yourself relinquishing your spot."

Emma nods and I deflate with anxious relief. Of course she forgot them. Deadlines aren't her thing. She's late for stuff all the time, and if anyone can get Bly to make an exception it's Em. I just hope it'll include me too.

bouquet of hues

THEO'S ON THE SIDEWALK IN FRONT of Bly after school when we spill out onto the steps.

Em spots him first, grabs my hand in her cold one. Two sharp squeezes until I follow her gaze and see him standing in the sun, skateboard in one hand, a collection of what look like pencils in the other.

"Hey," he says with a sly smile when I come down. "Brought you something."

He offers me a clutch of Caran d'Ache watercolor pencils, a bouquet of hues, tied together with a vivid rose-colored ribbon.

"The woman at the art shop said these ones are great for blending." He looks kind of embarrassed.

The pencils are Swiss, expensive. I have a few, not this many.

I can feel Emma's eyes wide on me, taking in this unprecedented male sweetness.

"They are! I don't know what to say." I never know how to receive gifts. I can hardly look up at him. "This is so incredible, thank you." I'm embarrassed, but then he takes me by the wrist, pulls me in to him, and gives me the softest kiss.

I finally understand what people mean when they talk about swooning.

When we part, Emma clears her throat and smiles at Theo.

"Hey," she says. "You're the guy from the Roebling House, right? The one with the black eye?"

Like I haven't already told her every detail about him, described his face right down to the tiny freckle by the right corner of his lower lip. I've forgiven her for Saturday. She came over Sunday and we spent the day sort of working on our Investigations but really raking over every detail of my night with Theo.

"Sorry." I introduce them. "Theo, this is my friend Emma."

"Hey!" She grins huge, tossing her shoulders back and thrusting a pale hand his way.

"Hey, how's it going?" Theo nods at her, keeping his hands on my waist.

Emma pulls hers back, smile dimming slightly.

Theo turns to me.

"Thought I'd surprise you," he says. "I only have a minute, but my family's going upstate for the weekend and . . ." His focus shifts to something over my shoulder.

I turn and look.

Jack and Alice are behind us on the steps.

Jack sees Theo, stops a second, then sprints the rest of the way down, brushing past us so close he almost shoulder-checks Theo. Alice hurries to catch up and slips her hand into his. She doesn't look at me.

"Um," Theo says, looking back at me. "So, Saturday. They're going and I'm not. Do you want to come over and watch a movie or something?"

Emma's acting really cool next to me, gazing at Theo almost like she's bored, but I can feel her psychically telling me to say *yes! yes! yes!* Excitement is sparkling up from her like bubbles in a fresh glass of seltzer.

"Yeah, that would be great," I say. "I'll have to clear it with my mom, but I'm sure it's fine."

Emma steps lightly on my toes for the mom comment. I

pull my foot back and look at the bundle of pencils in their rose-colored ribbon. Heat rushes to my cheeks.

"For your maps," Theo says. "Bring one when you come?"

Emma leans toward him in an ever-so-slightly beguiling and knowing way, her hand landing delicately on his arm.

"Good luck with that," she says with a throaty laugh, like they're already friends. "Evie and her maps . . ."

There's something in her tone. I sink inside for a second. I'm hearing her wrong, I have to be, but it sure feels like she's flirting with him, and kind of mocking me.

Theo looks at her, expressionless, then turns his face back toward mine.

"I've been thinking about you all week," he whispers, mouth at my ear.

My limbs go liquid. "You have magic fox eyes," I say without thinking.

Theo laughs, and he kisses me again.

"Take it easy," he says to Em with a nod once we part. He drops his skateboard and stops it with his foot.

She flashes him another flirty smile.

Theo winks at me. "See you tomorrow, Evie."

He sails off.

I turn to Em, my ears full of a blood-thunder rush.

"What was *that*?" I demand.

muddy well in the center

"WHAT WAS WHAT?" SHE ASKS, voice bright and tight even though she knows exactly what I'm talking about. She links her arm in mine and pulls me toward the subway. "Come on, let's go scour some sale racks. You need clothes for this date!"

I slip my arm loose from hers, follow her silently.

When you've been friends as long as we have there are two conversations running most of the time. The one you're saying and the other one, beneath the surface, the real deal. By the time we get to the subway I'm ready to cut through it all and say what I saw.

"You were flirting with him." I mean to sound resolute but my voice wavers instead.

"Run! I hear the train!" Emma darts ahead and I follow her down to the platform.

A woman rushes past us with grocery bags, then turns back to glare at Em. There's no train. From the looks of it, people have been waiting for ages. The platform's packed.

"Guess not," she says.

I glare at her, my question still hanging.

"What? Come on. No I wasn't." She juts her chin out. "God, you're being paranoid. You finally get a boyfriend and you're gonna act all jealous? Of me? Get over it."

She whips out her phone and turns away. A little kid on a scooter zips between us, close to the edge, his mother rushing right behind, yelling at him to *get off that scooter and walk*.

Tears sting the backs of my eyes. I should have kept my mouth shut. Even if she was flirting, it was automatic, didn't mean anything. Emma would never go after someone I like. She's right, I am paranoid. Flirty's her thing, it's how she is.

I look at her narrow shoulders, the back of her head. She looks small, standing there, turned away from me. Like someone to protect. Em's been crabby and tense since the Spain deposit was due, but she hasn't said anything to me about it and I can't make myself ask. I should never have said yes. It feels too weird.

"Jesus, where *is* the train?" Emma asks, whirling back to look down the tunnel.

"Signal problems," an older woman next to me sighs.

A group of middle-school kids runs through, loud and happy, all wearing overstuffed backpacks. One of them bumps Em and her phone flies from her hand and lands in the well between the tracks.

"God dammit!" she shouts. "Watch where you're going!"

Then, before I have a second to stop her, she looks to see if the train's coming and jumps down onto the tracks to grab it.

"Emma!" I scream. I can't help it. I can't believe my eyes.

She looks at me, at the shock that has to be wild on my face, and gives me this strange dark smile. She looks like a devil down there, like she's been possessed and is not herself.

We both hear the rails click.

"Get up here!" I shout, leaning over with my arms outstretched.

Emma pockets her phone and scrambles back to the wall and tries to hoist herself up. She grabs hard for my hands, but doesn't catch anything with her feet and falls back down, tripping over the track and sitting hard in the muddy well in the center.

"Oh my God!" She looks at me in disbelief and starts to laugh. Emma laughs when she's scared.

The rails click again. This time there's a slight breeze. I whirl to see the beam of a train's headlight just beginning to reflect along the far tiles of the station wall.

Everything's in hyperfocus. I look down the tracks. The headlight's there, but I can't see the train. Yet. If I don't help her, she's going to sit there laughing until it rushes in.

I drop my bag and jump down after her. People behind me shout but they sound far away. Abstract.

I wrap my arms under Em's armpits and jerk her into a standing position.

"What is going on?" she asks, as if we're experiencing something mystical.

I boost her up to the yellow platform edge until she can inchworm her body back onto it.

The rails click again, and now I see the train.

Time stops. Everything is silent, and for a second I'm nothing. Not Evie. No one. I'm absolutely gone.

"What the *fuck* were you thinking?"

A large man has me by the arms and I'm back on the platform. Words are flying from his face like bullets. The inside of his mouth is so red.

He lets me go and pivots to Emma. People are staring.

"You're a pair of *stupid* little shits!"

My arms feel like they've been torn out of their sockets.

The train rushes in, and he boards it with everyone else, and then we're alone.

My knees loosen and I sit down on the filthy platform, right on the ground, lean against the wall, and try to find my way back down into my body from wherever I went.

Emma crouches, muddy and silent beside me.

All around us new people filter in to wait for the next one. People who don't know what just happened. What we just risked.

"I'm sorry, Evie," she says finally, in a voice so quiet I almost can't hear it.

I look past her, beyond the outline of her face. This city is so packed with souls. I wish I could pin my heart to one of them instead, let it slip out, away from here, send it off safe, hurrying home with someone else.

hibiscus, delicious

EMMA SHOWS UP EARLY the next morning with a box of doughnuts and a tall coffee for me. The doughnut box inches over the top of my loft before her head appears, her smile not completely hiding the nervous look in her eyes.

"Wake up, sleepyhead. I'm here to help you get ready for your date. Your mom let me in." She lifts the coffee. "She said to tell you she's going in to work today. Something about inventory or audit? I don't know. One of those accounting-y words."

"It's so early," I moan, leaning against a pile of pillows.

"Sleep's overrated." She hands me the cup. "You can

sleep when you're dead."

"Poor choice of words," I say, closing my eyes again. I don't forgive her. Not yet.

"Who needs sleep?" she tries instead.

I do, I think. I barely got any last night, probably because I OD'd on adrenaline yesterday. I sit up with a sigh and pop the top on the latte so I can blow on it until it's cool enough to sip.

She scrambles up the ladder and sits in her usual place, perpendicular to me, her legs over mine, the box of fluffy doughnuts open between us like an offering. Their yeasty, sugary smell wafts up, making my stomach rumble.

"So, I was out running this morning," she says, instead of hello or I'm sorry. "And I passed this doughnut place I'd never seen before. Called Dough. Oh my God, Evie, wait until you taste this. They make them right in front of you. You have no idea how hard it was not to eat this whole box on the way over here."

She thrusts a gooey glazed doughnut my way and hands me a napkin.

I bite into perfection. It's still warm. The glaze is smooth, fresh, just the way I like it. The doughnut underneath's an airy cloud of goodness. She bought enough for ten people, the box is packed with a variety of rounds, but Em knows I like glazed the best and there are two more of them.

"Sublime, right?" She lifts a pink one out for herself. "These are officially doughnuts of apology."

"Mm, more like bribery," I say, closing my eyes. Even though I'm still totally freaked out, this mouthful of heaven is hard not to accept.

"Taste," she says, thrusting hers in my face. "It's hibiscus, delicious."

I try a small bite.

"Yeah." I chew, unconvinced. "It's pretty good, in a complicated kind of way." I shrug. "But why mess with perfection?" I finish mine in three more huge bites.

She leans against the wall by the top of the window.

"We shop today? Vera's Vintage and the sale room at Urban? Or you can come to my house and take anything of mine. You like those jeans I just got. They'll look great on you."

She has too much energy. I look at her closely. Emma's done this before, gone for days where she hardly sits still.

"You not sleeping much again?"

"I never sleep."

She eyes me like she's not sure if we're okay or not.

I'm not sure, either.

Before I can decide, she says, "You shouldn't have jumped down after me. Jeez, Evie. I was gonna get back up. It wasn't a big deal."

I am about to sip my coffee, but I put it back on the ledge instead.

"That was terrifying, Em."

"You made it that way!" she shoots back. "You're always so worried about everything. God. I was *fine*. It's not like I was going to stay down there. I'd have gotten up on the second try."

We stare at each other in silence. Emma can be persuasive. She's so confident sometimes, so sure she's right.

I sit up straighter.

She keeps her eyes wide, locked on mine, insisting I see this her way.

What if she's right? Maybe she would have gotten back up. Maybe I'm the one who made it dangerous. We've seen guys do that before, usually showing off for each other or for girls, and nothing's ever happened. It's possible to climb back up, like getting out of a swimming pool. You just have to be strong enough to boost yourself.

Only she wasn't.

She just sat there.

"No . . ." I shake my head slowly at her. "Emma, that was insane."

She looks like she's going to argue with me, then she doesn't. Her face goes from pale to pink and she starts to cry.

"I'm such a fuckup." She sets her half-eaten doughnut back in the box. There's a splotch of pink glaze at the edge of her mouth. "I'm sorry," she says. "Yesterday—I think Ryan is breaking up with me. . . ." Her voice trails off. She looks up at me. "He lives with someone!"

She widens her eyes. "I went over there on my free period to surprise him? And when he came to the door he acted super weird—I could see her in there, behind him on the couch! This woman in sweats and a T-shirt, not even beautiful, but there she was in his apartment like it's hers too." She exhales. "Oh God, it's totally hers too." She closes her eyes a second. "He made up this lie about a book he was going to loan me, totally pretended I was someone from school, like he barely knew me. It was awful."

I'm silent. There's no satisfaction in being right, but this whole Ryan situation never seemed like a good idea.

"No one ever wants to stay with me," she says, sounding so sad. "And then I get back to school, and Theo's there waiting for you, this totally cute, nice guy—do you know how lucky you are?"

My mouth falls open, then I close it again.

"Lucky?" I manage.

She nods, tucks her hair behind her ears. "Yeah, when I tripped on the rail yesterday and fell back into that muck between the tracks, all I could think was how perfect that was, you know? Like a metaphor for my whole life! I always end up stuck in some muck at the center."

She takes an uneven breath, balls my blanket in her fist.

"I mess everything up. You're so normal, Eves. You do it all right. I can't even get my parents to listen to me about Mamie's project, about anything, much less find some normal, decent guy! Guys only like me for sex. And then this cute one shows up at school and brings you a present." She stops and blows her nose on a napkin. "It was so romantic. And I'm sorry if I was a little flirty. I was jealous."

I move over close and give her a hug.

"Ryan is a loser," I say.

She stiffens.

"I mean for lying to you."

"I really like him, Eves," she says.

I want to scream at her, *You don't even know who he is!*

"You'll find someone better. So many guys like you! You just have to pick the right one. A nice one."

"Nice is so boring," she laughs, wiping a tear from her cheek.

"And Mamie—"

"Her show's coming up," Emma interrupts, shoulders falling. "My parents think we should go."

"Of course we're going. Fine, whatever. We decided that

already. We'll protest the show. Remember? We're going to make her see what she's doing to you." I'm acting like I'm certain about it now. I guess I am.

Emma looks like she's considering it again. Nods, slowly.

"We'll wear black and smudge ash on our faces," she says, turning to me, suddenly energized by the idea. "Oh my God, how cool would it be if we could get a bunch of people to join us, and, like, totally disrupt the whole thing? Mamie wants to talk grief and loss?" Her eyes widen at the thought. "We'll give her grief. We'll get Alice and Mandi and we can make noise like those women who wail at funerals! You know? Everyone in black? The ones who make that wrenching sad sound, what's that word?"

I laugh. "Ululate? Oh my God, you are a mad genius. We'll be Bly's first ululating group. Hey! Something unique for our college apps."

She smiles at me sideways. "Now you're talking."

I smile. "A night she won't forget."

"She's not getting away with making Patrick into art. She's gonna see us, *seeing her*." She narrows her eyes at me like she's assessing whether I'm really in or not.

"I'm in," I say.

"I still think we should pull the fire alarm," she says.

"We won't need to," I say as confidently as I can. "I have

your back on this one."

"YHMB?" She grins.

"IHYB," I confirm.

My stomach does a nervous shimmy.

kiss

THEO COMES TO THE DOOR light on his feet, in a pair of jeans and a dark-green T-shirt that says "This Is What a Feminist Looks Like." He meets my eyes through the window and grins, cheeks bright with color, hair wet like he's just out of the shower.

When he smiles like that, it makes me realize I need to have more faith in love. This is the rush people sing about, reach for, this feeling like you're falling into a wave. It lifts you high, pushes you out into something bigger and better than your small self. It's like discovering another type of force.

"So, your mom said yes." He grins, lifting the gate so I can step into the warm, dark shop.

"She did." I follow him up to their apartment. "What if she didn't?"

"I'd be disappointed," he says.

"Wouldn't you wonder why? Doesn't it bother you not to know?"

"If you're trying to make the case for a phone, it won't work. I appreciate the element of surprise."

I can't take my eyes off him in front of me on the stairs, his long legs taking the steps two at a time, the pale bottoms of his bare feet, the line of his shoulders, the shape of his back.

"Something smells great," I manage to say.

"I made pizza. Not too original, but I'm told I'm good at it. I hope you like lots of toppings."

"Toppings are great."

Suddenly I'm nervous. Not the kind where I'm about to start yammering a mile a minute about something irrelevant, but a bigger kind, a deep nervousness, the type you get when you realize you're home alone with a guy you like and anything could happen.

I try to breathe.

Their apartment is mostly dark, a few under-cabinet lights on in the kitchen, the oven light, and the bridge twinkling outside the windows.

Theo heads to the oven to check on his pizza.

"Another minute or two," he says, throwing a kitchen towel on his shoulder. "So." He breaks my silence. "The film people were here all night last night and into this morning, and they were using our roof. If you're cool with it . . . they left some gas heaters up there?"

"Okay?" I don't know where he's going with this.

He eyes me a minute. "How do you feel about a date on the roof?"

"Are you going to make me climb up there?" I ask.

"Ha!" Theo laughs. He opens the fridge and pulls out a bottle of water. Sets it and two glasses next to plates on a tray and opens a drawer for silverware. Laughs again to himself.

"We can watch a movie up there? It's a pretty sweet place to hang out, especially at night, if you're not freezing, which, thanks to the film crew, we won't be. My dad and I built a deck up there. During the summer we project movies onto the neighbor's wall."

"And there's no climbing involved?" I joke, but my heart's still skittering. Why am I doing this? Turning something amazing into something scary? Fear and excitement are kissing cousins.

"Scout's honor," he says, holding up two fingers in some

sort of honorable scout-like gesture.

"You were a scout?"

"Are you kidding?" he scoffs, laughing. "They would never let us do that. Way too bigoted and mainstream for the radical offspring of Margaret and Porter Gray. My mom takes Alo to this alternative scouting group now, but there was nothing like that around when I was younger."

I laugh with him and say something random about Bly's scouting retreat, but I feel like this can't be my life. I'm an imposter. I'm about to be found out and shown the door.

"A movie on the roof sounds awesome," I say, trying to sound like a girl who has nights like this.

Em and I spent the entire day shopping, trying stuff on, doing and undoing my hair until we decided to leave it tousled and down. I didn't really have money to spend, but I ended up buying a new lip gloss to wear with a pair of her jeans and a not-too-tight, just right Les Thugs T-shirt Jack brought back from Paris last year. Over the T-shirt I'm wearing Emma's cherry-red vintage sweater, the one with the pale-blue buttons.

Theo pulls the pizza from the oven on a wide wooden paddle.

"If you take that"—he motions to the tray—"I've got this. You won't need your coat up there. Those heaters are strong."

I follow him up through his house, along a third-floor hallway past their bedrooms, up more stairs to a small landing, then we climb a last set of narrower steps to a slanted door overhead. He pushes it open and we step out onto the roof.

I'm standing on a private deck beneath the Brooklyn Bridge. It's rickety, and made on the cheap, and totally marvelous. A low railing of mismatched wood encloses the three open sides. Someone's wrapped it in small-bulb string lights. At the far end is a white brick wall from the building next door, which is one story taller. A beat-up but comfortable-looking outdoor-style U-shaped couch faces the wall, with a big square table in front of it. On the table a few candles flicker in hurricane lamps next to two big bowls, one full of popcorn, the other a variety of movie candy.

"Okay?" Theo asks, setting the pizza on the table with a smile.

I am the luckiest person ever. I shiver a little and smile.

"This is . . . ," I say, awestruck. "It's like the bridge is yours."

I think about how many times I've tried to reorganize our apartment, arrange our old furniture in new ways to make it look better. My efforts seem small and unimaginative compared to this.

"Yeah." He grins. "Cool, right? My parents have no

money. They never have. The only smart financial decision they ever made was buying this building for nothing back when they met. It was a wasteland down here. They had no idea it would turn out like this, that they'd eventually be able to make some money with this place." He stops a second, looks around. "I'm gonna do the same."

"Buy a building?"

It sounds so incredibly grown-up I feel naïve.

"Well, real estate." He nods, taking the tray from me. "I've been saving for a few years. I want to get something, somewhere. I'll never be able to afford anything around here, but I'll find a place."

"You sound so confident."

"Yeah," he laughs. "I am. I mean, why not, right? Confidence is free."

He sweeps an arm toward the couch. "Pick your spot. There are blankets if you get cold. What do you want to watch? Boxing okay? I can stream a match through my laptop."

The look on my face must say it all. Theo breaks into laughter.

"I'm messing with you! I'm not going to make you watch boxing."

I take a spot in one corner of the couch and he sits next to me, the wind picking up his hair and blowing the scent of his shampoo my way.

It's breezy up here, and I'm shivering. But it's not only the cold, and not fear, either. This is excitement.

Theo wraps a blanket around my shoulders.

"I'll warm you in a second. First let me get these heaters going."

Aaah! What does *that* mean? *I'll warm you in a second?* Where's the implant that lets me record everything I see and hear? I'd be sending every byte to Em, asking her what I should do, what I'm supposed to do in a situation like this.

Theo stands and turns on the heaters, tall silver things he's placed on either side of the couch. Then he sits next to me, blowing on his hands.

"I think it got colder again this week," he says, pulling the blanket around his shoulders too and scooting in close. "Okay, so if we're not going to watch the fight, you have to choose the movie. I made a list of titles." He slips a small piece of paper out of his pocket. "Some old and some new. There's the ever-fabulous *Breakfast Club*. Or *The Perks of Being a Wallflower*. I put *Moonrise Kingdom* on it because, you know . . ." He looks over at me, flashing that crooked eyetooth, "It has maps in it. Did you bring one to show me?"

I blush. Shake my head. Theo doesn't press it.

Emma made me feel weird about them, like maybe

there's a good reason they're kind of private. I couldn't even make myself look through them until the last minute, digging them out of their hiding places in sketchbooks and folios just before I was supposed to be out the door. But none of them looked right, like the one I could bring to show someone else and say, here's this thing I do.

Theo looks from the list to me. "No takers?"

"Em usually chooses," I say, shifting in the corner. "I like almost everything."

Theo eyes me, skeptical. "Okaaay . . . well, Em's not here, so a few more options, then you'll have to pick."

I nod.

"How about *Safety Not Guaranteed*? It's a time-travel movie, I think. Or *500 Days of Summer*?"

He looks up at me.

"Go on," I say with a grin.

"Picky, picky." He smiles, running a finger down his list. "*Eternal Sunshine of the Spotless Mind*? Or if you were dying to see a movie about boxing, we could watch a classic, one my dad and I always watch, *On the Waterfront*."

I shake my head and try not to feel automatically jealous of him for having a dad to watch movies with.

"*Harold and Maude*?"

"No, not *Harold and Maude*!" I say it so fast I kind of choke on the name.

Theo looks at me, surprised.

"Way too sad."

"Sad? It's hilarious and liberating."

I shake my head, throat tight. "When I was like thirteen, my mom mentioned it was one of my dad's favorites, so I watched it after school one day."

"And?"

"And it took me weeks to recover." I close my eyes. "That scene where Maude throws her ring in the water?" I try to swallow past the tight spot. "Too, too sad. I'd had enough of death. Call me a sappy romantic, but I wanted love to be enough. I wanted Maude to stay."

"Love was enough. That was her point."

I pour myself a glass of water and take a sip.

"I'm sorry," he says, taking my glass and setting it back on the table. He wraps an arm around my shoulder, then presses his forehead to mine. "Someday we'll watch it together and you'll see how beautiful and positive Maude is."

We're close like that a minute, blinking blurrily at each other, then we kiss.

It might be the sky, or the twinkling lights, but it's most likely kissing that finally helps me relax. This is a night in my life. It's not a dream.

"So . . . what do you want to do?" he whispers after a bit, his lips hot on my neck.

I lean back against the cushions and stare up at the pillowy city-lit clouds. It's a question I can normally never answer, but tonight I know exactly what I want. I reach for Theo and we kiss some more.

reckless generosity

"YOU'RE LATE! I THOUGHT YOU WEREN'T coming and I was going to get stuck with these poopers!" Em laughs when I meet her on the corner. The Sullivans have a dog walker during the week, because Em hates picking up after Sam and Grizzle, but the weekends are hers now. The dogs were really Patrick's thing. But they're crazy for her, tugging on their leashes, all fur and energy, thrilled to be out.

"Sorry, sorry, sorry!" I unwind Marcel's leash from my wrist and let him greet his dog pals.

I'm late because my mom got up early to hear about my date. It felt weird telling her, so I kept it general, described the roof, the lights, the movie. I wanted to ask her why she didn't try dating, why she just gave up, but I made pancakes instead.

"Well . . . ?" Emma asks. "You look happy. . . ."

I grin at her and give Grizzle a treat from my pocket. He's an old, skeptical poodle with an underbite. I have a soft spot for him, messes and all.

"Oh my God, Evie, don't keep me waiting! Spill!"

I'm suddenly embarrassed because I want to say that it was the night of my dreams, but that sounds so cheesy. "I can't believe that happened to me," I manage, laughing.

"You had sex!" she shrieks, the wind whipping up and blowing her hair across her face. I look around to see if anyone heard, but we're alone on the sidewalk.

"What?!? No!" I look down and button my coat so I don't have to see if she looks disappointed or not.

We set off down the block. Despite the weird early spring, this morning the air smells like snow.

"Nice hat . . ." She reaches over and pulls it down over my eyes. "New . . . ?"

I straighten Theo's hat. He put it on me late last night, when we stood at the curb, waiting to find a cab. I pull the sleeves of my sweatshirt down over my hands.

"Details. Now."

"I almost don't want to talk about it—there aren't words—"

"Oh my God, Evie! Your eyes look all shimmery. You're in love!"

She bounces happily on the toes of her sneakers until the dogs get worked up too and tug her along wildly ahead of me.

Love. I blush at the word. A ridiculously grown-up concept, like *husband* or *dinner party.*

"I don't know . . . maybe . . . ?"

She waits for me to say more.

I don't know how to play this part, our roles reversed. I'm usually the one listening. For some reason my date feels impossible to talk about, private, not something I'm sure I want to share, not even with her.

Emma stops to let the dogs sniff and mark the base of a tree. Satisfied, they take off again. Marcel's in a mood, lingering near the tree and refusing to budge.

"Come on," I say to him, as lovingly as possible. "It's okay."

She turns back to me and circles her hand in the air. "More, more!"

I try a mysterious smile.

"No way, come on . . . !" she wails. Then she stops cold.

Looks back at me again. "Wait. Are you sure you didn't sleep with him?"

"I already told you, no. I didn't sleep with him."

Sam nips at Marcel's backside and gets him moving again.

"No?" She's eyeing me like she's trying to spot a lie.

I shake my head. "It was . . . I don't know, surreal, like something made up. Impossible and great."

I can still feel my hand on Theo's chest, his collarbone, the solid curve of his shoulder.

"He brought me up to the roof. I wish you could've seen it, Em. It's like something out of a movie. He had gas heaters and blankets and little bulb lights. . . ."

"Ooh!" Emma does a semi-ironic pirouette under her leashes.

"And we were going to watch a movie and eat pizza, but we kissed and talked instead."

She stops, letting Sam tug her in protest. Looks at me almost with awe.

"Wow. Sounds amazing." There's an edge in her voice. Envy, maybe. "I'm so happy for you! What'd you talk about?"

I let the dogs lead me along a second and zone out on the trees lining the sidewalk. They're covered in buds, small green knobs bursting bright against their stone-colored limbs.

"I don't know . . . everything. Relationships, his ex-girlfriend, what we want to do in the world." I close my eyes, remembering. "He's saving to buy a *building*." That part still impresses me. "We talked about how weird it is that some people have everything and other people nothing. He told me about going to buy a laptop a while ago, and when he left the Apple Store, he had to literally step over this homeless guy sleeping in the doorway. He said he still doesn't know what to do with that, but he feels like he has to do something."

"Deep." Emma laughs. I ignore her and go on.

"I could have talked to him all night. We covered snow, and music, and childhood." I pause so Marcel can sniff the bottom step of someone's stoop.

"Of course you'd have that kind of night," Em says, eyes bright.

I look back at her. Sam stops to do his business near the curb.

"What do you mean?"

"I don't know." She shrugs, pulling a bag from the little pouch on his leash. She wrinkles her nose as she bends to clean it up. "It's so you. Weird and cool and magical. I've never had a date like that . . . guys and I . . ."

She ties up the bag, her face a twist of disgust.

"You're so lucky." She shrugs and hands me the leashes so she can sprint to the corner to dump the bag in the trash. "It sounds too good to be true," she says, coming back.

Maybe she's right. Maybe that's why I don't want to talk about it with her.

"Oh my God!" Emma wallops me on the arm. "I'm not doubting you or anything. Lighten up. I'm totally teasing! You had a great date. Enjoy it, would you?"

But her face changes.

"What?" I know that look.

"I hate to be an *actual downer* after your dream night, but I can't not tell you."

"What is it?"

She bites the corner of her bottom lip, hesitant.

"I'm so, *so bummed* . . . my parents . . ." She drags it out, squinting at me, dark brows knit. "Evie, I'm sorry. Spain's not happening."

So she was right. Something was too good to be true. I just had the wrong thing. My heart sinks, even though I kind of knew it already. It's why I couldn't make myself ask her about it when the deposits were due. Why I didn't try to get a passport. Disappointment's hot in my throat.

"It's okay," I say as lightly as possible. My voice climbs

an octave higher. The dogs pull me along faster. "I kind of figured!" I feel out of breath, can't look at her for a second.

"Are you sure? You're okay? I'm so, so sorry."

I nod, embarrassed by how disappointed I feel, by the fact that I was stupid enough to think it would happen. Could. It's like I got caught trying to get something for nothing. No free lunch, I know that. I focus on Grizzle's underbite. He rolls his root-beer-barrel eyes up at me, like he knows what's happening and is totally sympathetic. Rescues gotta stick together.

"Evie—"

"No, it's fine.

She comes closer and puts a hand on my arm. "I wanted us to go together so bad—they don't even have the right to say no, I was using my own money—but when I tried to get the cashier's checks at the bank, they called my dad. Turns out you need approval on a youth account for transactions like that. Total bullshit. They've been telling me about my money forever; it's not like this one extra ticket was going to use it all up. I'm so, so sorry."

The bank called her dad? I need her to stop apologizing. I can't help her not feel bad about this. Not right now, while my face is so hot it's making me sick. Here goes the slippery world again. I'm never standing on anything solid, and when it all shifts I need a second to recover.

"But I thought you said they—"

She cuts me off. "It was me. I was taking you."

"Oh God. Your parents don't think I was asking you for it, do they?" I ask, feeling sick.

Mr. Sullivan's a self-made man and loves to talk about how he got to where he is in the world. He takes a dim view of people who expect something for nothing. Sometimes when he says that I feel like he's talking for my benefit, like he knows I'm at Bly on aid. They probably contribute to the scholarship fund. My stomach feels leaden.

"God, no!" Em says when she sees how I'm taking it. "Don't get all worried or mad, Evie, they'd never think that about you. Patty and Frank just didn't agree with my"—she take a breath and drops her voice into her father's register—"*sudden reckless generosity*."

The planned recipient of Emma's recklessness wishes she could disappear. If I were alone I'd draw a map of Spain on the ground, then erase it.

We walk in silence. Emma stays close.

"I'm sorry, Eves," she says again, her face a twist of what looks like real regret. "Besides, if we make a scene at Mamie's show, they're not gonna let me go, either."

"It's okay." I give her a smile. "Really. Don't feel bad. No biggie, you know? We'll travel together another time. In college or something."

I take a deep breath and force my shoulders back. I don't need Spain. I'm the girl who chalked a heart in the back of a cab crossing the Brooklyn Bridge at midnight.

She reads my thoughts. "When do you see him again?"

I smile. "This week, I hope! I only went home when I did because I didn't want my mom to worry. We kissed until the cab came."

Evie looks at me with respect.

"Shit, Ramsey. You took your time getting here, but look at you now. Way to *go*."

She's right. I'm lucky. I'll see Theo again soon.

cake

ONLY I DON'T.

Theo doesn't come over. He doesn't call. Not on Sunday, not the entire rest of the week. Not the following weekend. I walk Marcel by the churchyard about a thousand times, my heart beating wilder with each pass, but there's no sign of him.

"What if something happened? What if he got clocked in the head boxing and forgot my existence?" I shift my backpack to my other shoulder so I can pull out my keys.

Emma rolls her eyes at me, but she's having a hard time staying focused on my situation because she cut afternoon classes to find Ryan at the bar where he works.

"It's official," she says for the hundredth time, slurring her words. "I'm dumped. He freakin' dumped me."

"Nice of him to send you off with a bottle of champagne. He's high class." I'm sarcastic. It won't matter. She's too drunk to care.

But she shakes her head and gives me a sloppy smile. "Nope. That I took. I asked if I could use the bathroom before I left, and there was a whole case just sitting there."

I found her swaying on the corner a block away from school an hour ago, bottle in hand. I made her toss it in the trash, but it was already mostly empty. Then I looped my arm in hers and pulled her along to my place before anyone else caught on. We took the long way, stopping at the deli for a bagel and a gallon of coffee.

When we step into my apartment, the change of scenery seems to hit her reset button. She slides off her boots and drops her coat on the floor, then swings her focus back to Theo.

"A week and a half is kind of in*sane*," she says, leaning against the wall by the door. "I mean, that's effed up. Right? You have to do something. . . ."

"It's embarrassing." I moan, trying and failing not to feel low.

She pats me on the back.

"Tell me you're going to do something, because you're *nice*, Evie. And this is cute pencil boy. You need to know what's up."

"Don't call him pencil boy."

"Sorry, that does sound kind of weird," she laughs. She chews the edge of her lip, then closes her eyes. With my luck she'll fall asleep.

I kick my shoes off as noisily as possible onto the pile by the door and toss the mail on the table. I'm supposed to walk Mrs. Cohen's dog for her today when I take Marcel out, but the dogs will have to wait. There's no chance I'm leaving Em alone until she's had about seventeen more coffees and doesn't smell like a drunk debutante.

". . . but Eves, he *is* weird." She reanimates and drifts over to our low, wide armchair, her favorite spot. "I mean, who doesn't have a phone? You knew that, going in. You can't get all stressed out about it now."

Phone or not, hearing nothing from Theo after a date like that is making me doubt everything I remember. Maybe it was only dreamy for me, not Theo. What if I'm so self-absorbed I didn't notice he was hating it? The idea that I could have read it all wrong is horrifying but not outside the realm of possibility. What do I know about love?

"Here's what you do." Em spins so she's sideways in the armchair. Her hair falls so long over the arm it brushes the floor. "Oh my God, this is the best idea, *ever*."

"Yeah . . . ?"

She looks at me like she's super serious, but her eyes are bleary and her cheeks still drunk-pink.

"So, so simple," she says, as if enunciating more clearly is going to make it all right.

"What is?" I ask, exasperated.

"You're gonna ask him to come to Ben's party with you this weekend!" She lifts her head a second, energized by her plan.

I make a face, then try to erase it before Em sees. I flop on the couch and fantasize about repainting our dark apartment, brightening it up in here. Redecorating sounds way more fun than Ben's party, but the party's all Emma's been talking about. It's all anyone's talking about. Ben's parents are super divorced. Not the amicable shared-custody kind, more like the I-hate-you-so-much-you've-ceased-to-exist-for-me kind. Ben treks back and forth between them, and he's been forgotten by both more than once. When we were younger, he kept clothes at Jack's, because his parents were always leaving town, each assuming the other had him, leaving Ben locked out.

He's getting them back now. Ben's annual blowout parties are the stuff of legend. At the last one, kids from four different schools showed up. For Emma it's the best night of the year, a chance to meet new people on her turf, especially new guys.

"Hmm," I say, noncommittal.

"Hmm, what? It's a solid plan, girl." She wiggles into a slightly more upright position.

"And wouldn't Jack love that." I'm sarcastic. "If I show up with Theo, I'll never get him off my case."

"Jack," Emma scoffs. "Who cares what Jack thinks?"

I do. I think. Why do I?

"Let it go, Evie. You owe him nothing. Oh my God, you have Theo! So Jack's jealous. Who cares? Jack's not your problem anymore. Besides, he's got Alice, as long as she'll put up with him."

I'm dying to ask her what she means by that last part, but I don't want to talk about Alice. Not with Em. I'm pretending Alice doesn't exist.

"Evie, work with me here. It's a perfect plan and you know it."

"And how do I ask him? No phone, remember?"

She lets out a huff of frustration. "Jesus. You know where he lives. Go there, obviously. Grab what's yours!"

Grab what's mine. Emma's preaching against her own philosophy, but I don't point out the inconsistency, because Ryan dumped her. She gets wiggle room today. Besides, I know how her mind works. This isn't really about finding a solution to my problem. She thinks if I get Theo to come to the party then I'm guaranteed to go too, and she wants me there. Needs me. I'm not a party person, but she does better with guys when I'm around. It's like color theory. We're a complementary color scheme. Opposites on the wheel make each other look better. It's all about the contrast.

To be fair, I'd never go to parties if it weren't for Em, and some of them have been pretty fun.

"And that's not weird? Me showing up like that?" I can't tell if she's serious or just drunk serious, but she looks pretty locked in on the idea.

"Not at all." She shakes her head vehemently. "He lives in a public space. Aren't you still supposed to go pick out something, some thank you? You pick your gift, then casually ask if Theo's around. Piece of cake. I'll go down there with you. Tomorrow, after school, okay? If we don't go then, it will be too last-minute."

She'll probably flirt with him again.

As if he can hear my thoughts, Marcel puts his paws on Em's lap and whimpers pitifully at her until she says yes, then he lumbers up on her, leaning his head into hers and licking her face.

"Hello, fat weirdo. Ever hear of a toothbrush?" She scratches him behind the ears.

But I shake my head. "No way. Can't do it."

"You have to! Don't be such a chicken. He's obviously totally into you."

I press my lips shut tight. I can't tell her I'm scared I read it all wrong. I can barely think it. It's too humiliating.

This is so typical—me worried, her wild. I climb off the couch and flip through the mail. Another official-looking letter from our building owners. I stick it back with the rest of the mail and add it to the pending avalanche on the sideboard.

I stare at her a second, but it's clear she's expecting a response. A commitment.

"Fine," I say finally. She doesn't look like she's going to forget about this idea anytime soon.

She yawns huge. "Okay, buzzkill," she says. "Got more food?"

"Grapes okay?"

"Yeah."

I push through the swinging door to the kitchen, but the grapes aren't on the counter where I left them this morning.

"No grapes," I shout out to Em. "I'll find something else."

She doesn't answer.

I pour us both big glasses of water, grab a packet of spicy seaweed, and head back out. When I step through the swinging door I almost crash into my mom.

"Whoa!" I say, holding the water high so I don't douse either of us.

"Hello, girls. What's this I hear about a party?" She's standing there smiling at us both. It's disconcerting.

"You scared me!"

I'm shocked to see her. She's barefoot, in leggings and a T-shirt, flipping through the mail I just tossed on the sideboard. She looks flushed, like she just woke up or something.

Emma's face is rigid and fake-happy. I think she's trying to look sober, but she's making it worse, and distractedly petting Marcel on top of it all. He's going to snap at her if she doesn't stop. Marcel rejects distracted affection. All or nothing with him.

"What are you doing home? Are you sick?" I ask.

A wry smile crosses her face and she looks like she's about to say something, then changes her mind.

"Took a vacation day," she says, pulling her fingers through her hair. "I've been lounging in bed like a queen. Napping and reading."

She hands me a small stack of postcards and envelopes from various colleges, then sets the rest of the mail, scary letter and all, back on the mountain on the sideboard. I glance at the postcards. My SAT scores attracted a few schools, at least. I test well. It's the rest of it I find hard. The postcards are all idyllic photos of beautiful students laughing on lush lawns, like college is one big fancy picnic. I drop the stack on the table.

"You girls have a lot of homework tonight?"

"Almost none." Em shoves Marcel off her lap and sits up straight. It looks weird, extra formal. My mom reads Em like a book, and she knows it. She's panicking that my mom's onto her, that she'll tell her parents, or kill the plan to go to Ben's, or both.

Marcel flops near the couch with wheezy complaint.

My mom smiles at us like she's clueless about Em. I have no idea what's going on. Before I can think of a way to ask, she says, "We're low on groceries. Why don't you girls go out for shakes?"

No questions about the party. Or Em.

"It's my treat. You know I love having you here, Emma." She eyes Em apologetically. "But I'm pampering myself today and was still looking forward to a hot bath in a quiet house."

Em's off the chair and slipping on her shoes before I can answer.

My mom pulls a card from her purse and holds it out. I take it, incredulous. She's definitely been replaced by a clone.

"Maybe pick up something for dinner too?" she asks. "I was very lazy today and didn't do any shopping."

"Will do."

I eye her closely. She looks okay. But something's up. She's never home during the day like this. When I was younger I was terrified she'd get sick too. Like my dad. I'd lose her and then be alone in the world.

When I reach for the card she pulls me in for a quick hug and kisses the top of my head.

I try not to think about all those legal-looking letters or what would happen to us if she lost her job. It's just a day off. A worm of worry wiggles through me.

ha ha ha ha ha

EVERYONE'S BUZZING ABOUT BEN'S PARTY ON Saturday. Even in the library. Two quivering and pimpled freshman are stationed at the checkout desk, but they look like they're using what little muscle mass they have to keep breathing and don't seem at all likely to ask the people yammering at the top of their lungs in the library to shut the heck up so those of us who are, as Dr. Holmes put it, *tardy on our Investigation* can get a little work done.

Em came in this morning wearing this dusty blue sweater that looks super cute on her. Did she dress up on purpose? She and I are going to see Theo after school, and I'm a little tense.

I'm contemplating yelling *Quiet!* when my phone skitters across the carrel, because, hey, what's one more distraction?

"Yeah?" I answer, in a whisper I hope is loud enough to remind everyone else that's what they should be doing.

"Hey, *Evieeee* . . . ," Emma says, dragging my name out into something strange.

"Can't talk. In the library," I hiss.

"Oh, sorry. But, um, okay, can you do me a favor? Will you go to my locker and see if my wallet's in there?"

She's using her innocent flirt voice, and not for my benefit. This one's high and thin. Before I can ask what's wrong she laughs and says, "Um, there's been a misunderstanding?"

"Where are you?"

"It's *totally ridiculous*, but I'm in security at Urban."

"What?"

"Can you bring me my wallet?" More laughter.

I start throwing my stuff in my bag and clear out of the library.

"Like, now? I think it fell out of my bag in my locker this morning?"

"Emma . . . ," I say, checking my phone. "I'm only free

another twenty minutes."

"Okay, thanks! I'm in the one by Union Square."

She laughs, staccato. *Ha, ha, ha, ha, ha.* A girly machine gun.

I rush past Dr. Holmes and Ms. Vax talking in the hall outside his office. I nod a polite hello when I dart by, but he shakes his head at the phone I still have stuck to my face, and Ms. Vax holds up a hand like she's going to catch me and make me stop avoiding her. I mouth *sorry* to them both and keep going.

"It's a mistake, *obviously.* I explained it to them already. When I didn't see my wallet in my bag, I panicked and shoved the shirt in there a second so I could have my hands free to look for it?" Weird breathy laugh. "They're making me wait here until you can come . . . so I can pay for it?"

She's totally stealing. I don't know why I'm surprised. Something was bound to happen. Emma's like a kettle, the water gurgling up the spout until it starts to shriek.

"On my way."

I race down the stairs two and three at a time. I have math next. If I run I might make it. I don't bother checking her locker. Emma doesn't use a wallet. She's not that organized. I'll give her mine.

banned

I DON'T KNOW WHY I'M NERVOUS, it's not like they caught *me*, but still, when I walk in the store, my knees feel loose. I find her in the back corner behind the fitting rooms in a dingy office under overbright lights. No hipster sound track in here. Just two bearded dudes in skinny jeans and wool hats, who, when you look a little closer, have this take-no-prisoners hardness in their eyes. They're saying something about calling the police when I walk in.

With her dark hair twisted in a topknot and her cherry-red lips, Emma doesn't look nearly as tough as she's trying to. I hand her my wallet and stare them down while she rifles through my cash like it's hers and pays for the contraband. I have four dollars left when she's done. With one guy in front of us and another in back, they march us up and out through the store under the blatant stares of other shoppers. I'm wondering if they take lessons in how to totally humiliate people when I see Emma's hand flash out like a mad bird toward a spinning rack of jewelry, then come flying back toward mine to press something sharp against my palm. Feels like a bee sting. I close my fingers around hers, because the whole thing happens in a millisecond, but then it feels like time slows, and my insides turn to liquid.

"If we see you in this store again, we will call the police," the smaller of the two says as we near the door.

"This is *such* bullshit!" Emma shouts before we're even out the door. Still holding my hand tight, she does this defiant little skip-stomp thing, like it's 1980 and she's a punk-rock rebel kicking her way out of the Chelsea Hotel and not a sixteen-year-old girl who's just been caught shoplifting in a hipster clothing conglomerate.

I feel like I'm going to throw up. Whatever Em pressed into my palm is biting my hand. My face is hot and I'm light-headed. The cold air hits me like a slap.

"AS IF!" Em shouts, gripping my hand harder and rushing

us down the wide sidewalk toward Union Square, cackling like a hyena. She looks back toward the store. "BANNED!"

Like she's proud.

"Open up." She grins, uncurling my panicked, fist-tight fingers from hers. "Let's see what we got!"

A small cardboard earring card sits bent on my damp palm with two tiny pale-blue studs glittering on it. I whip my hands back like they're hot, which I guess in a way they are.

"Nice!" Emma says, catching them before they fall. She holds up the small square and inspects the earrings she grabbed.

Correction.

The earrings she made *me* grab on the way out.

"You made me steal those," I say slowly.

"Shut up. I'm the one who took 'em. Wasn't that a total rush?"

Her coat's open and her hair is whipping wildly around her face in the arctic wind that rolled in again and has everyone waddling around in jackets as big as down blankets.

"Quit looking at me like that. You were an innocent bystander. Besides, if they'd seen it, they'd be out here by now!"

She laughs, then takes my hand again, pulling me along

so fast we're almost running.

I blink back tears the cold wind is stripping from my eyeballs.

"Fucking awesome!" she shouts, not noticing the glare she gets from a nanny passing with her charge.

I'm speechless. My tongue dried up and blew away.

She breaks away from me and does a little skipping twirl, her arm aloft, curving over her, delicate in a way that reminds me of the ballerina in my old jewelry box after I bent the spring she was on, dooming her to Swan Lake in a wonky oval.

She laughs again, maniacal. "Oh my GOD! That was so *freakin'* close!"

I laugh then too—it's the adrenaline—even though this is so not cool. I hate her in this moment and I wish I felt as free.

"What were you thinking?" I ask, when I finally get a grip. I stop in the middle of the sidewalk and let people push past. "You made me steal something and you owe me fifty bucks."

"Oh, Saint Evie," she says, slowing when she hears the edge in my voice. She rolls her eyes. "Are you sure you're not Catholic? Jeez. Stop acting like I did something horrible. Do you know how rich that company is?"

I march up, grab her arm.

"Listen, Peter Pan—"

"Ha! Robin Hood, you mean Robin Hood!" she laughs.

"Whatever." I look her right in the eyes. "Seriously. What the *hell*?"

She makes this face almost like she pities me, like she's been trying, but I obviously don't get it, and for a disorienting second I'm swayed.

"Jesus, Evie," she says. "You and money. It's not the most important thing."

"Easy for you to say," I mumble, feeling simultaneously outraged *and* like a stick in the mud. A lot of people steal. Maybe I'm making it into too big a deal.

"Come on . . . I even got something for you. . . ."

Before I can reply to that utterly clarifying information, she unzips the front of her coat and reaches into her shirt, extracting another pair of stud earrings on a card. She hands them to me. Tiny compasses, each with a real spinning hand.

"Ta-da!" She holds them out to me on her small white palm like a thoughtful gift.

I'm speechless.

"Map girl, they're for you!" she says, like I don't get it. "Perfect, right?"

"What else do you have on you?" I stomp my foot on the sidewalk so hard it hurts my jaw. "What if they searched you? Or called the police, or your parents? Emma, *what the hell*?!"

She blinks at me a second, then pockets the earrings, disappointed.

"Oh my God, Evie. Jesus. Relax. I know my rights. They can't randomly search a girl like that. They only had those two guys on duty. They had to find a female clothes-folder person to come sit by the open door while we waited for you to get down here. There are laws and stuff, you know? And they didn't call my parents. So stop freaking out. I needed a rush, but you're still the voice of reason. And you saved me, poor Emma the fuckup. You had my back this time. Please, please don't make this into a thing."

I pinch the frozen bridge of my nose.

"Besides, that shirt was *not* worth fifty bucks."

Her logic.

"I wanted something new. For Ben's," she says, sounding slightly less rebellious.

I don't point out that she could have easily bought something new.

She hops up and down on her tiptoes, renewed by the thought of the party. Apparently I'm not the only one still supercharged with adrenaline.

We stare at each other a second.

"I'm missing math," I say.

She rolls her eyes. "One class. You'll live. I have a good feeling, Evie. Things are changing. You're going to ask Theo, and I'm going to meet someone, and Ben's will be *fu-u-un. . . ."*

She links her arm through mine and turns us back toward school.

"Mandi says Ben's dad's got a new place, some glassy penthouse. A bunch of her LaGuardia friends are coming. Guys too."

I'm still speechless.

She makes this little *tsk* sound with her mouth. Lowers her chin and looks up at me with those innocent eyes.

"Evie." She pats my arm. "Don't be such a grandma," she pleads. "Come on. We can't go to Theo's with you all in a snit. It was stupid. I'm sorry. I was bored. I won't do it again, I promise."

But she will.

She will one hundred percent for sure do it again, and I know because I'm looking at her. She isn't the slightest bit ashamed by what happened. Emma's high from this, totally flying. She's out here smashing things and I'm running after her trying to fit it all back together. Her body's here, walking next to me, but the rest of her is somewhere else, free, dispersed, and thrumming. I can hardly spot her, she's vibrating so fast.

where the world falls away

"EVIE, HOLD UP!" MS. VAX CALLS out of the art room when I slink by. She's got Otis Redding cranked and no class at the moment.

I whip a U-turn, quicken my pace, but she comes running after me. "I know you heard me," she laughs, pushing her huge, round red glasses up onto the top of her head and placing a hand on my arm. "Got a second?" There's this weird glint in her eyes.

I check my phone. "I'm—" but I've got nothing. I'm free right now, and I only came up here because I was hoping to find her studio empty. "Yeah, sure, I guess."

I follow her into the room and over to her corner near the front. She sits right on top of her desk and crosses her legs, a huge grin spreading across her face.

"Sit," she says. "I have some news!"

I perch on the edge of a stool.

She rubs her hands on her knees like she's dying to tell me something.

"Of course, you know by now, I'm a meddler," she says, like we're already in the middle of a conversation. "And I sincerely hope you're thinking about art school after this." I open my mouth to say something, but she lifts a hand to keep me quiet. "And, I know you're reluctant to go public with your maps, but they're so wonderful!"

I have a sinking feeling. "Yeah . . . ?"

"But, honey, that TeenART call for submissions was too fabulous an opportunity for you to miss." She beams at me and clasps her hands. "I submitted on your behalf. Teachers can do that. We're encouraged to recommend a student. I sent them some of your work."

"What? How?" I don't know what she's talking about. Ms. Vax has none of my work right now.

She brushes my question away like a fly, the silver bangles on her wrist clanging.

"But that's not the best part, and I'm so excited to tell you this! The grant officer called me this morning to let me know they've selected three students from Bly as potential candidates, and my dear, you are one!"

If she were a fairy, which when I was littler I used think she might be, her wings would be fluttering so wildly right now she'd lift off her desk. But she's no fairy.

I stare at her. She's always worn a ton of makeup, her eyes encircled in lavender shimmer and her lips a color that can only be described as tangerine pink. Her face is a palette.

Her words sink in.

"Wait, you did what?"

"I sent them one of your maps. You'd written 'Where the World Falls Away' on it? I found it on the table near the back."

She laughs then, a big ridiculous-sounding *Ha!* like this is some kind of miracle.

When I don't laugh back, she pulls her glasses off her head and fiddles with the frames.

"Well, okay, not exactly *on* the table. It had slipped into recycling, but it was so good, Evie! It is so good! Oh, honey, say something? You look so serious!"

I don't know what to say. My first instinct is to run out of here and find someplace to hide. Then anger bubbles up instead and I open my mouth to attack her, to hurl something at her like, *Is your life so empty you have nothing better to do than mess with mine?*

"I don't want to do this," I choke out instead.

A million feelings crowd me out of myself. My fear of showing my work to people, being expected to make it, of being held to some kind of invisible standard. What if they hate it? Reject me? Or worse, let me in? My maps are real to me. They're mine. Places I don't need to worry about anyone else.

Her eyebrows are lifted so high right now they're about to merge with her hairline. TeenART's already shoving me into the glare of accountability. And art school? I'd have to tell my mom I'm not good at anything else, that I don't have a plan, nothing practical in mind for the future.

I press my lips together tight and take a deep breath through my nose.

Ms. Vax clasps her hands near her heart. "The nomination guidelines were straightforward. One or two images, a small amount of general information about each student, and a paragraph about how you think they'd benefit from this opportunity. Evie, I wrote about your talent *and* your reluctance to . . ." She hesitates, looking for the right words. "To express it to the larger world."

Black spots dot my field of vision. I've never fainted before, but I'm wondering if this is how it feels.

"That was my *private* thing!" I say, louder than I mean to. "I *recycled* it."

Her face falls. She nods. "I took a chance. Possibly overstepped. I know that, and maybe it was even a little sneaky of me, but hear me out. Dr. Holmes and I have been talking, and Evie, this is something that would be so good for you. This is a risk worth taking. You need this."

The light coming in through the huge windows behind her is bright, then dim, then bright again, like the clouds are pulsing through the sky as rapidly as my panicked synapses. I feel like I'm moving, flying faster through light than I'm ready to go.

"A representative from the foundation is coming to visit. She'd like to interview the candidates for final selection. Beyond thinking about how you might want to talk about your work, there's no real preparation. It's not a test or anything, they just want to meet you, Evie. See who it is behind the work."

I can't make myself say it out loud yet, but sometime soon I need to tell her art can't be my path. I'm not a rich kid. I need a better plan, some kind of work, job, *career.* I'm made of panic. I cover my face with my hands.

"My maps are for me."

She hops off the desk and plants her hands on my shoulders. She means to be encouraging, but I feel pressed in place, trapped.

"I'll send you the details. This isn't the kind of thing to

walk away from. They were enthusiastic about your work. You deserve this opportunity, Evie."

I lower my hands and look at her. She's so close it's like she's trying to stare inside me.

"This foundation is well-known. They are rigorous supporters of art in general, and women in art in particular. If they offer you a spot, you'll have a stipend, a mentor, a studio space. Evie, it's a dream. You'll learn so much, and it will be so good—just what you need on an application for college. I can see by your expression that you're freaking out, but honey, you have to listen to me when I say there's no risk here."

Everyone's risks are different.

She leans forward and with both hands squeezes my shoulders again, the tension in them hot. "All you have to do is show up and see how it goes. As soon as I have the date and time for the interview I'll let you know."

I get up and leave her room without another word.

want or yes or

“OH MY GOD, GET IN THERE! This is *so not* a big deal.” Em gives me a little push. “Evie, you *never* go for what you want. Wake up, girl.” She steps close and pats-slash-slaps me lightly on the cheeks like she’s trying to get me to snap to.

I’m frozen in place outside the door to the Roebling House because none of this feels right. This whole day’s a mess. Or maybe Emma’s right, and I’m looking through crap-colored lenses, exercising my bad old habit of holding back—but I don’t think so. Something is off, and I still haven’t forgiven her for the whole Urban deal. I don’t know why I let her talk me into doing this, coming here.

Visitors and tourists come and go around us, the door jingling open and shut, and for a second I think I'll turn around and get out of here before it's too late, but then Em has me by the shoulders, and she steers me in.

Margaret's at the register wrapping up a ticket reservation.

"Evie!" she says, sounding thrilled I'm there. "I was just asking Theo if you were ever going to come in and pick something out." She smiles warmly at me. Em's made herself scarce, and I have the weird feeling she's disappeared entirely. She'd better not steal anything in here. I'm so nervous I'm clenching my teeth.

"Hi," I say, feeling overly polite. I keep my voice low. "Um, I actually came to ask Theo something. Is he around?"

"Upstairs," she says, lifting her bright eyes to mine. She's a fox too. "You know the way. He'll be happy to see you!"

I turn to look for Em. She's over by the books, watching me.

"Wait here." I mouth to her. I don't need her up there with me, flirting with him.

She gives me a fake pout, then smiles. "Don't take no for an answer!"

I blush at the thought of Margaret hearing her and step around the register, through the door marked "Private."

"Hello?" I call out as I climb the stairs.

"Hi?" Theo's voice comes back a question.

He's at the dining room table working on his laptop, shirtless, in gym shorts. When he turns to look at me, I gasp. His left eye and cheekbone look like uncooked meat, red and purple, and his eye's nearly swollen shut.

"Your eye! What happened? Are you okay?"

Theo's face is like a time-lapse of feelings, each expression racing over the next until he shuts it all down. He pushes his laptop aside and stands.

"My stupid brother thinks he knows what's best for everyone, but he really needs to mind his own fucking business."

"Lazarus?"

"No, *Alo*," he deadpans, then shakes his head, lips pressed tight. "I don't want to talk about it."

Every instinct tells me to turn and leave.

"Hi, so, um, I hope it's okay I'm dropping by like this," I stammer instead, "but I didn't know how else—"

"Sorry I haven't come around," he says, looking down. "A lot's been going on."

"No problem!" I sound like an eager idiot. So much for Emma's advice to play it cool. "I mean, I figured you were busy, and I have been too, and I wouldn't even be here, show up like this normally, but, um . . ."

Chester gets off the couch behind me and comes loping up to sniff my crotch.

"Chester! Back off, dude," Theo says, rolling his good eye at me apologetically, then wincing. "Dog has no manners."

I set my bag on the arm of a big squishy armchair and try to gather my wits. He looks so hot in those dark gym shorts. Even with his swollen face. God, his *knees* are cute, and his straw pile hair—the mess of it, and those icy eyes, well, the one still visible. I can't believe I kissed him. He kissed me. We did that together. For a second I remember the taste of his lips, and something starts vibrating deep inside me, and I have to clear my throat or else I'm going to laugh or cry or generally lose control. Love's terrifying, but Emma's right. I have to go for it, take a risk. Reach far, then further.

I close the distance between us, step up close, and slide my hands into the back of his hair, pulling his wrecked face down to mine. I press my body into his and we stumble against the edge of the table. This is the kiss he gave me, the one I've been wanting to give back, the kiss I've wished for ever since our last one. My lips act like I know what I'm doing, like I'm even better at this than I was before, until it's crackling between us, electric, monumental. I kiss Theo like there was never a time I didn't know how to do this. His skin smells good, clean, and we're so close to each other, closer.

Only then he steps aside. Stiff, uncomfortable. Moves so there's an arm's length between us.

I'm a collection of sensations, my lips tingling, my heart racing through me so madly my fingers twitch. Theo's moving his mouth like he's going to say something, and then he starts to talk, but I'm kiss deaf, my ears all blood and thunder, so I interrupt him, barrel forward and say what I came for.

"There's a party this weekend. I came to see if you want to go to it with me? Together?"

My voice comes out weird, though, like my body's read his body language, assessed the situation before my brain's had a chance to catch up.

Theo's face freezes.

A map of this moment would be schematics. Robot girl misinterprets human boy.

He turns away, looks at his laptop screen, then looks back at me again.

"It's a Bly thing," I say fast, trying to sound human. My jaw's tight and my teeth feel ready to chatter. Theo's face is so closed he looks like a stranger, not the guy from the roof, the one with the warm chest, the thudding heart. It's like we've never met, much less kissed for so long my lips went numb.

"Everyone will be there," I forge ahead. "It's kind of an annual deal—this kid, Ben—"

Theo shakes his head, cuts me off.

"Hey, can you sit a sec?" He motions to the chair next to him. "I want to show you something."

I look at the chair he's pulled out, but moving through space requires a strange amount of concentration, like I'm new to this body or something.

We sit. Why does he smell so good? The only words to describe it are *want* or *yes* or *mine*. Other words start to bang around in my head too. Like *run!* and *stupid girl* and *good-bye*. And then Theo turns toward me, and there it is, in his eyes.

This was a mistake. Coming here. He's not happy to see me and he's about to say something I really don't want to hear.

I swallow. Cross my arms over my chest, then cross my legs, try to remember how people sit in chairs.

Theo takes a breath, like he's trying to figure out where to start.

"Remember when I told you about that day I walked out of the Apple Store and stepped over a homeless guy?"

I nod.

"The whole way home on the train I felt sick. I couldn't figure out what I was supposed to do. I wanted to go back and hand it to him. Or return it and give him the money. Instead I just sat there, holding that slick silver and white bag—I couldn't reconcile it, the experience of shopping like some aristocrat, this pricey, sleek machine . . ."

He trails off. Thinks a minute. Shakes his head.

"I mean, this is the same equation we face all the time, right? Especially here, in this city full of kings. We have so much and some people, most people, have so little. Agonizing is selfish bullshit. The real question is, what can we do about it?"

I'm quiet. I don't know what he wants me to say, where this is going.

Theo sighs, drops his head in his hands a second, then looks up at me.

"My family's having this debate. What should Theo do with his life. My parents say I have to go back, finish college. Laz too—like it's even *up to him*." He clears his throat. "Last week they staged this . . . *intervention*. I'm supposed to stop boxing. They think I'm drifting. Wasting my gifts." He fiddles with the curling edge of a sticker on his laptop. Shakes his head. "But it's not up to them. Especially not Laz. He's the worst. He needs to mind his own freaking business. Just because he does everything they tell him to doesn't mean I have to too."

He rubs his face. Bounces his knee up and down.

"I don't know, Evie. I was going to tell you, but . . ." He takes a deep breath. "I want to do something *decent*, you know? Use my skills to help out. Make a difference for someone else. The night before we met, I stepped into this fight—this guy was in that alley in SoHo, the little dark one between Lafayette and Crosby, and he was knocking his girlfriend around. People were walking by like it wasn't happening, and I almost did too, like it was private business, but then I realized that's bullshit, so I stopped. It didn't seem real, you know? I was amped from sparring at the gym, and when I saw him yank her hair another time, I told him to knock it off. Leave her alone."

He's animated, talking faster, his face flushed.

"Then the guy turns to me with this, like, *murderous* look"—Theo's eyes darken— "and he beat the shit out of me."

His head jerks back like he's just taken a hit. He looks at me. I don't know where this is going.

"And the girlfriend?" I ask.

"She ran into the bar and called the police."

"That's why your face looked like this when we met?"

He nods and absentmindedly touches the scar on his lip.

"So you helped her."

"Yeah, and everyone was all pissed at me for it! The cops, my parents, even Father Joe. They said domestic violence is the worst and I could have been killed, but I felt incredible after that night, like I did something *real*—it meant something to someone in the world, more than all this day-to-day crap we call living."

I start to relax a little. None of this is about me. He's working stuff out.

"So you're going to . . . what?" I ask. "Be some kind of superhero vigilante? Start a school and teach self-defense?"

Theo's quiet a long time.

Then I get it. He's saying good-bye.

"Evie, you're so great, and I—"

My heart sinks. I blink back at him, hold my breath.

"I shouldn't have started something, this, with you," he says quietly. "I can't do it. It's the wrong time for me, a mistake. I'm sorry."

There it is.

It was too good to be true. I know this lesson already. I can't believe I'm learning it again. The whole thing was a dream. And not the kind that happens to me.

I slump back against the wooden chair, gutted. Why is it so painful to get your hopes dashed? It's embarrassing. If Emma were here, she'd tell me to buck up, act like I don't care, at least until I'm out of here.

Those schematics would look like a maze. Leading to an off switch.

Robot girl powers down to avoid total circuit disintegration.

"So, no college." But I don't even know why I'm talking. My voice is all desperation, and when I say it, I realize a small stupid part of me was hoping we might end up facing The Future somewhere together.

"No college."

My bag falls off the chair and Chester starts snuffling through it, pulling stuff out.

"Chester, leave it," Theo says, stern. Chester ignores him.

We sit there a second, listening to Chester push his wet muzzle through my things, then Theo leans back in his chair to grab his collar, get him out of my stuff.

Chester eyes me sadly, then shuffles off.

"Sorry." Theo crouches down to gather it up.

He hands me my bag.

"It's okay." I hold it on my lap like a shield. "He smells Marcel."

Theo rubs his forehead and looks up at me out from under his hand. The angle of his eyes, apologetic, tentative, makes me feel like pleading with him not to do this, how can he not see he's supposed to be mine?

"I need to do something that *matters*."

I nod, even though I'm betraying myself.

He opens his laptop and a page pops up. A picture of a

public square somewhere ruined-looking. Destroyed buildings alongside some ramshackle reconstruction.

"This is Haiti," he says, following my gaze. "Port-au-Prince. Remember that earthquake a while ago?"

"Yeah," I say, my throat tight. I hate him for this, for making me like him more even when he's saying good-bye.

Theo pushes his hair out of his eyes.

"They're still slammed. And now with the hurricane . . . ? There's a school there, an orphanage, and a lot of work to do. Father Joe goes every year. I'm going too."

"How long?"

Theo looks at me, then shrugs, like it doesn't matter.

"Six months at least. The plan is for me to join a building crew, but I'll probably also tutor in math and maybe a little boxing." He cracks his knuckles, then looks at me. "Joe says love's a verb. You know? Action."

Haiti. I don't know what to say. I can't compete with that.

"I don't want to hurt you, but this . . . this isn't right for me. You took me by surprise, but I can't be anyone's hero right now."

"Hero?" I jerk back like he's hit me. The word sears.

"That came out wrong," he says, trying to backtrack. "I broke up with Lindsay because . . ." Shakes his head. "I really like you, but you seem like you have some stuff to figure out, and we—I'm not the one for you to do that with. I don't even—"

"Got it." I'm dying from shame. He thinks I want him to take care of me. I push back from the table so fast the chair nearly topples over. "It's okay, no problem. Sorry I showed up like this." The words are rocks in my throat, and I hug my bag tighter. "Good luck in Haiti."

Reach for more than you have coming and get your hand slapped.

"Evie . . ." Theo's chair scrapes the floor as he comes after me.

But I'm already pretending he doesn't exist. That I don't even care. I've had practice. It's what I do when people talk about their families, the future, vacations, their dads.

"Wait!" he calls out.

I run down the stairs, right past Em, right on out of there.

map the black

BEN'S HOUSE IS A GIANT PULSING HEART. At least, that's what I chalked on the base of one of the slate-gray walls in the hall when I got here. Anatomical and throbbing. Hearts are on my mind since mine turned ghost at Theo's. Or maybe it's whatever's in this red plastic cup. Emma gave it to me and I've been drinking it, and right now I swear the wall of windows is flexing and bowing with the bass thump of whatever EDM Devon's playing through Ben's dad's powerful speakers. They're built-in everywhere, so it feels like you've climbed right into the mouth of the sound and have become part of it. I've totally lost track of time, but people are starting to hook up with each other, and I'm pretty sure I've been here at least one lifetime.

I don't need a hero. My cup's almost empty. Here's Evie breaking her own rules. I fumble for the chalk in my pocket again, but I'm too drunk to draw handcuffs, open or closed.

I'm wandering, weaving my way through hot bodies, smiling and nodding at people drunker than I am, red-faced girls who want to hug and say stupid stuff like, *Why aren't we friends?* or guys who nod with their chins and try to press against me when I pass.

That was not love. It's what I'm telling myself, but two dates with Theo and I'm wrecked. I get why my mom gave up. Curse love and hearts and stupid hope. Curse rooftops and kissable lips. Curse fox-eyed boys with straw-colored hair, boys who lift their fists. But most of all, curse me for reaching out so far and falling.

After Theo's, Em took me home with her. We sat toe to toe on her window bench until I ran out of snot and tears. I totally get it—why she does what she does—I'd do anything to stop how this feels. I'm keeping the hero part to myself. It's too humiliating. Theo saw right through me to the sloppy mess, a lost girl with a long way to go.

I'll map the black. If you're messed up, you may as well know where you are. I'll need really big paper. Dark poster paint. Every shade of gray and black.

Emma parts the crowd with uncanny grace, sexy in her crop top and ruby lips. She's making her way across the room to me, two more cups held high over her head like emergency flares.

I try to bring myself back. Who knew time was made of so many overlapping planes? I down the last of my drink. Whatever it is burns my throat, tastes pink.

Ben's dad's penthouse is a bad-dad castle in a hedge-fund kind of way. Lots of leather furniture, tall windows, black lacquer. Feels like the Death Star. The air's all wet and sweaty from everyone dancing.

I lean against the wall in my corner and look down at the black hole I markered like a sucking funnel on my arm. A few silver stars float near the event horizon. Sorry, stars.

"Here." Emma hands me another cup, her face flushed. "Roman's over there." She shoots an exasperated glance in his direction. "If he talks to you, ignore him. He won't stop texting me."

I glance to where Roman's standing, staring at us, then sniff what she's brought me. More pink. "What is this?"

She raises her dark brows, sticks her tongue in it, and laughs. "Who cares? Vodka and something sweet. I don't know. Mandi poured. Drink it."

Over her shoulder I watch Jack and Alice slip in the front

door. I'm forgetting to forget her, thinking she looks pretty, when, as if on a magnetic trajectory, her eyes fly to mine. I look down at my cup.

"I'm so drunk," I say to Emma, not even sure if the words are coming out right.

She snorts at me. "Lightweight. This is, what, your second glass?"

"Is it? I lost count." I pull up the dress she made me wear. This is one of the reasons I hate parties. All the girls whip out credit cards and show up in something no one's seen them in before. Not super dressy or anything, but new. That's the key. Parties are for showing each other the new stuff they got. At least Em's dress looks good on me, even if it's a lower-cut V-neck than anything I'd ever buy. I drew looks when I first crossed the room, which I both loved and hated. Em's always telling me to work my assets. I don't really think of my body in terms of assets, and I usually never listen to her about dressing sexy, but since Theo cut me loose, it's clear I've gotten everything about being a girl wrong. Might be time to try it Emma's way awhile.

"Parties are easier when you're drunk," I say to Em, feeling philosophical.

She rolls her eyes. "Most people call that fun," she says. "Come on, Heartbreak Hotel. Stop looking so glum."

She downs her cup and pats my arm. Motions for me to

do the same. I do. Some of it bubbles up my nose.

"We dance!" Her hand firm on my arm, she drags me back into the throng.

I don't even like EDM, but somehow it becomes me. Or I become it. Pink. Trippy. Effervescent, like my drink. I am free from myself for a while, and it's incredible. It's like I'm seeing sound, my pulse in sync with everything around me, all of us one giant connected network, a human organism, everyone jumping and pulsing and whirling together.

Someone plants a wet kiss on my neck, but I don't see who because Mandi pulls me over, and I dance in a small circle with her and Sonja and some girl from LaGuardia named Sage, who looks vaguely familiar, like I might have seen her in a movie. Next to Sage are two guys whose names I don't catch, but they're part of the dream too, faces angular and sweaty, teeth overly white.

I move in and out of circles of people for so long, I feel like everything's circular, and I start to wonder why we don't just make maps on balls, then I remember we do, and they're called globes. I get the giggles, and then I think of maps on balls, just the word *balls*, and laugh even harder.

"I have to pee!" I announce, midgiggle, to where I thought Emma was, but it's actually Sage, who gives me a thumbs-up. I start to make my way through the crowd for the bathroom.

Em's at the far edge of the room near the door to the kitchen. Roman's standing at her side, kind of bent over her. His hand's on the wall behind her head and he's saying something super intense. Em looks trapped, or sad or something, her features staging a mutiny, abandoning party-face, threatening to slide down into their old territory of despair.

"Evie." She breaks away from Roman when I near. "Can you talk?" Her fingertips press into my arm with a weird desperate strength.

I'm not sure if she means am I capable of speech or can I talk to her. I almost laugh at this distinction, which has never, before tonight, occurred to me.

"Yes, but if you keep squeezing me like that you're going to make me pee my pants!" I laugh, working my arm loose from her grip. "Come on!" I say, trying to cheer her up. "This is what people call fun!" Her face falls further. "Oh! Don't look like that! I pee fast. I'll be *right back*," I promise, bouncing on my toes a bit.

Roman makes some remark about Emma and her *hench-bitch*, or at least that's what I think I hear, but before I can laugh in his face or say anything back, Em puts an icy hand on my arm again, tight, like she's drowning and I'm a buoy, but I'm seriously going to wet my pants if I don't find a bathroom now. I look around a second, then do what she did for me earlier, grab a full-looking cup and stick it in her hand.

"If I don't pee now, I'll die. But I'll be right back, I promise."

I feel so weird, so sure, so emphatic, like everything is really intense and full of much, much deeper meaning. I sway down the back hall of the penthouse, which is a gauntlet of closed doors. It ends in a set of glass steps. I climb them to a lofted mezzanine, a see-through tree house high over the action, a weirdly quiet space with a love seat and bookshelves and best, best, best of all, a small bathroom in the back.

Cold water on my face snaps me back into myself. I sit cross-legged on the vanity and stare at my face in the mirrored wall. This is who I am, right now. Bright-cheeked and kind of sweaty. A rosy-faced girl in a dress. The wisps around my hairline that looked so carefree earlier are twisting into ringlets. More water on my face and I break away from the larger cosmic being. I lap water from the faucet like a cat and land back into myself. I'm not made of music. I'm bones and guts. Finite and brokenhearted. The party sounds far away. Probably time to head home.

"Hey." Jack's voice surprises me from the dark love seat when I step out of the bathroom.

I don't know how long I was in there or if he was sitting

here before I went in. Time is still a little slippery.

He pats a spot next to him. "Got a sec?"

"I guess." I squint around the rest of the dark space for Alice. I'm totally not up for another surprise attack.

"Saw you dancing down there," he says, standing when I don't sit.

He comes close. God help me, he still smells so good.

"Didn't know you danced."

"Life's full of surprises."

"That's, ah . . . nice dress," he says, his eyes staying resolutely on my face. Then he steps back an inch and runs his hands through his hair. "God, Evie. Are you trying to kill me? What happened between us? Did I do something wrong that night . . . ?"

I open my mouth to say our near-miss kiss was me—my stupid worries, my fault for wanting it too much, for thinking too hard—but he lifts his hand close and touches my lips.

"Wait. Don't tell me," he says, green eyes wide. "I don't wanna know."

I stay there a second, his fingertips against my mouth. I fight the urge to kiss them. Kiss him. I could totally do it now. But everything's already ruined. I pull my face back slightly and Jack lets his hand drop. I'm definitely still drunk. And what is this, happening here, now? Is this why

Emma gets messed up all the time? Everything is so loose, blurry. Without worry, it's all possibility, so few cares.

I lean close to him again. My head against his chest. Evie, stop overthinking.

Then Jack wrecks it. "I'm glad you're done with Gray."

"What?" I say, taking a big step back.

"Yeah. Emma told Alice he broke up with you? Uh, you guys broke up?"

Emma told Alice. Even though I asked her not to, begged her to keep it to herself. Alice probably loved it.

I stare at him with my mouth open.

"It wasn't some big secret, was it?" Jack sounds tentative, like he's just realizing he probably shouldn't have said anything.

Just then a balled T-shirt flies over the glass loft railing. Lands near our feet. We both look down.

"Dude!" Ben shouts up from the center of a group of guys. "Come shoot baskets with us. My dad hung a sweet hoop on the roof."

Behind him and off to the left, Alice is standing in a group of girls, staring up at us. When we see her, hurt breaks her face in pieces.

"Down in a sec," Jack shouts back to Ben, eyeing Alice nervously.

"Hey, wait." I grab his wrist, look him in the eye.

"What?"

"Why'd Theo ask if you'd confessed?"

Jack's body lurches slightly, like he's been hit. He bends down and grabs a cup on the floor near the couch. Downs whatever's in it.

"It's snowing," he says quietly, pointing to the huge windows in front of us.

I look out. Papery white flakes flutter past the glass, like someone's shredded a love letter, let the pieces fall.

prickle

IT'S ALL THERE ON JACK'S FACE.

He turns and sits on the couch. I sit too. Everything is weirdly clear. As if in one heartbeat all the vodka I drank burned off, and I figure something out, something so obvious I can't believe I didn't see it before. Theo was never a problem. Jack's mad scramble to get me away from him was about protecting himself. He did something bad, and he was scared I'd find out.

I shoot him an I-know-what-you-did stare, feeling suddenly terrible with power, even if I don't know, not really. Then I look away, back down at the crowd. Alice isn't there anymore.

Jack stares straight ahead another minute, like he's trying to figure out how to start. He shifts and his thigh brushes mine.

I angle my legs away, ever so slightly.

It doesn't go unnoticed.

For a second, I feel righteous, badass. I never hold people in thrall like this.

Then I steal a glance at him. He's sweating a little, and beneath the party-chill he's cultivated to perfection, I can still see the real Jack, the one I've known forever, interested eyes taking everything in, stupidly open heart, his easy goofy smile. Something near the middle of me does a little turn, longs for him, but I shut it down.

He's hiding something. I use Theo's word.

"Confess."

Jack lifts his chin, defensive. Looks at me through those dark lashes, his eyes twitching at the corners, mouth forming, then holding back words. His face is an evolution of dread, guilt, resignation.

"He told you."

I keep my mouth shut.

He picks at a loose thread from a small hole in his jeans near his knee.

"Did he?"

"You know he didn't. He has more class than that. I'm asking you."

Another long minute. Jack stands a second and I think he's going to split, go shoot hoops with Ben and those guys, but he sits again, shifting, uncomfortable.

Snow keeps falling. So much for spring.

Jack plays with the loose thread, then snaps it off.

"Why'd he break up with you?"

I shift, uncomfortable.

"Maybe because of you. Because I have terrible friends." I feel guilty the minute I say it.

Jack's shoulders fall.

"I'll break up with Alice."

"What? Grow up." I lean back against the love seat, queasy. It is way too easy for people to hurt each other.

He bends forward over his knees a second, arms around his waist, then he sits up, squares his shoulders.

"It's not like I did it yesterday," he says, looking at me, pleading. "Remember that, okay?"

"Okay."

"Gray left camp in the middle of the night because we peed on him."

If the death of a crush made a sound, it would be like the last guttering gasp of air from a balloon.

"What?"

"We thought it would be funny."

I make a huff of disgust.

"He was asleep." Jack's voice is full of misery. "Jeb said we'd do it so it looked like he'd peed the bed."

"He slept through it?"

Jack looks at his feet. His face gets redder than I've ever seen it. He shakes his head.

"They held him down."

"They?"

He shakes his head, defensive. "*They.* It's not like I wanted to. Christ, Eves, don't look at me like that. I stopped as soon as he woke up. And for what it's worth, I tried not to hit him. It wasn't my idea. It was all of us."

I'm screaming at him in my head but can't seem to make any of it come out of my mouth.

"You know me. I'm not some asshole."

"What you just said is, like, the definition of asshole." My voice is so tight my throat hurts.

Jack shifts, faces me. "That kid was clueless. He acted so superior, totally unbelievable, like SciTech was beneath him, like we were, the rest of us were a waste of space. I was so sick of people like him. Looking at me like I wasn't good enough. And that was the summer it was all changing. Then he came along. And he was this cocky little guy too, not like he is now. I mean, what the fuck did he have on me?

He took a swing at us, started to fight back, so Jeb pissed on his face."

I can't believe what I'm hearing. I jump to my feet. Jack reaches out and tries to pull me back down. I shake myself free.

"Wait. Please, Evie. I tried to leave the room then, I was going to get the floor monitor, but Jeb stopped me. Before I could shake him loose, Theo grabbed his stuff and left."

"You're a hero," I say as witheringly as possible, my posture rigid. "What the hell, Jack?"

Jack deflates. "I'm sorry. I know it's messed up. You have to believe me. I tried not to be part of it. I pretended I was asleep at first, but Jeb knew I was faking."

His face flushes deeper red, and he can't look me in the eye.

"And you couldn't, oh, I don't know, do the right thing? Stand up for him? Say no to Jeb, wake up your dorm floor counselor or something?"

Jack shrinks. "It could have been me. But it wasn't. I just wanted those guys to like me. To be one of them."

He looks at me for some kind of encouragement. All I can think is how ugly everything is. I run my finger over the black hole on my arm. Jack's falling into it too, compressing faster than I can say good-bye, turning into a nothing little dot.

"He's an angry guy, Eves."

"Are you kidding me right now?"

"He is."

"Well, I wonder why."

"You weren't there. He was such a dick, acted like we were his intellectual inferiors."

"You were his intellectual inferiors," I say quietly.

A second ago I wanted to say mean stuff to Jack, to hurt him the way he hurt Theo, but there's no fight left in me. Everything is complicated. There are no villains. No heroes. Just us.

Jack drops his head. I look at his neck. It's weird how plain it looks. Skin with little hairs poking out of it. Like any other neck. A week ago I would have had a hard time catching my breath with him stretched out next to me like this, exposed. Now it's just another body, vulnerable, stupid. Between the glubs and thumps and other odd galloping contortions my heart is doing, my idea of Jack falls apart.

"The wasps . . . ," he starts again, but with no conviction.

"Theo had nothing to do with those wasps, you idiot," I snap, my skin prickling with something, my own kind of storm whipping up. "You made that up."

He reaches out like he's going to grab me, try to make me believe him, but his plan dies in his eyes as it hits him. The idea that Theo planted those wasps is how he let himself off the hook all these years.

"I'm sorry," he says, defeated.

I turn for the stairs because I just remembered Emma. She was upset about something and I promised to be right back.

Jack stands too. "Evie, please," he pleads.

But I'm not listening anymore.

stiff and bitter

WE MEET ALICE ON THE STEPS. Her face is blotchy, like she's been crying.

"Alice." Jack reaches out for her, but she shrugs his hand away.

"Emma was trying to find you," she says to me before I can slip by her.

"I know," I say, looking over her shoulder to the hallway. Em's not there.

Alice stays planted in my path. I close my eyes a second and lean against the wall. How long was I up there? This is why I don't drink. One sip and time turns sly, ready to betray. The memory of her fingers pressing into my arm, the look on her face when she said she wanted to talk. Dread gathers in me, slow, heavy.

"Where is she?" I demand, scanning the hall again.

Alice shakes her head, her face stiff and bitter. "She left. A while ago."

My shoulders drop with relief. It's a first, Em heading home before me, but maybe she's starting to figure it out. I whip out my phone to text her.

Wait up! I'll join u.

It bounces back, undelivered. Her phone's off.

"Thanks, Alice," I say, trying to pass her again. "And it's not what you think. Jack and I were just talking up there."

She presses her lips together, tight. Says nothing.

I look at her another second, then step away.

Before I get more than a few feet, though, she catches me, wraps her fingers around my wrist. Squeezes it, tight.

"Wait. I think you need to go find her. Emma was pretty messed up. She left with a group of guys from Columbia, Ben's brother's friends?"

"What? When? Alone?" I demand.

"Yeah. Ages ago. When you went upstairs with Jack."

"Why didn't you stop her?" I ask, with a sinking feeling. "You're the one who came with her."

I swear Alice looks the tiniest bit happy when she says it.

nowhere

SNOW KEEPS COMING DOWN, DOWN, DOWN.

How did I let this happen? There are a few basic rules, and one of them is, if you go to a party together, you look out for each other.

Emma's nowhere.

I circle Ben's block, then wrap back, circle wider. Almost no one's out, even though it's a Saturday night. The sudden lurch back into winter has a few people darting and scurrying from bar to restaurant and cab to building, but mostly I'm alone on the quiet, whitening streets.

Even though Ben's dad's is in TriBeCa and Em and I

are a good mile and a half up, I pull her short jacket in as tightly as I can around myself and start to walk home, willing myself to find her, spot her out somewhere and whisk her away from whatever group of guys she's using to erase herself.

But the city's quiet, Emma's block deserted. No one's even driven down it since the snow started to fall. There are no footprints anywhere near her stoop. By the time I round back down to my own corner, my feet are stiff blocks in my shoes.

I fight back panic and let myself in to get warmer clothes. The apartment is dark and my mom's bedroom door closed. I'm in my room, pulling on jeans and thick socks and a sweatshirt, when my phone rings. The number's strange. I answer anyway.

Emma's crying.

"Why am I such a worthless person?"

There are too many *s*'s in worthless. Her speech is super slurred.

"Em, where are you?"

"I didn't want to bother you. I saw you with Jack. Are you still in love with Jack? You should be. He's nice. Who cares about Theo? You should definitely go out with someone Evie, you really should. You're not all messed up like me."

"Emma, where are you?"

Silence.

"Em? Don't hang up. I'm coming, but you have to look around, tell me where you are."

I'm hopping around on one foot, pulling on a boot, phone crushed between my shoulder and cheek. I can hear cars. They sound like they're going fast.

"Em? Where *are* you?"

"Evie, you're never lost, not like this, like me," she slurs. "If you mapped me, I'd be in a garbage dump." She takes a jagged breath. "Did you know they gave away his *heart*?"

"What?"

"Patrick's heart. Someone has it. An old guy. And his retinas." She can hardly say the word *retina*. She's starting to scare me.

"Emma, stop. You're drunk. It's making everything seem worse. Tell me where you are."

She drops her voice to a nearly unintelligible whisper.

"I lost track," she breathes. "Some guy passed out on me, and then . . ."

A loud rustling sound crackles in my ear, like she's going away or is being dragged somewhere. I start to panic. Where *is* she and what are those guys doing to her? "Em?!"

More rustling, then she's back.

"This is *his* phone! I'm so messed up. . . ." More rustling noise. “Oh my God, where are you? You should see this, with the snow and the lights, the sky is all swirly like the guy without the ear did it? Who’s that guy?”

Before I can say Van Gogh she drops to an awed whisper. “It’s not the sky, it’s water.”

Jesus.

I have to find her.

“Emma, I’m coming to you, but you have to tell me where you are.”

“I don’t know . . . ,” she wails. “Where are you? People are always leaving me. I needed to talk to you. Roman said I was heartless and selfish and a bad person.”

“Em, who are you with? Are you still with Ben’s brother’s friends?”

“She was in my house.”

“Who?”

“Today before the party.”

“Em, tell me how I can get to you.”

“Mamie was in my house!”

There’s a snuffling sound and I can’t tell if she’s laughing or crying. She’s totally out of control and I have to figure out where she is.

“Is someone else there with you? Can you put someone else on the phone?”

I slip out of my apartment as quietly as I can and start

pummeling the elevator button, then skip it and fly down the service stairs, one hand on the railing, taking multiple steps at a time.

"You're the only one who really knows me," she sobs, sloppy. "I wear everyone else out. I don't want to wear you out."

"You're not wearing me out. Em, are you with someone else?"

"Why am I like this? I'm such a fuckup. You'd never make your mom wish you died instead of Patrick."

"Emma. Put someone else on . . . ," I beg. I have to get to her. What if she's wandering in and out of traffic, hating herself?

"I'm alone," she whispers back. "Oh my God, Eves! I'm barefoot! What did I do with my shoes?" She laughs, loud. It hurts my ear. "My feet aren't even cold!" She laughs again. "This is *so cool.* Why aren't we like this all the time?"

I stop midflight and rush back up to our floor, slip in again, and pack a bag for her. I stuff it with a sweater, leggings, thick socks, and a pair of Vans.

Something really loud rumbles by. A truck or a bus?

"Jesus. Emma," I hiss. "Focus. I need you to listen to me. Stand still and look around. I hear cars. Tell me where you are."

She *ahhs.*

"The river. It's so black and beautiful. It's like a fat snake. Why don't we do this all the time? The river's so pretty. Why do people say there's no nature in New York? Remember when we made those little birch canoes for Lewis and Clark?"

I hear what sounds like a group of drunk guys catcalling her, hooting and cheering. Their voices are loud at first, then fade.

Cars and the river. Before I ran out of Ben's, Mandi said she heard his brother's friends talking about an NYU party in the West Village. Maybe she's on the West Side Highway?

I run back out to the elevator.

"Hang on," I say. "I'm coming."

"Evie! If you spin *yourself*, the other spinning stops!"

"Emma, find a place to sit. Are there any street signs near you?"

I hit the stairs again. The rubber soles of my boots bounce and echo lonely against treads on the steps, the shiny industrial green-painted walls. My phone's signal is weaker in here and I'm scared I'll lose her.

I'm not religious and usually feel too stupid to pray, but I start mentally begging someone. *Please don't let her fall into traffic. Please keep her out of the river.*

Emma starts crying again.

"I'm always alone." Her voice is very small. "Does everyone feel this alone?"

I rush out the door to find a cab.

hard lemonade times a million

THE DRIVER GUNS IT DOWN the West Side Highway. I beg him to go slowly so I can look for her. We almost blow by her when I spot someone sitting next to the Christopher Street Fountain, wrapped in a ball, knees hugged tight to her chest. It's Em, and she is indeed barefoot.

She's too drunk. It's like watching her drown. She throws up when I try to pull her into the cab with me.

"Stupid bitches," the cabbie curses, tossing my bag onto the street next to me. He guns it, the door swinging shut, leaving us in the snow.

"I'm sorry," she repeats between heaves. "You hate me. You should hate me."

I hold her hair back and wait until she's done. Because of the snow, the West Side Highway is nearly empty. Emma's shivering terribly. I walk her down the path a bit until I spot a bush big enough to block her while I help her slip out of her puke-covered clothes and get into the clean, dry things I've brought. She smells like vomit and hard lemonade times a million. I stuff her ruined clothes into my bag and breathe through my mouth. When I was little I threw up whenever anyone else did. Maybe love grows you out of things like that.

"My phone!" she says when it clatters onto the ground from the back pocket of her jeans. "Oh my God, I stole that guy's phone for nothing!" she laughs.

I pick hers up. It's powered down. I turn it on again to check for texts. It vibrates with a thousand of them, all from her parents. My stomach lurches at the thought of her dad showing up.

Em throws up again. Neater this time. Then she slumps over like she's passed out. I slip her phone in my pocket and lean to help her.

"Em?" I shake her shoulder. "How much did you drink?"

She looks like she's having trouble opening her eyes. I've

never seen her this messed up.

"I can't—I just wanted everything to stop," she mumbles.

"What?!" I try to sit her up. She's like a rag doll. "Em!" I shake her some more.

She drowsily opens her eyes, sits up. "Doesn't matter. S'gone now." But she seems too out of it.

"Where'd the other phone go?" I don't know where she's been or what might have happened to her. What if we need it for evidence?

She looks around, unsure. Opens her eyes a little wider. Raises a shaky hand to wipe her mouth. Her makeup's smeared in ghoulish circles under her eyes and the lipstick's mostly gone from her lips. She turns away from me and vomits a third time.

I'm panicking. This is the worst I've ever seen her, and thinking of her, like this, with a group of guys—I have to get a handle on myself, on the situation.

She straightens up and wipes her mouth with her hand. She looks more alert, like that one woke her up.

"Did you find it?"

"Forget it. You called me from it. I still have the number."

She looks ready to lie down on the sidewalk for the night, so I wrap an arm around her waist and drag her over to a bench. I can barely hold her up, she's noodle-kneed and hanging off my shoulder so heavy it's hard to walk. We slide through the snow.

My phone buzzes in my pocket. I stop to check it. Mrs. Sullivan. My heart lurches. We're in so much trouble. I panic and click Ignore. I'm getting her home as fast as I can. We'll be there in no time and they can talk to her then. There's no covering up this situation.

"I wreck everything," she says, dropping her head to my shoulder.

I don't know what to say, so I hug her a second. "You don't wreck everything. But we have to get out of here." I stand. "I'll grab a cab. Okay? Do not move. Got it?"

She grabs my arm. "Wait." Her grip is hard on my wrist. "Patrick was using Adderall. My Adderall. That night, well, for a while. I gave it to him."

Her teeth start to chatter when she says it.

"What?" I look at her but also keep an eye toward the largely empty street, hoping to spot another cab.

"You have to listen to what I'm saying," she says, shaking. "No one wants to hear this part, but it's my fault, Evie. You know how he was about grades, so competitive. I hated that stuff, but Patrick liked it. He used it that whole spring. It made him tense. Remember?"

I do remember. Patrick changed. He was always a little

righteous, like his dad, but this was different. He snapped at us a lot. Mamie smoothed things over. I steered clear and assumed being kind of ticked off all the time was his response to the remaining few months of life at Bly.

I look at her.

"He was high that night at the beach." She sounds more sober now. "He's dead because of me. I fuck everything up."

I drop back down onto the bench next to her.

"Em, it's not your fault. Patrick was beyond drunk when he died."

She starts to cry again, but less like a drunk and more like a person who knows something terrible has happened that can never be undone.

"They all say I'm wrong, but they act like it's true, like I'm such a bad person," she wails. "And when Mamie came over to talk about her show, she filled our whole house. . . ." Em shakes her head like that's not quite right. "Like she was breathing up all the last little bits of Patrick hanging around. Totally erasing him."

Snot runs over her lip and I'm worried tears are going to freeze on her face.

"My mom wanted us to hug," she says quietly, her eyes two sad holes darker than the river behind her.

She starts shivering and shaking so violently, I wrap my arm around her shoulders. What if this is never over?

She can't move on? What if there's no pulling Emma back together again?

"They weren't expecting me to show up," she says. Bitter. "I surprised them in the middle of their feel-good-fest." She's doing that weird hiccup-breathing you do when you cry so hard you can't breathe right. "They were in Patrick's room! And this show . . ." She makes a small fist and hits the bench so hard her knuckles bleed. I grab her wrist before she can do it again. "It's happening on his birthday."

It's a sucker punch.

Patrick's birthday has been somber since he died, unmentioned, a day to get through, and until now his room has been a sealed archive. A mausoleum.

"Em, you have to tell them what this is doing to you."

She shakes her head. "They don't listen. All they care about is forgiveness. They want to forget it and move on, but you know what? Forgiveness is a total lie, don't believe anyone who tells you it's not. It's a lie people tell so they can go back to not caring."

She's so messed up, and nothing I say will make any of it better. This is how she feels. Emma sags like all the life has gone out of her, and for a second I check to see if she passed out. But she leans against me, opens her eyes again, and says in a near whisper, "My mom let her take one of his shirts."

Before I can find the right words for that, a car pulls up on the curb. Mrs. Sullivan's in the passenger seat, her face lit blue from the glow of her phone.

They tracked us.

Mr. Sullivan leaps out, barking Emma's name. He rushes over to us, rigid with fear or fury, and yanks Emma to the car by the arm, eyes wild.

••• — — — •••

SNOW.

Mountains of it melting. Blue, blue skies and ice pods clasped like little glass hands around the green buds on trees. Everything's messed up.

Emma's gone.

Mrs. Sullivan called my mom first thing this morning.

"She didn't want you to worry," my mom explains, pouring me another glass of water. "They're taking her out of town for a little while."

"How long?" I down the glass. I've never been this thirsty and my head feels broken.

My mom shakes her head. "She didn't say." Then she makes this face and I know whatever's coming next is going to hurt.

And it does.

"Honey, they asked that you not call."

Because we went to that party together.

Because we were both drunk.

Because I let them down and didn't get help when I knew she was in trouble.

I stare at the wrinkled egg on my plate. It quivers there, a blurry yellow eye holding me in its gaze.

When I start to cry, my mom says, "What if I call Patricia . . . ?" But then I look at her and she quits talking.

Everything's wrecked. Theo. Jack. And now the Sullivans hate me. I will never forget Mr. Sullivan's rage-filled face when I told them she'd been throwing up. I thought it would make them feel better, but that's when he yelled so loud his voice cracked.

When your friend's in danger you call for help!

Like we were repeating what happened with Patrick. I don't know. Maybe we were.

And Mrs. Sullivan, so freaked out, trying to keep the peace, waggling her phone at me, and saying how grateful she was for tracking, how the minute I turned Em's phone on they knew where to come.

I push my plate away. My mom clears it without a word.

In psychology class last year, Ms. Jesme said that on a scale of human emotions, shame hits the lowest note.

It rings deep in me all day long.

I hide in my bed. My mom murmurs outside my door, her voice quiet through the heavy wood.

You're a good kid. People make mistakes.

I'm sure you thought you were doing the right thing.

Emma might be going through something friendship can't fix.

When the heat kicks in, the air in our apartment shrinks. I force myself to get up, put clothes on, and take Marcel out into the snow.

I walk to Emma's block. It's the only place I feel like going. I travel a mental timeline back to when things were less out of control. That Evie was so innocent. She had no idea what was coming. I make her brave enough to stand up to Emma's parents and tell them Mamie's project is messing with her head. How in Em's mind everything is brighter and darker than it is for other people. Needle-peak highs, fathomless trenches. I explain that the rest of us have to help her keep it all straight.

A fantasy. All of it.

I unwind Marcel's leash from my wrist and wrap it around my other hand. He stops and looks up at me like, at least to him, I'm still among the decent people of the world. I give him a treat. While he snuffles it up, I glance back at my tracks.

A map of my route could be made in Morse code. Stuttered starts and stops along the snowy street. I would make it more distinct, like an SOS, while I try to figure out what I'm supposed to do. Emma needs someone to stand up for her. Why am I so scared to be the one to do it?

Their house is dark. No dogs. No lights.

I brush some snow off their stoop and sit. The steps are biting cold. I press my hand into the snow and watch it melt away from my fingers.

Mamie's show's at the end of the week and Em's going to miss it.

broadcast from another plane

EMMA'S VOICE IS THIN, like she's made of air.

"Why am I like this?"

I was dreaming. Deep. Something about looking for Emma in water, or maybe under ice, and now she's here in my ear sounding like I found her, near the bottom and only barely gathering herself together long enough to form words.

I fumble with my phone, drop it in the sheets, grab it again, and struggle to make out what she's saying.

"You're the only one who really knows me. All the ugly parts, and you don't care, you love me anyway. Right? You love me no matter what?"

"No matter what," I whisper. I force my eyes to focus. Check the time. It's 4:40 a.m. Marcel's asleep on a pillow below me, his breath a steady whistle-snore.

"Emma, can't you sleep?"

"I want him back," she says. "I want to start over, undo every stupid fight we ever had. Keep him the hell away from her."

"Mamie?" I'm trying to follow her, but I'm still waking up, a little disoriented.

Marcel makes a small senseless sound, like he's watching a squirrel at the window.

"Why'd he die? Patrick was *perfect*. I'm the one who messed up. Every time my mom tells someone we *lost Patrick* I think maybe that's the way to find him—lose myself too."

"Em, stop."

Mapping the distance between us would be like trying to bridge infinity. She's out of reach. This is a one-way broadcast from a nowhere plane.

"They've been a part of it since the beginning." Emma's voice rises, a little louder, higher. "She *started* the whole thing with my parents, painting them holding a picture of Patrick. My mom says she needed to be part of it, even if I wasn't *ready to understand*. She says it made her feel closer to him, and if I could stop blaming people I might feel close to him too."

Her despair has infinite mass.

"I thought at least if we went and messed up her show I might feel better, like I did something. Because nothing makes me feel close to him."

Electromagnetic waves traveling through the vacuum of space.

"Emma—"

"You have to help me, Evie. Why do people like her?" she cries. "Why is Mamie back? Why is everything I do wrong?"

Before I can respond I hear a voice in the background. Low tones. Her dad. My limbs buzz hot. He's going to yell at me again.

"Emma," I whisper quickly before he can. "I'll help fix this. I promise."

There's a rustling sound, then the line goes dead.

topo map of nebulous force

I'M WEDGED DEEP IN THE SOFTEST, saggiest part of the couch. Nights like this usually make me feel better. Mom and me together, watching TV. She's in the corner with her legs across my lap, scrolling through the menu of options. I keep my eyes on the screen, like I care what she picks, but I'm all over the place, bouncing between Emma and Mamie's show and Theo. Stupid Theo. I've started a fight with him in my head. I tell him I don't need a hero, I *am* the hero. Then my mind loops back to what he said about anger poisoning you when you keep it in. *Oh yeah?* I demand in my head. Well, what happens if you're not sure how to let it out? Or what it's even about?

He never has an answer for that one.

I shift on the couch and bite a particularly satisfying hangnail from my middle finger.

"Your dad did that too," my mom says, keeping her eyes on the screen. "When he was worried about something."

I drop my hand to my lap. She says that every time she sees me do it.

"This looks good, right?"

She's picked a British legal thriller. When my dad got sick, my mom deferred law school, and she loves these. She's grinning at me, so I grin back. It's obvious she's super invested in thinking I'm feeling better, that she's the only one who secret-cries in the tub, that this week without Emma is flying by and soon enough everything's going to go back to normal.

"Looks great." I reach across her and click Play on the remote.

We hunker down under this crazy pink, green, and black zigzag afghan my great-grandma made and balance the huge bowl of popcorn between us.

Some people go upstate or have big family dinners. This is our version, the two of us on the long couch—well, me and mom and the space where Dad would be. She digs into the popcorn, but I'm not hungry. My stomach's been tight for days.

"So, what are you worried about?"

When I don't answer, she goes on. "Honey, Emma's parents know all about her . . . struggles. They're trying to get her to turn her attention to more positive things."

I snort. Take a handful of popcorn. "Positivity is like using a bandage when surgery's required."

My mom pauses the intro to our show.

"I think it's pretty clear now to Patricia and Frank that they need a better plan." She tilts her head so she can see my eyes. "Emma's been in trouble for a long time now—long before Patrick died—you know that, right?"

I nod, blinking fast so I don't cry.

My mom starts the show, but now I can't focus on the screen, so I picture us from overhead instead, outlined like a topo map, our blanketed bodies lumpy mountains on the couch. I'd draw us green and blue, like eroded hills, then blur in some white pastel mist for the Ever Missing, our nebulous force. But this is annoying.

I slouch down low and pull a pillow to my chest. I'm sick of drawing my way through stuff, tired of trying to see anything at all, of being myself, of always looking for more than what's right in front of me.

My phone vibrates. It's been buzzing all week with texts from Jack. He follows me through school, begs me to meet him for lunch or coffee.

Only it's not Jack. A Photogram notification pops up instead. @WrenWells accepted my follow request. I click her name and images appear. Nothing personal, pictures of paintings, street art, a few small strange abstractions.

After that night on the beach, she disappeared. It felt like she died too. But Emma's right. Here she is getting a do-over. Mamie's made a new life, and it looks pretty great. My stomach forms a fist.

"Oh no! This is that one where the girls die," my mom gasps, covering her eyes with a buttery hand. "I didn't remember the title."

We skip the shows that feature long-haired girls tossed like litter in bushes.

"Tell me when I can look again."

She pulls the afghan over her eyes.

I tell her I will, and lean in to her like I can shield my mom from TV misogyny. But my head's somewhere else.

The sound track vibrating the plastic speakers on our TV is percussive, urgent.

Do. Some. Thing. Do. Some. Thing.

criminal

SO I DO.

After school, I trek to the far edge of Chelsea to scout Mamie's dad's gallery. The whole way over I'm out-of-body, someone else, a girl who plans and executes. I'm definitely off the map, and people off the map are fearless. My skull's a noise box, Public Enemy's "Fight the Power" blasting between my ears. I'm a disrupter, a defender, stomping in imagined combat boots.

The gallery is midblock. I shoulder open silvery windowed doors and step into a silent white space. The gallery's an empty blank between shows. Before I can ponder what it means, the silence, all this whiteness, a pencil-thin young man with severely combed hair and black glasses bigger than his head looks up from his desk and says in a crisp tone, like the irritation of addressing me is terminal, "We're not open—there's nothing to see."

I stand and gape for a second because in the larger space, just past his station, as red and crackling as a burning bush or some other portent, I see it.

A bright-red box, its lever marked "PULL."

Emma was right. It's simple. I could pull the fire alarm. Clearer instructions have rarely been offered.

I lift my eyes. The ceiling is studded with flowerlike sprinklers. A field of them, metal daisies ready to rain Mamie's paintings away.

Gallery Man sniffs, irked by my continued existence, and informs me the gallery's preparing to host a private event. Then, he says, they will close for a week to mount the next show, sculpture by Rachel Someone. He taps a bored finger on the top of a stack of colorful postcards. I feign interest, take one.

Because snapping a phone picture of the space would be too weird, I thank him and stand there another minute, memorizing the room. It's empty, waiting for something to happen. Concrete floors, white walls, and that beautiful shock of red, that powerful little box with its lever sticking out like an invitation, and those silvery sprinklers dotting the ceiling, apocalyptic, ready to rain.

Exhilarating.

I can totally do this. Sometimes you have to go big to get people to pay attention. That idea alone makes me feel more like Emma. Less thinking, more doing. Like that day at Urban. I suck in air, like I'm surfacing in water. The rush is intense.

The *private event* Mr. Pointy mentioned has to be Mamie's show. Her dad's a big deal, and this is his gallery. It will be crowded. The never-ending nepotism kids at Bly take for granted is going to smack her back like the biggest karmic boomerang ever. The shelf behind the reception desk is heavy with monographs, a few of which bear her father's name. He'll pack the house for her. It's what fathers do. Jealousy bubbles in me, volatile.

Fathers. Unknowable creatures from the country of men. One time at the Sullivans' when I was around ten, Mr. Sullivan sent me up from the basement to ask Mrs. Sullivan to bring him a beer. We were down there building a soda volcano, but the mesh kept collapsing under the weight of our clay. When I went up to the kitchen, I couldn't figure out how to say it, what to call him when I relayed his request. I stood there tongue-tied, clearing my throat and blushing a painful crimson, because the words *your husband* were impossible for me, too intimate or adult or something, and my mouth couldn't shape itself around the words *Emma's father* any better. I finally settled on *Mr. S* and avoided referring to him altogether after that.

The gallery man makes a raspy throat-clearing sound like he's trying to sweep me out. I shake off the memory and straighten up. I'm not that girl anymore. I'm someone new. I take my time, refuse to scurry, lingering at the door to look once more. Ms. Vax has taken us to art openings before. Clusters of people stand in clumps, wearing dramatic clothing and clutching plastic cups of wine. It'll be easy to lean against the firebox, catch it with my shoulder blade. I'll reach for it if I have to. I'm nobody. I'll go unseen. No one will notice me, and honestly, I don't care if they do. It'll be like civil disobedience, only emotional. That lever's coming down.

kick-ass ninja

I WEAR BLACK. BOOTS, tights, and a skirt. Button up a weird blouse Emma gave me for Christmas last year, which I never put on because I thought it looked more like her than me. She's always doing that, giving me gifts she'd like, but I'm grateful for it now, the strange silky material, little puff shoulders, and long ties at the neck for making a droopy bow. It makes me feel beautiful like her. Only strong. Strong and anonymous. Sometimes the forces of anarchy need to blend in. I keep the ties undone, let them hang, then check myself in the mirror.

Nailed it.

Kick-ass ninja, Emma-style. I check my last texts from her. Two bubbles at four a.m.

Did you mean it?

You'll fix it?

I pass my mom on the couch on my way out. Part of me wonders if she'll comment on my outfit, but that's stupid, because she never does. She trusts me to make good choices. She looks up from her book for less than half a second. Blows me a kiss. No questions about where I'm going. It's super lonely being trusted all the time.

By the time I walk up to the gallery I'm perfectly no one. Another New Yorker out for art early on a Friday night. And I was right about the crowds. Mamie's dad's packed the place. I can't see her, but she's here somewhere, a star in her constellation of important people.

I slip in as quietly as possible, another face in a white box full of faces. Someone's speaking near the center back wall, but the room's all a-murmur and I can't make out what's being said. I grab a flyer from the reception desk and hold it in front of my face, like I'm reading the stupid stuff some Anna woman has written about Mamie's work.

Then people quiet down.

I look up.

Mamie's talking.

Seeing her is a shock. I've been so focused on stopping

this event I didn't really work through what it would feel like to see her again. The memory of how badly I wanted to *be* her rushes back. She looks small up there, stammering, terrified, more human than I remembered. Less cool and perfect. I'm deaf with embarrassment for my younger self until I hear her say *Patrick*.

His name hits me like a slap and my whole plan slithers out from my imagination and into the real. Today's his birthday. I scan the room for the Sullivans, but they're not here. One small victory for Em, at least. I take a shaky breath. There are more than a few Bly faces. The dean; Ms. Hennessy, the photography teacher; and next to her, Ms. Vax. People who will hand out extra-special punishment if they see me pull the lever.

A thin trickle of sweat runs down between my breasts. The room is close, too hot, overcrowded. My blouse clings to my back. I raise the info sheet in front of my face again before anyone sees me. My hands are trembling, but I take a deep breath and work my way toward the wall with the firebox.

I have a job to do, and I'm done letting fear hold me back.

When I get close, I lean against the wall, then inch over casually until I'm in front of the box, the metal cold through my thin blouse, the contours of the lever right under my shoulder blade. I give it a little test nudge. The lever doesn't act remotely like something that's going to budge without being deliberately pulled down. Possibly with both hands. My heart thunders.

Evie. Commit.

Mamie's voice warbles. I lean against the chilly metal and look at her a minute. Her name's on the wall behind her, spare, all lowercase, "wren wells," like some small bird fluttered in, modern, fortunate, innocent.

I close my eyes. Bitterness ratchets up my throat. No one's innocent.

Patrick's dead.

Emma's a wreck.

I'm telling myself revolutionaries do not let fear hold them back when something in her voice changes, drops. She's going down all on her own, an epic fail without my help. I shift my footing a little, move a step away from the firebox and out from behind the tall man in front of me so I can see her better. It seems only fair on behalf of Emma to let her suffer as long as possible before I pull the lever.

She's standing next to the painting of the Sullivans. It's life-size, like they're up there with her, and it takes my breath away. The image is distorted, but she caught them. Living in it. Their faces. The look they have now that Patrick's gone. How did she do that? It's so strange, but they are *here* in paint, Patricia and Frank in Patrick's room, near his window, by his still unmade bed, holding a photo of their son.

I retreat to the wall again, unsettled.

My eyes flash from the painting to Mamie's face, and for a second I don't recognize her. Her expression holds none of the entitlement I'd imagined. She looks as lost as I feel.

Right then, a motorcycle thunders by, the gallery door opens, and a guy steps in. Mamie hesitates, the space momentarily filled with the roar of the thing.

A few people cough. Everyone's waiting for her to go on, but she doesn't.

I try to shrug off the weird feeling gathering in me. Everything's changing, somehow. Mamie's obviously losing it, and because I'm so porous I catch other people's moods, she's making me lose it too.

Mamie makes a sound that's not words.

I stare at my boots, muster the confidence pulsing through me a minute ago, try not to feel for her, but it's hopeless.

I look up. Her eyes are on the guy who stepped in. He's tall, with dark hair and glasses, wearing a slim navy suit and leaning slightly on a suitcase handle. Obviously a surprise arrival. The way they're looking at each other makes me feel lonely, like I've missed the point of something huge, complicated, something I've refused to consider.

I clench my jaw. Take a deep breath. Will myself to look away from them. Whatever's going on between Mamie and that guy is beside the point. I'm an insurrectionist on a mission. *Focus on the mission.*

Mamie starts talking again, but not about art. She tells what happened instead, why she made these paintings.

I get myself into position. Press my back hard against the firebox to root myself in the here and now—but Mamie's words pull me through time until I'm back on the beach that night with Em, watching her scream and scream in the flashing blue light.

My eyes fill with tears. I blink them away, looking around the gallery while Mamie's painted people tower over us, lost and haunted.

Just like Em.

She explains why she started with old film, the first images already partly imperfect, like memory. How she scanned, enlarged, and projected them until they were as distorted and indistinct as she felt after Patrick died. Then she painted what she saw. All those lost people living blurry within us.

A painting of me and my dad would be mostly white.

I squeeze my eyes shut tight. My inner rebel feels like dress-up. I glance around the gallery, hoping for a sign.

Something to help me recommit to my mission. The guy who came for Mamie is still by the door, listening to her like she's speaking to him, like they're connected.

Mamie's in love.

And I've been mean. Naïve. Why am I so small?

She's a thousand times braver, standing up in front of all these people, telling what it means to hold someone only in your heart.

She keeps her eyes on the guy by the door while she talks. He's in love with her too. That fact alone would kill Em if she knew.

The alarm box is cold against my back. Doesn't feel like a solution anymore.

I clench my teeth, press against it hard, harder, like I can wedge it through my ribs to the place where I'm supposed to have a working heart, and not the dark hollow echoing there instead. How can this be what Emma needs?

The gallery is full of people from the paintings. Real people. Not the villains I had in my head. Victims of alcohol-related accidents. People who know loss, like Em and her family. Like Mamie. Like me.

Small on the wall next to each canvas are her original photographs. The one closest to me is a family of four on a beach, holding a picture of a girl named Sabrina.

There's no way I can wreck this.

Not for Em, not for anyone, and not because I'm scared.

Mamie's doing what she can, trying to live with what happened, trying to make something anyway, to go on.

Being scared is what got me here in the first place.

The only wrong thing about tonight was me.

endless possible mistakes

I SIDLE OUT, PAST THE BLY COHORT, past Mamie kissing that guy, and start to walk downtown. I don't know where I'm going, but for the first time in days my head's a cathedral of silence. No more sound track, rebel or otherwise. The gallery had something big in it, like when you see a whale, and it's bigger than your wildest expectations, so big it seems impossible, and you realize the ocean is full of magisterial creatures you forget about because you've limited yourself to only what you see. It left me with an electric shiver that's getting stronger, like walking is charging it, charging me.

It was in Mamie's paintings—I've been looking at love all wrong, wanting it to fill me, when I should be trying to serve it instead. I'm not sure how we got here, but I don't think friendship is supposed to be like this, to mess with your head, to make you see things from the wrong angle.

I picture for a second what I almost did, the chaos and pain I would have caused, and my body vibrates with relief, with the conviction that not only did I dodge a bullet, but one from my own gun.

This part of town is covered with posters and graffiti, people making their marks where they can, inside galleries and out. I stop at the end of a block, pull chalk from my pocket, and draw a gun on the ground. Hearts exploding from the end of it.

Place where Evie got another chance.

The light changes and I straighten up, cross the street, and keep walking.

This night is nicer than any other spring evening, and I don't want to keep my head down anymore. I've been hiding, paying attention to the wrong things. I want to be open to everything—the air full of river and the beginning of green, and all that love in the gallery—families that are still families after something unspeakable blew them apart, and Mamie making images, and all those people there to support her—I want it all—God, even that guy who showed up, especially him, the way they looked at each other—I want *that.*

If that's what my mom had with my dad, maybe that's why she won't look for someone else.

I'm tripping along, loose with relief and the idea of wanting. I'm thinking life is full of endless possible mistakes, and I sidestepped a big one tonight, when my phone buzzes.

I dig it from the bottom of my bag.

Emma.

Are you there?

I stare at the screen, unable to respond. Her question seems bigger than she means. Unanswerable.

Something comes loose inside me. Breaks away. When this relief dies down I'm still going to have to tell her how *wrong* we were. But not yet. I power my phone off and drop it back into my bag.

Tonight was so screwed up. I'm so screwed up. And love is super confusing. I wanted to help Em, get rid of what's been making her so sad, but I had it all wrong. I almost made a huge mistake, an unforgivable one.

My knees go weak. I stop. People sluice past me on the sidewalk.

I should have stayed and talked to Mamie instead of

slinking out like a coward. Then, like I'm a magnet orienting to a new field, I turn and walk back to the gallery. This pretty night's not for me.

I have to go find her. Tell her what I almost did.

no one else can do it for you

MAMIE AND HER GUY ARE OUT on the sidewalk when I get back up there. They're leaning against the gallery wall, her arms inside his suit coat, slipped around his waist, their foreheads pressed together.

I stop and watch them. They look so happy kissing and smiling and talking. Then I turn back. I'm not going to mess with that.

I only make it a few paces before I hear Mamie say my name.

"Evie Ramsey? Is that you?"

I try to keep going, walk another step or two away like I

didn't hear, but I can't leave. She remembers me. I turn to face her. They're side by side now, both a little flushed, leaning against the gallery wall, holding hands. She's smiling, her face open. She even looks happy to see me.

"I'm sorry to bother you," I say, taking another step back. Why is my voice so tight? "Just wanted to say hi."

"Come here!" she calls, waving her arm toward me like we're in a swimming hole and she's stirring the water.

I stand there another second, my heart banging around inside my chest. Then I walk to her. Her guy's supercute, even if he's kind of squinting at me like he might be annoyed. If I were Mamie, I'd chalk a bed on the sidewalk and pull him down on it. Place where everything's as it should be. That's how they look standing there together.

"I haven't seen you in so long!" Mamie's voice cracks a little when she says it.

She drops his hand and pulls me into a hug. I let her do it, but can't lift my arms to hug her back. I am officially the world's worst human.

"Still making your maps?" she asks quietly in my ear. We pull apart.

She smiles into whatever expression my face is making. I can't tell because every feeling I've ever had is whirling inside me and my face is so far outside the swirl, who knows what it's up to.

"Evie, this is Cal." Her eyes shine when she looks at him. "Evie was like a little sister to me. She and Emma—" She pauses a second, takes a breath. "Patrick's sister—we all used to hang out."

"I think I've seen a few pictures of you." Cal nods like he's genuinely happy to meet me. He steps forward with a hand outstretched. I take it. Up close his eyes are this dark winter-ocean color. He's even cuter than Patrick.

And that's it for my throat. I drop his hand. One of ours was shaking, probably mine. My throat narrows like I'm strangling myself from the inside out. I step back from them both, and before I can choke out a good-bye, burst into tears.

"Hey now!" Mamie puts a hand on my shoulder. "It's okay, Evie. I know it's weird. It's been a long time, and I left so abruptly—I didn't—couldn't—"

"Don't be nice to me," I interrupt. "I came to wreck it all. Tonight. This." I tilt my head toward the gallery. "Your work." Mamie's face freezes, her hand falls back to her side. Cal comes closer.

"Emma's *so* hurt," I say. "Mamie, she's so mad at you."

"Emma . . ." Mamie's voice is small. She shuts her eyes like she has a headache. Lifts a hand to her cheek.

The dam breaks and all the ugly rushes out of me. I'm blubber-crying, not making sense, but I can't stop. I wrecked something essential inside myself tonight, and now there's nothing left to hold anything back.

"It's so messed up. She thinks I love you more than I love her, and I wanted to show her that I didn't, that I don't, but nothing I do . . . she thinks *everyone* does, loves you, not her, like she's bad or something, and her parents . . . and you, *look at you right now,* tonight . . . with *him* . . ." I turn my snotty, teary head in Cal's direction. He's stopped looking surprised and is kind of glowering at me now. "It's so unfair that you—"

Before I can say more, Cal lifts his hand in the air to stop me.

"Hold up," he says firmly. "Take a breath." He steps right next to Mamie so they're one person standing in front of me. "What are you saying?"

What am I saying? How can I be this lost? It's like Emma and I were some kind of flimsy structure, holding each other together, and now she's gone, and I'm flapping, empty. I don't know anything. None of what I could say to Mamie would sound right. I don't know how I thought it ever would.

Silence drops between us like a heavy barrier with me on the wrong side. The outside.

"Okay, okay, it's okay." Mamie's face is very pale and she sounds a little bit like she might start saying that over and over again and never stop. She takes a deep breath and tucks her hair behind her ears. "I know Emma's mad. I know it. I—"

But Cal cuts her off too. "I still don't understand what's going on here. What are you saying?" he asks me again. His voice has lost all the kindness it had for me a minute ago.

I cry harder.

"I was going to pull the fire alarm, the sprinklers—"

Mamie's body jolts a little, like I hit her.

Cal puts his hands on her waist, draws her close. "The alarm wouldn't trigger the sprinklers. They're heat activated," Cal says in a low voice.

"Emma wanted me to." Not true. Not the whole truth. I shake my head. "I mean, *I* wanted to too. I was ready to make chaos, for her, you don't understand, she . . ." I'm flailing. "I—"

Mamie cuts me off, points to the curb. "Wow. Okay. We should sit." She takes a deep breath. Smooths her dress.

I walk over to it and drop down, my forehead on my knees. The street is dusty under my boots. Someone's lined the curb with Riot Grrrl stickers.

I'm the only one sitting.

Mamie's boyfriend's probably calling the police. I close my eyes, put my wrists behind my back. Easier to cuff when the cops pull up. The least I can do is go without a scene.

I peek back at them. They're standing close, speaking so softly I can't hear what they're saying. No phones. Then Cal nods slowly and I catch, "Okay, if you're sure." He takes her face in his hands and looks at her—no one's ever looked at me like that. It would kill Emma. Mamie's living everything Patrick's missing, everything he'll keep missing.

But it's not Mamie's fault. Life gets to go on. Love does too. That's the part Emma can't face. I pick at a loose piece of rubber on the bottom of my boot and pretend I'm not watching.

"Go be with your dad. I'll be in soon, I promise." She pops up on tiptoes and gives him a quick kiss.

He glances down at me on the curb, his face not quite a scowl, but pretty close. When he turns back to the gallery he's unsteady a sec, like he's had a little too much to drink. Mamie watches him go, then sits on the curb next to me, so close our arms touch. She draws her knees in to her chest and lays her cheek on them, looking at me sideways.

"Evie, I feel guilty about so many things," she says after a minute. "I'll never not feel guilty. And Emma . . ." She closes her eyes. When she opens them again, they're watery. "What happened with me and Patrick made everything a million times worse for her. But I don't know what to do about that. I don't know if there's anything I *can* do."

"I was trying—Emma just needs—"

But I don't know how to finish my sentence. For so long I thought I did. I thought I knew what she needed. How to give it to her.

"She saves me too," I say, only that's not true anymore, either.

"If I've learned anything since Patrick died, it's that you have to figure it out for yourself. No one else can do it for you."

So many things are rushing through me I can hardly slow any of them long enough to figure out what they are, who I am, even. But I need to explain it to Mamie.

"Em and I, it's like we're both missing the regular toolkit. I'm, like, this *freak*"—I wipe my nose on the back of my hand—"mapping, frantic, like I can force the future to give me a hand with direction, or at the very least describe a recognizable present, while Em's running around finding every way she can to explode out of herself. I'm . . . Bartleby or something, my face to the wall, and she's a blown dandelion."

Mamie laughs when I say Bartleby, then nods like I just made sense.

"There is no regular toolkit. And if there were, you

wouldn't want it. It'd keep you from seeing things like Emma blown out like a wish. And you're not Bartleby, Evie. You're just not."

I wipe my nose again.

Mamie puts an arm around me.

"I'm sorry I disappeared," she says. "I was messed up for a while. I couldn't really handle much."

"I can't believe you're apologizing to me after what I just told you."

I am a worm. Smaller. A microscopic worm in a worm's microscope.

"Well, I'm glad you didn't do it." She sighs. "I don't know, Evie. I always thought if you used half the energy you spent trying to fix Emma on your own life, you'd be unstoppable."

I don't know what to say to that.

Mamie squeezes my shoulders.

"It's impossible to run away from yourself. Believe me, I tried. Hiding from what scares you feels like a solution, but it really only deepens the fear. My dad's partner, Zara, is always reminding me the only way out is through." Mamie sighs again. "And she's right. Also"—Mamie looks me right in the eye—"art helps. Art's a place you can work on ideas and feelings when you have nowhere else to put them.

That's what you were doing with those maps, right? Please tell me you're still making them? I always thought they were cool."

Nothing turns out the way I expect. I'm on a curb in Chelsea with Mamie Wells, and even though I told her I came to destroy her work, she's talking to me like we're made of something similar, like everything's maybe going to be okay.

"Did you really change your name?"

It's all I can manage; it's going to take time and practice to start saying what's really in my head.

"It's a childhood nickname. It's a . . . it was a way for me to . . ."

"You don't have to tell me," I choke out, but I want her to tell me everything. I want to ask her how anyone knows what they're supposed to do next, but my inner and outer selves will not connect.

"This night is super intense," Mamie sighs. "I changed my name because I wanted to feel like myself, if that makes any sense. I wanted to be done being the person everyone expected me to be."

"That's how I feel. Split, particulate, unable to assemble."

This is exactly the kind of remark that would earn me a blast of exasperation from Emma. A laugh. Or both.

Mamie just squeezes my shoulder again.

"I don't know what you're thinking for college, but art school's in there, right? God, I remember how competitive and awful Bly is junior year, everyone scheming, working their connections, walking around making themselves sound golden."

"Pretty much."

"Don't let them get in your head."

Too late.

I sigh.

"Come up to Providence. You can stay with me, do the official campus visit. You'll love it. I'll show you around."

I start to do what I always do when people suggest someplace I know we can't afford. Close up shop. Lights on, no one home. But then she adds, "And there's financial aid. Not just loans. Bring your portfolio. I can look at it, help you pull it together if you want. Deal?"

"Um, yeah." I came to mess up her life and she's planning to help me.

Mamie gives me another quick squeeze, then stands and offers her hand.

"I've gotta get back in, but really, I'm glad you came tonight. It's like the Blake engraving Dr. Holmes loves. That one line always stuck with me: 'Cruelty has a Human

Heart.' We need to be tender with each other. With ourselves." She pulls me up and hugs me. Whispers in my ear. "None of this is easy. Uncharted territory. But Evie, *you* make the map. You save *you*. Okay?"

unbridgeable distance

MAMIE'S WORDS FOLLOW ME around the apartment.

You save you.

I'm alone for the weekend too, my first time, a unique circumstance. My mom's never had anywhere to go. She's at some Brucker Candy Company retreat upstate. And I'm not exactly alone. Shame and regret are constant company.

While I can't really picture my mom backward trust-falling into the arms of Vera from production or confronting her fear of heights on a ropes course, her absence means I can be miserable and no one will mind. She was weirdly excited when she called to check in, so I put an extra-bright smile in my voice, but now the apartment's darker and lonelier than ever. I'm pacing, practicing what I'm going to say to Em, trying to figure out how to tell her we were wrong, but there are no scenarios where it comes out well.

I throw myself into cleaning, like I can buy inner peace through external order. I used to do it a lot, rearrange the furniture, pretend I was hired to stage it, make the place look appealing, happy, boho chic meets free-spirited intellectual.

I dig coins from the couch, almost four dollars, vacuum everything, dust the tops of shelves and the legs of all the chairs. I sift through piles of mail, even the random pieces of junk that come addressed to my dad, the ones my mom has a hard time recycling. I take down slippery stacks of magazines, catalogs, legal journals. I sort the letters from the building people by date and prop them next to the tray of perfumes on my mom's dresser. I scrape the toothpaste from the bathroom mirror and scrub the tub. I empty the linen closet, start a donation bag with my Powerpuff Girls sheets and beach towel. I toss the tiny wrist splint I wore when I was eight after my cast came off. My mom saves *everything*.

I tackle the fridge, scrubbing shelves and dumping the stuff in the far back that looks like a new and sinister lifeform. I empty my closet, adding all the clothes and coats

I've outgrown to the donation bag.

Shame's headlamp hits every dark corner, and Regret is a cutthroat antisentimentalist. Between the three of us, every aspect is inspected, hideouts dismantled, the smudge of inertia erased. I purge my laptop, read a "READ ME, PLEASE" from Jack and three emails from Ms. Vax reminding me of the time and date for my TeenART interview. That one stops me for a second. I imagine myself showing up, giving it a shot, but then my stomach starts to flop around like a fish on a hook so I reorganize my Investigation and finish what I was writing about engineering and imagination. Roebling faced his skeptics and resisted the idea of an "unbridgeable distance" to make a seemingly impossible connection. He took us all someplace new.

I pull apart my room, gather every sketchbook and journal I can find and sort through them, making a pile of every map I've still got. I have enough for a small atlas, a weird compendium. I'll call it *World Atlas of Being Lost* and sell copies to no one. This is me saving me.

I bathe Marcel, suds him up until he looks like a snowball and smells like coconut oatmeal, then we curl up together on Mom's bed while I sift through old photos. I linger on one of my handsome dad. We're at the Union Square Greenmarket on a fall morning. I'm on his shoulders, eating a candied apple. My mom's holding his hand. She looks a thousand years younger. All around us are buckets of mums and baskets of apples.

The thought of talking to Emma makes my stomach go cold. I don't know what I'll say to her, but everything's changing.

Even me.

astral

SOMEONE KEEPS CALLING MY NAME. The weird thing is that it sounds like *my* voice. I blink at the clock. It's ten to six. So much for sleeping in. I lie still a minute, until I'm sure it was a dream and I'm alone, no one's actually in here with me. My mind's full of bridges. No, more shivery than that, the edges of images and words popping the way they do when a map starts to come. I close my eyes, and maybe it's afterburn from the sun angling through the blinds, but I see cables and spans, the faith it takes to build into space, to trust your math, the need to connect one thing to another.

I slide in thick socks down the hall to my mom's room

and hoist my grandmother's sewing kit from of the back of her closet. Destruction's no part of love. Em's forgetting that. I was too. It was everywhere in that gallery, between all those people, between Mamie and her guy. Love just *is*. Our lives are made of it, even if we're too lost to see it.

My mom keeps the sewing kit for me in case I decide to learn. My grandmother made my clothes when I was little, dresses with smocking and delicate collars. She'd approve, one maker to another, of an alternative use of her things. I carry the heavy box to the dining room table.

I open it and stare into an altar of making: wooden spools wound with bright thread, silvery needles with delicate eyes, snaps, pins, and small metal scissors. I sit with the kit and try to make sense of the images in my head. Narrow paper rings slip easily off vivid fingers of embroidery floss. I pull some of it straight, stretching strands from a center point out. I start to wonder if anyone's ever made a star-shaped bridge, multiple decks reaching for different destinations. Then I know what I'm missing, what I need to get started.

I run back to my mom's room and sift through the pictures again. I'm looking for one in particular, a black-and-white my dad took of me two months before he died. I'm in the V of a tree, my hair long and wild from an afternoon in the park. The sun's cutting through leaves near my face. I remember the day because I was wearing my favorite overalls, the ones with big pockets. I had them stuffed with pinecones and acorns. In the photo I'm still wholly myself, not knocked flat by the loss of my dad, my fading mom. I'm staring at something outside the picture, my small hands clasping each other tight like I already know to shore myself up. My mom told me he loved this picture so much she kept it tacked on the wall near his bed. The little holes in the corners from the pins are what made me think of it now. I bring it back out with me and sit down to work.

This one has to be big. I look through my paper until I find the right piece, then lay the picture near the center. Near the bottom right corner I pencil-sketch a compass rose. True north's an anatomical heart. Arrows mark the cardinal directions.

I inspect the thread, tangled and rainbow generous, select candy-apple red, and start to stitch right through the photograph, a line from the center of me radiating like sound, a rhythmic undulation. I pencil connections, me to Emma, and Jack, and Marcel, and my mom, even Mamie. Future routes to stitch. Colors reaching like cables from me into the unknown, off the edge of the image, onto the bordering paper, and out to that edge as well.

It'll look like a star-shaped bridge, an aster, a multipoint constellation, bright thread lines linking everything together. I grab the photo of my family at the Greenmarket and add it too. I stitch a small silver spiral, like a nautilus shell, near my dad's head, then another for Patrick, and beyond them both I use a brush pen to make ink-blue waves roll into undefined space.

Maybe I'll try for TeenART. Maybe this is something I could bring. Map where Evie starts trusting herself. I'll call it *Starbridge/Constellation.* It will be astral, an explosion of stitches.

love, theo

AFTER A FEW HOURS OF PLANNING, sketching, inking, and stitching, Marcel and I are beyond ready for fresh air. The dining room table is littered with snips of thread and pencils and paint, but what's starting to take shape makes me happy. If Robert Rauschenberg can paint on a quilt, hang it on the wall in a frame, and call it *Bed,* I can make a self-portrait star-bridge celestial thread explosion and call it a map.

My mom said she'd be back late afternoon, but I leave her a note just in case, saying it's noon and I'm heading out for a few hours to breathe some real air and play with Marcel at the dog park.

We swing by Mrs. Cohen's to see if Dominic wants to join us. Mrs. Cohen's always happy to see me, opening her door after I do the light knock she taught me, a private rhythm, hers and Mr. Cohen's from back when he was alive. Mrs. Cohen is the definition of birdlike, the knobs of her spine visible through her thin cranberry sweater. I decide to visit her more. I want her to last forever.

I suck on a lemon candy from the dish she keeps near her armchair and wait with Marcel while she stoops to slip Dominic's dainty feet into his tiny sidewalk boots. Marcel eyes him with pity. Dominic looks at the ground. He cocks his ear to the side, though, and listens while she has a little chat with him, reminding him to behave himself. Love is complicated. Dominic always behaves himself.

The minute her door is closed he adjusts to us, boinging up and down in his little boots near Marcel like a Super Ball, trying to get a rise out of his fat compatriot. Marcel pretends he's above all that, but by the time the elevator opens to the lobby, they're both dragging me toward the door. I spot something taped to our mailbox. A postcard of the Fort Lauderdale airport and its crowded runway, planes lifting off and landing. A sticky note on the picture reads "Came to us by mistake."

I flip it over. Dark boyish scrawl crowds the small white square.

Evie—I'm waiting for my connection to Haiti, but I can't leave without telling you I'm sorry. I fucked it up between us & then I didn't even say good-bye. I'm going because I have to, it's as simple as that. My family is always so sure they know what's right for me, but my choices are mine to make. Your choices are too. I hope you figure out what that means for you & you do it.

Evie, you're the light. I wish I'd told you that one last time, but I didn't because I knew if I saw you again I'd want to stay.

Love,

Theo

Love Theo!

For a second I fixate on the word, then I let the dogs rush me out into the day. I follow them wherever they lead while I read and reread Theo's postcard. They sniff and mark and show off for each other, pretending to eat random crap on the ground while eyeing me nervously. After a block or so they figure out I'm not paying attention.

Theo's sorry.

For what? For saying I needed a hero? For dumping me? For starting something when he knew he'd be gone? For going? I can't tell what this postcard means. It's like he slipped out but left the door open behind him. After reading it so many times I have it practically memorized, I shove it in my coat pocket. Maybe I'll add it to my map.

Marcel's a creature of habit, so I should have expected him to lead me to Emma's block. What I don't expect is to see Alice on her stoop with a book. It's nice out, almost summery, so I don't know why it's surprising, other than the fact that I've pretty much managed to erase Alice from my mind altogether when not confronted with her continuing existence. I stop a second while reality and the world inside my head stitch themselves back together. It occurs to me that people call this kind of split denial, and that it's exactly what my mom does when she ignores the legal letters in the mail.

I follow the dogs.

"Hey." Alice lifts her eyes from her reading when I walk by.

"Um, hi," I say back. So much for slinking past unnoticed.

She's wearing a pale-pink sundress, milky and pastel, like her skin. I wonder if she put it on for Jack. She looks beautiful sitting there, the sun moving through the new leaves above her, painting a pattern of light on her face.

Before I can chicken out, I say, "Alice, I'm sorry."

I'm ashamed it's taken me this long to say it.

She raises a brow and lays her book in her lap.

"For?"

Dominic snuffles in the dirt at the base of her boulevard tree. I loop his leash tight around my wrist.

"For . . . everything? Pretty much. For being threatened by you all the time, for treating you badly, for wishing you'd disappear. You were right about it all."

Including Jack. But that part I still can't make myself say out loud, not yet. I don't know what's going to happen with Jack. I slip two dog treats from my pocket, crouch, and let the dogs slobber them from my palm.

She eyes me skeptically. I don't blame her. I thought saying I was sorry would kill me, but it's having the opposite effect. I feel lighter, more alive. Maybe gravity's a question of regret. Do the right thing and feel yourself lift up a bit.

"You're burning," I say, straightening up and pointing to her shoulder.

"Global warming," she sighs, pressing her skin with a narrow fingertip. A bright circle appears like an inverse shadow.

The dogs start to tug, impatient.

"Well . . . okay then . . . enjoy your book." I turn to leave. My stomach's growling and I forgot to bring money for lunch. I'll have to go home to eat, take Marcel to the dog park later.

"Wait. Did you do something to wreck that show?"

Her question stops me in my tracks.

"What?" I whirl around.

"Mamie's show. Emma called. She said you were planning something."

At the mention of Emma's name, I'm heavy again. I've been hiding in my map, ignoring her texts. I don't know how to tell her I didn't go through with it.

"No. I didn't. I couldn't."

The dogs work circles around my legs until I'm tied up in leashes.

"That's good." She nods, her features softening. "Well done."

Over us both, two lazy clouds turtle by, make time visible, white against the blue.

"I went, though." I hesitate, not sure what I'm going to say. "It was . . ." I go for the truth. "Her show blew me away." I realize as I say it that I have to try for TeenART—really go for it—no chickening out.

Alice sits up a little straighter, surprised. She smiles.

"I can't explain it. The paintings were huge, strange, beautiful. They were like telescopes that looked back through memory, and time, and pain. . . ."

I stop talking. My words sound stupid and don't come close to describing what I saw in that room, how I felt when I heard Mamie talk, what it was like to see her in love with someone new.

I shrug. Untangle myself and turn to leave.

"I broke up with Jack," Alice says to my back. It's a statement. No emotion.

I face her again. She looks resolute.

"Alice, we weren't doing anything at that party, I promise."

Marcel must sense my distress, because he leans against my leg so hard he almost knocks me over.

"I know." Alice picks up her book again.

I look at the cover. *How to Build a Girl,* by Caitlin Moran.

She follows my gaze, flutters the edge of the pages. "I mean, I didn't know at the time, at Ben's, but I believe you. Anyway, it doesn't matter. That's not why."

"Then why?"

"He's not a good boyfriend. He needs to grow up. You should know that, in case you guys . . ." Her turn to shrug. "I deserve better."

She smiles, wry, one side of her mouth up. She looks how I wish I felt, what I'm trying to figure out. Like someone pulled together, proud of herself. I file it away for later.

A squirrel skitters past Dominic and he goes nuts, barking, lunging, tugging hard on his leash. Marcel starts to get worked up too, yanking my arm from the socket. I give in, let them drag me away, tossing a quick good-bye over my shoulder. But then I stop. I call back over to her.

"Hey, Alice!" I'm not even sure about this.

"Yeah?" Her face shifts, defenses back up.

"Do you want to, um, would you maybe want to get coffee sometime?"

Her face shows no emotion and she lets me stand there, waiting.

Finally she looks down at her book, then back at me again.

"I don't know," she says slowly, but she's nodding. "Maybe . . . I guess. Maybe?"

It's good enough for now.

I twist Marcel's leash around my wrist again and try to smile at her even if she's not ready to smile back.

more in common with air

IT'S SAFE TO SAY THE LAST THING I expected to see after I dropped off Dominic and let myself back into the apartment was this trail of clothes.

I stand there blinking a second, key in hand, wondering what kind of break-in looks like this. But it's not a break-in. It's clothes. At one p.m. on a Sunday. Mom's and someone else's, strewn as if from an explosion that started near the front door, with a contrail leading through the dining room, down the hall, and into the open door of her bedroom.

I freeze, confused. Marcel starts sniffing the Levi's. This

is such an unexpected household equation. Apartment early afternoon is supposed to equal empty. Not big shoes and navy boxers.

I walk toward the hall.

"Um, hello?"

The minute my eyes spot some skin, I start taking fast steps backward. I'm pretty sure all I saw were the bottoms of a pair of bare feet, but those large soles were more than enough.

A bra, which cannot be my mother's because it is made of a lace that has more in common with air than clothing, is caught on one of her fern's leggy fronds.

"Evie!?" My mom sounds frantic. "Is that you? Honey? What are you doing home? Don't come in here!" The last part sounds a little bit like a scream.

Like I'm an intruder, storming the place.

I drop Marcel's leash on the floor and turn to leave. This is one thing too many. Gotta get out of this place.

I look around the apartment, at all the work I did to clean it and how it still looks dark and shabby. I hate it. It's stuck in the past. And my map on the table. It's a mess. Nothing here to show me what I do with this, where I'm supposed to go next.

I tug open the heavy linen drawer in the sideboard and

pull out the envelope of cash my mom keeps for household emergencies. This is definitely an emergency. I'm just not sure what kind.

I walk out the door.

small falling parts

I SPEND A FEW PANICKED MINUTES looking up trains out of New York before I realize running away from your life only makes sense if you have somewhere to go. I sit on a curb a second, crushed. Then I text Jack.

Are you home? Can I come over?

His reply is immediate.

Door's open.

I turn off my phone. I don't want to be tracked.

When I get there, Jack looks so glad to see me that he opens his mouth and no sound comes out. But then I start to cry, and he comes back into himself, taking me by the hand, pulling me gently into their penthouse.

By the time I manage to choke out why I came, and why I'm holding a random wad of cash, he's pulled it together, and for a minute at least we pretend nothing's weird between us.

"Evie," he says, when I've finished talking. "You have to go back there."

I stare at him, but he's serious.

"Did you not hear what I said? I just walked in on my mom having sex with some guy, like she's the teenager and I'm the parent!"

Jack blinks at me a minute before hugging me, tight. Then he pushes me back, his hands on my shoulders so I have to look him in the face.

"I'm totally hoping you coming here means we're still friends, and we need to talk, I've been trying to get a hold of you, but you have to go home. Face your mom. You're not mad about this. It just scared you because it was unexpected, but lots of things are unexpected, and some of them are good."

We're standing in almost exactly the same spots we were in when he tried to kiss me. He waits for me to say something, and when I don't he goes on. "Do you know how long you've been telling me you wished your mom had a boyfriend? For*ever*. You've been saying that forever. And if you left the way you said, you know she's freaking out."

Jack has a soft spot for my mom, but he's right. I'm full of a thousand emotions, disoriented, spinning wildly on my axis.

"There's nothing wrong with what she's doing, it just caught you by surprise."

"I'm a snow globe," I say.

Jack doesn't even blink. He's used to this kind of statement from me. He knows I mean I'm shaken up, transparent, and full of small falling parts.

"We'll always be friends," I add, because I need him to know that, and it's the truest thing I can think of right now.

Jack throws his arms around me again and hugs me so close for a second I can't breathe.

"Oh, snow globe, I've missed you so much."

I hug him back. Things are messed up between us, but I've missed him too.

He lets me go, steps back with a sigh, then puts his two warm hands on my shoulders.

"Don't run away," he says. "Face this."

I hug him one more time, then turn to go, so I can.

no rule book

MY MOM PRACTICALLY RUNS to the door when she hears my key in the lock.

"Evie! Thank heavens!"

I step into the apartment and glance around really fast in case there's still some guy in here. There isn't.

I'm stiff when she hugs me. Then I drop my defenses and hug her back. Tight.

"I'm sorry, Mom," I say, my mouth in her hair.

"No, honey, I'm so, so sorry! I don't know what we were thinking, honestly!" I can feel the heat of embarrassment rising off her. "I feel terrible! David and I saw your note—we thought we had—but you don't want to hear that."

She takes me by the hand and leads me to the couch.

"David? Did you meet on your retreat?"

Her face falls. "Oh, honey, no. I'm so sorry. I did this all wrong. I wasn't at a retreat this weekend, I was with . . . we . . ."

"You lied?" I stiffen, move away from her a bit.

She's quiet a second, then nods. "We wanted to protect you. In retrospect, it wasn't the best decision."

I turn my head away.

"I don't understand. What's going on? I'm so confused."

She sighs. "You know, I dated someone after your dad died."

"You did?" I swivel to stare at her.

She smiles, but her mouth goes down at the corners.

"You were so young—he made your loft for you."

"What? Why do I have no memory of this?"

She looks really sad for me and pushes a strand of hair from my eyes. "It was a terrible time. We'd just lost the condo."

But we'd lost so much more, and that's the part I push away all the time. I've tried so hard not to be like her, but I'm exactly like my mom. I refuse to face the hard things. I don't make a sound, but tears come, run down the sides of my face and pool in my ears. I'm not sure why I'm crying, if it's because we lost my dad, or because she has this life I didn't know about, or if it's maybe from relief. I keep my lips pressed tight.

My mom pulls me back into the cushions. I let myself relax against her.

"He was a kind man," she says after a while, wiping tears from my cheeks. "Paul Opie. Mrs. Cohen used to come and sit with you when he and I went out."

This fragment of my childhood rushes forward from wherever it's been hiding. Mrs. Cohen in our kitchen making beet soup. We used to stain our lips with the cut beets.

"Opie?" I wipe my face on my sleeve. "God, what if you'd married him? I'd be Evie Opie."

She smiles. "I know. Funny name. Funny man. He was so kind—I was completely lost without your dad." She sighs. "You know, your dad's cancer—" She stops a second, swallows. "It was so fast. He was gone before we knew what was happening. It took me a long time to feel anything beyond clamoring panic every time I opened my eyes."

She's quiet a minute. Kisses the top of my head.

"Paul built your loft for you. I felt so lucky! You were thrilled, so happy to scramble up there, so high, every night." She laughs, but it doesn't sound happy. Exhales. "I was terrified you'd somehow fall out the window in your sleep. Evie, for the longest time it felt like anything could be taken from me, at any time."

I know the feeling.

"But you didn't stay with him."

"I didn't." She touches her necklace. I look closely at it. It's new. A small round diamond set in gold. It's delicate. Beautiful.

"I couldn't imagine opening my heart up again, not really, not the way I did with your dad. It was all so much, raising you alone, looking for work. I needed him more than I felt for him. It didn't seem fair to Paul."

She eyes me closely. "There's no rule book for any of this," she says, wistful. "I decided if I was going to see anyone else, I'd do it in private. I'd shelter you from the whims of my heart until I met someone worth bringing into your life too. You'd had enough loss. But today—"

Color climbs her cheeks.

I look at my hands.

"I'm so sorry we surprised you, honey, I really am. We were getting ready to tell you—"

"Tell me what?"

She twists the necklace again.

"David and I are planning to move in together."

My mouth falls open.

"Are we losing our apartment? Those envelopes—"

She shakes her head. "No, honey. I mean, you know how things are here, they'd love us to go, but that has nothing to do with it." She turns my chin so our eyes meet. "He's a good man, Evie. I love him."

"Love?" The word hangs there a second. My mom's in love. It's a shock.

"We've been seeing each other for almost a year, spending time together when we're not with our kids. We're not in a rush, but we want our families to meet."

"Families?" It's a lot to take in.

She smiles at me, huge, and I swallow past the ache in my throat.

"David's divorced. His kids were at Bly when you were little. Ezra's your age. Do you remember him?"

Small kid. Nervous-looking. A shock of white-blond hair.

"Oh my God. Ezra Maddox was a crayon-breaking, play-dough-eating devil."

"From what David says, he's come a long way," she laughs. "He and his sister are at Auden."

I snort. Auden. Boarding school kids. I fiddle with the string on my hoodie while I process everything. Suddenly her late days at work and weekend inventories make more sense. "Oh my God, that day I was here with Em and you were home . . . ?"

She nods. "We almost told you then, but Emma was here. He and I took a day off to talk about things, our future."

"Your future."

Her eyes are on me. I close mine. This is moving fast. Jack's right, I wished for this, but now that it's here I can't really make sense of it.

"There's no rush," she says softly. "We can wait until you're all off to college. Ingrid's only in tenth, and she may want us to wait. It might be a while."

Her news goes off in me like one last bomb. The weird buzzing emanating from my mother when college comes up is about her, not me. She's electric with love and I'm holding her back. I draw my knees in tight to my chest, drop my head, and sob.

"Oh honey," my mom sighs, wrapping around me again and rocking me a little. She lets me cry a minute.

"I'm sorry," I whisper. "I want you to be happy. . . ."

She shushes me, but I need to say what I feel. Keeping it in hasn't been getting me anywhere.

"Everything's changing. Em and I . . ." I stop. Start again. "I can't picture the future. I don't know what to do about college and I'm scared I'll disappoint you."

"Honey." Mom strokes my forehead, her hand cool. "You never disappoint me."

"I'm a screw-up, Mom," I say, pulling my hood around to wipe my face. "I'm not gonna get in anywhere. I mean, what school's going to take me, much less give me money?"

She lets me cry another minute before she clears her throat and starts again.

"Evie. Your grades are not *that* bad." Her voice is low and calm, the way it was when I broke my wrist. She strokes my hair. "I didn't realize you were so worried about this. Bly's competitive, I know. Has the pressure been terrible?"

I shrug.

She sighs. "We're good at not talking about the big things, aren't we? We'll have to work on that." She leans back and points toward the dining room table. "I was looking at your project over there, and it seems pretty clear that art school is the first place you should look. Evie, you're so talented."

I start to object, talk about money, but she shushes me.

"We'll figure it out. You can do work-study, we'll take loans."

She's quiet a minute. I look up.

"I've been depressed and leaning on you." She whisks away a tear with her fingertip. "And I'm endlessly sorry for that. But I'm trying. I'm getting help . . . and if you'd like, you could see a counselor too? Maybe we could work on talking about some of the more difficult things?"

"Like you meeting guys," I tease, feeling guilty for making her cry.

She tilts my chin up and looks at me with a rueful expression. "Like how you always try to spare my feelings, try to make me smile. But yes, we can also talk about David. I wish your dad were here to see you. You're so much like him. Practical, capable. I'm sorry I've been so bad at all this."

I cover my face with my hands.

We sit there like that, me wrapped in her arms, our hearts beating together. Marcel lumbers over and lies on the floor by our feet. He settles in with a sigh.

"Em's been leaning on you too."

My eyes are a river. "I thought she'd be okay if I were a better friend," I say, ashamed by how naive it sounds.

She wipes my tears with her palms and kisses me on the head again, like she can kiss away every hopeless thought I'll ever have.

"Oh honey, I'm sorry. Em's problems aren't yours to fix. I've shown David a few of your maps, Evie, and he says—"

I move my head away from hers.

"What? Mom!" I squeeze my eyes shut tight. Tighter.

"He's a graphic designer. He says you have a great eye."

I moan.

"He suggested that next year you could do an internship

at his firm? For your Senior Endeavor? You're talented, so visual, he thinks you might—"

"Slow down!" I put my hands up.

"Yes, okay." She nods. "Of course."

My stomach growls, loud and long.

"Hungry?" She stands and pulls me up by the hand.

"Starving." I let her tug me to the kitchen. I don't remember when I last ate.

"Let's see what we've got. How about cake toast?"

Cake toast. One of the few memories I have of my dad, his treatment for middle-of-the-night growing pains. It involves canned frosting and lots of rainbow sprinkles.

"Oh my God, cake toast sounds perfect."

My mom opens the corner cupboard, then crouches on the countertop, twisting sideways to reach into the very back of the pantry.

"Hang on . . . ," she says. "Aha! Take this." She hands out a dusty jar of martini onions. "I can feel it!"

In her soft rose-colored T-shirt, and with her hair gathered in a loose ponytail, my mom looks so pretty reflected in the window over the sink. Happy. She should be in love. Why did I think she was done with that, somehow? That love was something a person could be done with, do without? Suddenly I want more than anything for it all to work out, for David to be decent, to make her happy.

"Ta-da!" Mom turns, victorious. She holds a red-lidded tub of vanilla cream-cheese frosting high, seal intact. "See? A more organized mother could not offer you this."

I grab a jar of sprinkles from behind the rest of the spices and we clink them together like champagne.

"Never let it be said I didn't cook for you." My mom laughs.

"I never will."

"To Daddy," she says, popping the top and lifting a frosting-covered finger.

"To Daddy," I echo, dipping my own finger. "And to us."

We'll move forward. Be done with the ways we've held ourselves back.

rebecca & enid

MY MOM AND I WERE UP late last night, practicing what I'll say to the TeenART people about my maps. And, after a last-minute freak-out session slash pep talk by the bathrooms with Jack, I'm finally ready to hike up to Ms. Vax's room for my interview. When I showed him my *Starbridge/Constellation* and ran through what I planned to say, Jack leaned back and looked at me with total admiration. He let out a low whistle and said, *Wow, Eves, that's one cool celestial event.*

Then he left so I could nervous-pee one more time, check and double-check the bobby pins holding my hair twist, and put on some lipstick for luck. I'm as prepared as I can be.

It's not until I'm rounding the landing to the fourth floor studios that my phone buzzes in my bag.

I pull it out.

Where are you?

It's Em.

I stop and blink at the screen. Her timing's surreal. Then I drop it back in my bag. Before I can get my bag back up on my shoulder, though, it buzzes again.

Stop avoiding me. I need you.

I can't breathe a minute. Stand frozen in the stairwell light.

You're back? I text, my thumb hesitating a few seconds before I hit Send.

I'm here, at school. Mandi said she just saw you and Jack on 3rd by the bathrooms but that's where I am and it's empty.

I lean against the wall in the stairwell and chew a hangnail from my thumb. What am I supposed to do?

???

I can't talk to her now, not yet, not until my interview's over. This is too important to mess up, and thinking about what I need to say to her makes my stomach hot. I can't do both. We never even talked about TeenART.

???

I take a huge breath. Let it out slowly. What am I doing? This is insane. I have to get up to the studio.

Sorry! I'm busy! I write. **Call you later.**

Then, after a sec, I add **XO**.

No!

Eves!

Please!

I have to talk to you now. It's important. Can't wait.

I stand so still when I read her words, I think for a minute if someone came through here they might not even see me. If only I could become invisible like that.

Need u. I'm desperate.

I check the time on my phone. The background image comes into focus. It's a photo of Emma and me from Halloween. We went as Rebecca and Enid from *Ghost World*. Yes, I was Enid. I used fabric markers to make my own Raptor shirt. Emma smolders at me from behind my apps, the perfect Rebecca.

Evie?

I check the time again. The other two candidates are probably both in there by now. Maybe they can go first.

On my way.

I run down the stairs.

floating like faraway moons

WHEN I PUSH OPEN THE DOOR to the third-floor bathroom, Emma's sitting in the window, on top of the heater, with her shoes up on the sink. The window is flung open high and wide behind her. They're supposed to be locked, only able to open like four inches or so, but Bly's in an ancient building and this one's been broken forever. They keep painting it shut, but as soon as it's warm out, people chip it free.

"Hey . . . ," I say, not wanting to startle her. "You're back."

She lifts her head and her face is all red and splotchy. Her eyes are swollen to small slits.

"They're pulling me out," she says, blowing her nose into a ragged tissue.

"What?"

"My parents. That's where we've been. A friendly little tour of schools for crazy girls. They're meeting with the dean and Dr. Holmes right now. I'm done here. They're yanking me and sending me to Our Lady of Screw-Ups in the mountains of California."

The news stops everything in me, and I sag back against the door for a second. I don't like the look in her eyes. I step closer. There's so much empty space behind her, so far to fall.

She lifts her hand like a cop. "Stop. I know you didn't do it, at the gallery. But tell me you did something, at least? Made her squirm? She felt some pain?"

She pulls the hair tie from her ponytail and runs a hand through her hair to shake it out. All I can think is, *Please don't fall.*

Em nods like I've spoken.

"Oh. You totally got charmed by her again, didn't you?"

She turns sideways, pulling her legs up onto the radiator, and whips her head toward the gaping space. She's silent a minute and I inch closer.

"You don't care about me anymore." She sounds so sad.

"That's not true." But the rest is out of my mouth before I can think. "If anything I've been caring too much." I set my bag on the counter and keep creeping closer.

"Stay back," she says, still turned away. Her voice is tiny in all that open air.

I think I can reach her if I lunge.

"Em—" I struggle to keep my voice calm.

"I mean"—she turns to look at me again, wiping her eyes with the heel of her hand—"it *was* a lunatic idea, right?" she says, nodding. "We would have been arrested pulling a stunt like that . . . it's not like we'd ever have gone through with it, but I thought you'd at *least*—"

It makes me sick, how ready I was. I cut her off.

"That's what's so messed up, Em. I almost ruined someone's work and hurt a bunch of people. It was selfish, and stupid, and destructive, and I was *still* going to do it for you." My voice breaks.

She narrows her eyes at me, straightens her back.

"You put people on pedestals and pretend they're perfect, but then you can't bear it when they turn out to be who they are, who they've always been."

Her words cut into me, but I don't care. Not with her sitting in the open window like that.

"Em, will you please get off the radiator and close that window?"

She swings her legs out into the open space until I gasp, then laughs. It's small and joyless, the laugh of someone who knows things have totally gone too far.

"Never play poker," she says. "It's all on your face." She pulls her legs back in. "I'm dust at the base of my pedestal, but Mamie . . . she's still up there, isn't she? Marble, perfect? God, Evie, what is it with Mamie? What the *fuck*?"

I reach around her and yank the window shut. My elbow's near her cheek when I latch it tight. She doesn't move away. It's like she's daring me to make contact. I lean back against the cold bank of sinks and face her.

"You're probably right. I need to start seeing people for who they are, not be blinded by some vision of perfection—but Em, I'm not like you," I start. "I've been looking to other people to try to figure out how I'm supposed to be. *Who* I'm supposed to be. I still don't know how anyone knows that. But I'm trying to figure it out."

"Ah, and clearly I don't have it down at all. You must be so disappointed." Her face is a picture of sarcasm.

"Stop twisting my words. That's not what I'm saying, but you wouldn't know what I'm talking about, because we never talk about me anymore. I'm scared of everything, all the time! You cut through life like you have a right to be in it, like you're not waiting for someone to give you permission to exist. If you start taking care of yourself, you're going to be so strong. And Mamie's like that too, only she—"

"Only she's not a major fuckup." Emma's trying to sound accusing, but her voice wavers. She rubs a bit of salty grit from the corner of her eye.

We stare at each other a minute. She's determined to hear it like that. To make it bad.

"Things haven't been right between us for a long time," I start again quietly. "We used to be more equal, you know? But somehow it's slipped, shifted. I feel like you're in charge all the time, and I'm your shadow, your helper."

"My brother *died*."

"It started before that."

"You mean when I started getting guys and you got jealous." Emma stares at me. Her eyes are distant, impenetrable, floating like cool violet moons in the top of her pale face.

"It doesn't have to be like this," I say. "I think you're in your head judging yourself so harshly all the time that it's starting to spill out of you, make you seem mean to other people—Roman—"

She flinches when I say his name.

"Roman!? Seriously? What do you care about Roman? He's a jerk—you said so yourself."

"Maybe that's because he feels like crap all the time too."

"Nice." She shakes her head at me and kicks the edge of the sink by my hip with the toe of her boot. "You are a total hypocrite, you know that? You've cold-shouldered Alice since, like, forever."

I catch sight of myself in the mirror. My hair's still holding. My lips are bright. I don't look nearly as small as I feel.

"You're right." I face her. "I did. And it's because I was jealous and judging myself all the time too, but we keep passing this shitty feeling around, dumping it on each other, and it has to stop. I'm sick of feeling so lost and afraid. I have no idea how to fix it, but it seems like loving myself a little better might be a good place to start, you know?"

"What?" Emma scoffs, loud. "Are you breaking up with me?" She sounds bitchy and mean, but deep-red splotches have appeared on each cheek. I'm serious, and she knows it. She snaps the hair tie from her wrist and reaches up to braid her hair, tight.

Tears heat the corners of my eyes and I drop my voice. "I keep thinking maybe you need me to open my heart wider or be more fearless—like if I stick close you'll believe in love. Because Patrick—"

"Shut up."

I keep talking.

"—that was random, an accident, and you know what? I think it's all random, and you're not the only one who has to live with it. My dad died and my mom's been a ghost most of my life . . . God, Em, I think this is just how it is."

"I see," she says, voice louder. "One little Mamie sighting and suddenly you're Evie the wise."

My heart starts doing this thing that I'm pretty sure means *get out of here now* in heart language. While I'm standing here, trying to get her to listen, I'm missing my interview with the woman from TeenART. An actual opportunity. My hands go cold, clammy. I fumble for my phone to check the time.

"Am I keeping you?"

"I—" My voice comes out weird and froggy. I clear my throat, try again. "I have to be somewhere."

"Whatever." She flicks her hand at me like I've been keeping her. "Don't let me stop you. By all means, go."

"I'm going," I say, crying for real now. "Because it's what I need to do. Emma, you are my best friend. But I can't figure this out for you. It's not good for either one of us."

I pick up my bag and walk to the door. Before I open it, I turn back to look at her again.

She's leaning against the window, facing out.

But it stays closed.

sprint

I SIT IN THE COOL, TILED stairwell and take a minute to pull myself together. Emma's hurt, and mad at me, but I meant what I said, and I needed to say it. I dry my face on my sleeve. Despite my racing heart and clenched fists, I feel strangely solid. Like I did something right for a change instead of something desperate.

I look down at my hands. I'm clutching my bag and my maps like a tough grip will make the difference. I'm afraid for Emma, and fear locks me up. I don't know what's going to happen with her, but I'm pretty sure I can't save her from whatever it is. She needs real help so she can save herself.

I set my things down and work my hands loose. Maybe staying sane means sometimes letting go. Ride the current instead of fighting it.

Another map starts to take shape in my mind. Something I'd like to animate. I whip out my sketchbook and make a few notes. A river with a girl floating down it, stars in her hair. She's on her back, her face to the sky. Somewhere near the edge of the map, the great mouth of a sea. She can use the constellations for navigation.

Time for me to go. Get up there. See if I'm not too late.

I stand and gather my things, then take the steps to the fourth floor three at a time, my bag and tube bumping against my back. Could be the adrenaline pumping through me, but each leap makes me lighter. This is me, reaching for a future.

Ms. Vax's studio's bright at the far end of the hall. She's hovering near the door, like a worried bird, glancing at the clock and pacing, talking to someone else in the studio just out of sight.

"I'm here!" I call down the length of the corridor. "I'm coming!"

She looks out at me and her face breaks into the kind of smile that tells me I'm not too late. A chair creaks and scrapes on the old wooden floor and then another woman comes into view, also looking glad I've come.

I still have a chance at this thing.

"I'm sorry I'm late!" I say, my face breaking into a nervous smile.

I sprint the length of the hall toward the studio, ready to open my strange atlas, share *Starbridge/Constellation,* myself.

Jack called it a celestial event.

I think I am a celestial event.

I think we all are.

acknowledgments

Books come into the world on a tremendous wave of support. I owe thanks to many people, but I want to begin with readers. Hearing from you after the publication of *Lovely, Dark and Deep* was the best surprise. Your connection to story, your enthusiasm and kindness mean everything to me. Thank you to all the book fans, bloggers, cover enthusiasts, and reviewers who make noise when they read something they like.

I owe endless thanks to librarians and teachers. When I was a lonely, awkward girl, you helped me find books by Lois Lowry, Paula Fox, Madeleine L'Engle, E. L. Konigsburg,

S. E. Hinton, Betty Smith, Norma Klein, John Knowles, and J. D. Salinger. Their stories carried me through the hours and filled me with the promise of new places and other lives. The first time I saw my book on a library shelf was a dream come true. I'm so grateful for the work you do and for your support.

Thanks to all you wonderful booksellers for your passion and your ability to put the right book into the right reader's hand. Bookshops are community treasures, and I'm so happy to see them come roaring back.

To my agent, Sara Crowe, and my editor, Alexandra Cooper—writing is solitary, but I never feel alone because I know you're in it with me. Thank you for your generosity, intelligence, wit, energy, and patience. You challenge me to make things better and never forget to listen to the language. I am so lucky to work with you.

I'm thrilled to be published by HarperCollins under the editorial direction of Rosemary Brosnan and the spirit of Ursula Nordstrom. Thank you to Alyssa Miele for your cheerful replies to my many emails. Thanks to the whole team at HarperTeen, to Erin Fitzsimmons and Catherine San Juan, the visionaries behind this gorgeous cover. To Jon Howard, Gwen Morton, Bess Braswell, Mitchell Thorpe, Vanessa Nuttry, and Kristen Eckhardt for your transformational magic. You turn a collection of words into a book and get it out into the world. Thanks to copy editor Megan Gendell for teaching me that no one calls the temple arm of eyeglasses a "bow" and for keeping me from looking like a total doofus. Equal thanks to Rosanne Lauer for your eagle-like proofreading eye.

Thanks to the design and illustration studio Maricor/ Maricar for sharing your art and for stitching my beautiful cover (all those hand-tied French knots!).

Thank you to the Garramone family, who turned their Paris apartment into the world's best writing retreat three years in a row.

Thanks to painter Allyn Howard for the studio visit, for loaning me books on maps, and for the long conversation about the technical details of making art.

Thanks to Jessica Dineen, Kath Jesme, Medbh McNamara, Noel McNamara, and Kim Purcell for reading drafts and offering thoughts.

A fair amount of freaking out seems to be part of writing a book. All my gratitude to family and friends for loving me anyway.

Finally, thanks to Medbh and Noel. You make me proud. And to Doug, I'm so lucky in love. *Forward!*

note

The Emily Roebling House, its gift shop, tours, and apartments exist only in my imagination. They are inspired by the very real and wonderful Tenement Museum on Manhattan's Lower East Side. I thought Emily Warren Roebling deserved a place of her own. After the death of her father-in-law and original engineer of the Brooklyn Bridge, John Roebling, and the subsequent disabling illness of her husband, Washington Roebling, Emily Roebling oversaw the completion of the Brooklyn Bridge. She acted as liaison between her husband and the engineering team and as an engineer herself. Emily was the first person to cross the bridge when it opened on May 24, 1883. The physical location of the building imagined to hold the Emily Roebling House exists in Brooklyn on the corner of Water and Old Fulton Streets, where it houses a Shake Shack and some apartments.